2030

LAST CALL FOR

HUMANITY

R SCOTT REATH

2030 LAST CALL FOR HUMANITY

Disclaimer:

This book is a work of fiction. Any similarities to any person or persons, living or dead, are purely coincidental.

Copyright © 2023 R Scott Reath

ISBN 978-1-7388757-0-2

Dedication

The following words are dedicated to anyone who sees through state and media-sponsored lies and to those who've had to speak an unpopular truth when the world wasn't ready to hear it. This book is meant to honor those who have suffered injury or unfair punishment at the hands of tyrants. A great debt is owed to all podcasters who've had to navigate a risky and shifting balance between truth-seeking and being demonetized or de-platformed. They inspired this work and all the gratitude I could ever possibly hope to share.

Contents

Chapter One

A BRIGHT FUTURE

A semi-dislodged brain chip meant Keith Molière was being hunted by the government, the police, and drones. Suddenly estranged from friends and family alike, his options were dwindling before his eyes as every news feed, every computer, and each city-wide public monitor system showed images of fugitives from the state. The state-funded media never told what became of those who were rounded up, but only issued bulletins about those being sought. Any questions or reports about illegal activity by the police were met with inflated charges of misinformation. No store, restaurant, or medical facility could be attended to without the prospect of being turned in immediately. How had it come to this so quickly? He pondered this for a moment before he heard his door suddenly pounded upon with a series of hostile raps.

"Open up! This is the police!" His improved memory immediately told him every detail of how this moment arrived but offered no solution to his impending dilemma. He had to consider how gradually the systematic disruptions in democracy were devolving into totalitarianism. When law-abiding citizens were being hunted over their brain-chip status as though they were an infestation of insects, it was no longer a democracy, regardless of how often they tried to convince us. For all their bleating about threats to democracy, the real threat came from electing the wrong people.

It began as innocently as any day might in Oxenberg, with mundane irritations and simple joys to balance them out. He'd always enjoyed the view and feeling of being free in his elevated loft that protruded into the sky. The engineering design left his unit protruding outward, adjacent to the rest of the building. While not a luxury suite, it was spacious, and his balcony gave the feeling of being suspended in the air and was a great vantage point to watch a thunderstorm. Despite having programmable windows that could reveal any type of weather as a mood benefit, he preferred witnessing what nature brought his way. He had three spacious bedrooms, a kitchen, a bath, and a living room that merged with a den. It was all he needed, and he got a break on the price for doing repairs, but most of all, he loved that balcony, which burst forth with sunlight every morning and pumped him full of free vitamin D. The city of West Oxenberg was revealed from his living room window with all its unique regions.

There were vertical farms, high-rise towers, and alleys that bustled with dubious activities at night.

There was a use-at-your-own-risk bike trail with few takers that Keith had mastered. Around the city's perimeter, one could see all the trees planted in wide patches of green that surrounded the parks, and way off to the west were Lake Mills and the Egress.

The Egress was a nickname for any uncultivated part of a city that became a stopgap dwelling for the dispossessed, disenfranchised, and homeless. Every city had its own version of an egress, and Oxenberg's denizens could be seen beyond the lake area. Since the 'Human First' government had taken over, most areas known simply or collectively as "the Egress" had grown about five times their original size. As other similar vacant lots and properties emerged into communities of the hungry, addicted, and lost, they were viewed with more contempt than pity by gated communities and governments. This was rapidly becoming a worldwide phenomenon. Too much spending on buying votes and overpaying media sources for favorable government spin would leave a deficit that would rival the amount spent on the military-industrial complex.

Oxenberg was a pleasant place to live that had few problems other than a growing Egress like any other city. It was within a collection of city-states that rivaled some of the best places on the continent of West Volcaria. They had been at war with Morgania which had better resources and a population that tended to vote conservatively. This was the main reason they were at war with West Volcaria. The left-leaning Volcarians tended to vote liberal and despised the Morganians with great fervor. All of this troubled Molière, as he was a civil libertarian who found both the right and left extremes to be too hateful of their counterparts for his tastes. Instead, he clung rigidly to a "Live and Live" credo.

Keith had begun to question his place in society as he put on his exercise suit, which electronically stimulated and developed his muscles as he relaxed via fiber-optic microsensors. Ideally, one was supposed to meditate during this time, but Keith listened to old-school rock music to relax and often found that meditation only frustrated him. He instructed his monitor to create 10 new folders for his favorite defunct band, "The Miltons" based on projections from samples of their previous works. He programmed different groups that had emerged, decades later like "The Millers", and placed them into the influence's category, and listened to the result of a device that consumed a great deal more of his time than he cared to admit. The mixing and matching of bands with different influences yielded a wide range of results, from brilliant to revolting, but the gems he discovered always felt completely unique to each person's taste, as the possibilities were all but endless. As he listened, he contemplated his life and his place in society.

His successes had been intermittent. He very much liked the idea of the new brain chips, as he could play music in his head as loud as he liked without risk of any hearing loss. He knew how much his exercise bike and suit helped him manage the excess weight he'd carried around as a child. In top shape now, he never commented on people's builds and felt immense guilt that it was always the first thing he noticed in others. He also knew that the steady calm in his life that he enjoyed had been interrupted a few too many times. At work, he had been involved in some heated debates and a few fistfights with bullies when he was younger. He wanted very much to quash that side of his personality that he had spent years suppressing. He wondered how much more productive and wealthy he would have been had he not spent so much time and energy biting his sarcastic tongue to be a bit more user-friendly in the workplace and society at large. The real incentive for him, however, was the improved memory. The fear of forgetting important things plagued his mind at times, and the prospect of improving his recall sixfold was more than he could imagine.

A commercial came on his monitor promoting the very product he was contemplating. A voice asked, "Who makes the best brain chip available? Why, the only people who make the brilliant brain chip, Thinkplus! Whether it's Tom building more extensions to his house, or Aunt Marjory going back to complete her university degree in just a month, you can't go wrong with a brain chip from Thinkplus! A trusted company that's been making people brilliant since 2026! Be better, be smarter, and be brilliant. Buy a Thinkplus brain chip today. Don't fail or get left behind, only to find yourself in a tent in the egress with zero advantage. Smart people stay employed, and brain chips make for smarter employees. Don't get stumped by questions about the modern world or be caught working too slowly to keep your job. You want that new car, a better house, and a better life with all the perks you deserve!" Extravagant pool party scenes flicker as the type at the bottom of the screen is read. A new, more serious voice read: "Any side effects from dislodged chips are easily fixed with just one visit to your doctor. Such cases are extremely rare and mild. Don't believe any misinformation to the contrary. Safety reminder; the spreading of any misinformation regarding the safety of brain chips is punishable by law and carries a ten-year sentence. Thinkplus brain chips are safe, efficient, and will make you smarter and a more desirable employee!"

Well-timed, he thought, as he decided to go ahead with the procedure and become smarter and calmer. He would make a better income and garner more respect. He'd never be troubled by forgotten data, and he had a promising job interview coming up. He was excited to nail his job interview, aided by a superior memory.

Keith planned to go hang out with his pal Mick to watch the robot fights, and finally, get some of the respect he felt was due. He was healthy and in good spirits, and the future bore the promise of a better life. This was bound to be a shimmering "yes" moment in a lifetime full of near misses and partial successes. He beamed with the anticipation of tomorrow and all that would come thereafter. He took out his Torpedo bike and rushed through the symmetrical streets and alleys filled with dubious activities. He had the painless procedure performed a day before his job interview with Casual Corporation to ensure he was at his best and had no negative side effects. Ten minutes early for his big job interview, he was ushered in by a friendly concierge with a thick, well-groomed mustache, and some well-traveled facial lines that supported a pair of deep-set, steely eyes.

"Mr. Molière," he said, smiling.

"You're just a touch early, but there is a viewing balcony; you can watch the other candidate complete his interview to get a sense of how things work around here. Surveillance is ubiquitous, right?" the concierge asked rhetorically with a chuckle. After thanking the gracious man in uniform, he studied his surroundings intensely.

Molière noticed a large two-way monitor above him playing another chip commercial. A well-dressed and attractive man and woman eagerly pitched their product.

"Has this ever happened to you?"

A man pictured at a job interview is asked a difficult question and struggles to provide an answer. He is asked to leave.

A second candidate wows his interviewer with crisp facts and impressive recall. As he walks past his defeated competitor, he is hired on the spot.

"You should have bought a brain chip!"

"Don't limit your chances to make an impression by fumbling or forgetting information you already know. Get a Thinkplus brain chip and remember everything you know, today!"

The camera pans to the dejected man telling his wife the bad news.

"Don't let this happen to you. Get the only competitive advantage that will ever matter. Your brain chip not only makes you smarter and more informed, but it also rids you of any negative emotions. You can impress at that job interview and perform your duties without being impacted by negative emotions like anxiety, nervousness, and contempt. Be a better corporate soldier, fighting the good fight, the positive way that companies prefer. Get a Thinkplus brain chip today!"

Molière strained to hear his competitor's conversation over the advertisement but got most of it. A medium-sized man in a pressed black suit with short black hair and brown eyes perched over sharp cheekbones answered.

"I am sorry, sir, my thoughts have been redacted in that area."

"It seems as though you've had a lot of your thoughts redacted; do you think maybe you're something of a problem?"

"I had my chip readjusted, and they couldn't salvage a lot of information on my nature until the new chip had more time to assess my thoughts,"

He explained this to his interviewer with a sheepish half-grin.

"Why would I want to take a chance on someone like that? You might do anything or even question the government. Did they redact your thoughts or your memories as well? It's hard to get a read on you if you can't remember why. Harmless questions are dangerous questions! We don't pay people here to think private little thoughts while they're on the clock, you know."

His interviewer was middle-aged and carrying a few extra pounds but had a stern look about him. He had his mettle tested more than once, as seen by the steely blue eyes and rigid expression, yet he started out very gently.

"Well, what about your experiences at Macro Craft?"

"I recall a lot of processing... large amounts of data, but my thoughts in that area have also been redacted."

The two stared at each other for a second, as the tension between them grew. The man seeking employment collected himself and altered his approach.

"I understand, I'd just like to express my commitment to following any and all directions given. They redacted some thoughts from my chip and the only things I can't remember are surrounding the redaction process as far I can tell as I was being operated on and under anesthetic."

With no humor or irony in his voice, the interviewer pressed his subject further.

"A test then. HR is here as a witness. Smack yourself across the face.

HARD! ....NOW!'"

"Alright!"

The man instantly struck himself hard in the face twice, with the second strike being audibly louder than the first. The woman from human resources was dressed conservatively in a chestnut-colored long skirt suit with a blue blouse and save for the cold expression on her face, looked a little bookish. No one needed eyeglasses anymore but some, like her, still enjoyed the presentation effect. From beneath her upturned hair, she spoke flatly.

"You were only told to strike once. You did not follow instructions correctly."

The man in the black suit pivoted rather effectively given the sudden stillness of the air in the room.

"Forgive my enthusiasm, I was just wanting to show a high level of commitment."

The interviewer pulled his stomach in a measure and revealed a hint of dominance in body position as he widened his seated position and leaned forward with his hands on his knees while elevating his jaw just a touch.

"Compliance is king — no deviation is tolerated. Do you understand?" "Completely."

Still pressing, he studied his prospect for weakness.

"We'd have to put you under heightened thought surveillance for a few weeks. Wear this on your lapel; it'll read your emotions and monitor any independent thinking triggers. We won't tolerate deviance."

"Understood."

The interviewee spat the word out quickly, but there was a trace of defeat in his voice. This seemed to intrigue his interviewer.

"You won't mind if I check what your chip is displaying about you over the last few days, or, do you?"

In an approval-seeking tone, the job-seeking candidate asked politely: "Please, sir, the doctors had to readjust my chip, and it's possible they redacted more than I thought. Did you say you could read my thoughts over the last few days?"

"Don't play dumb; we'll check anyway. C'mon, let's go."

The interviewer escorted the prospect from the interview room down the hall to a boardroom with a massive monitor that had miniature frames on a touch screen displaying colored thermal images of all the employees' thoughts. There are two stone-faced, square-built observers pouring over the data, displaying emotion beyond a palpable coldness and rigidity.

Molière had to reposition himself to compensate for his obstructed view.

"This is Dietrich, and Makimbo, they ensure that staff is following our emotional guidelines and policies."

"You mean behavioral guidelines?" with a lighthearted half-grin, the man inquired.

These two men did not speak, not even to say hello. The first, a clean-shaven black man of rugged build and sour expression in his recently fitted fine suit, glared about, while the other had very pale skin that contrasted his decidedly dark features and a five-o'clock shadow that seemed all but permanent. The dark-haired man appeared somewhere between bored and irritated. The interviewer continued; "No, here we maintain the certainty of positive-minded employees, and those with the most positive thoughts over a month get a small bonus. Of course, those who fail in this area tend not to be kept on. We pride ourselves, as most companies do, on providing a happy atmosphere, and we won't tolerate anyone who can't follow the program."

"But what about involuntary thoughts? People can't control them."

"Wrong-minded people, you mean? They shouldn't have been allowed in the door in the first place, but if they have thoughts of disinformation, anger, resentment, jealousy, or general negativity, they are out the door, and you know how tough it is out there once you've been let go from a corporation, right? The options range from prostitution, homelessness, and starvation to suicide. We don't make the rules, but we sure do enforce them. Now, I am going easy on you due to your recent redactions, but honestly, this kind of talk isn't going to bode well for you. Companies don't like questions, because if you ask any, you will be reported to the government for spreading misinformation."

"Over mere questions?"

"One question might be OK, but two puts you into conspiracy theory territory. Conspiracy theories are illegal and carry a ten-year sentence. I'm telling you all this, so you'll keep your thoughts clean during the test. Good luck!"

The interviewer touches the screen, which reveals all kinds of sorted images with colors indicating the prospect's emotions. Green, as it showed now, indicated being nervous. While scanning the room, the job candidate gets slightly angry, and this triggers a change in color to red on one of the monitors, setting off an alarm. The startled short-haired man began again.

"I am sorry, please let me try again."

"We don't permit negative thoughts in this company, and you were told. Pack your things. We have to inform the police, you understand."

"But..."

"They're on their way."

"Maybe my chip is faulty." "Whaa-aa--at?"

The interviewer bellowed in astonishment, followed by a high-pitched shout.

"He questioned the brain chip! Have fun in *jail!* And... get away from me!"

Within a few moments, the police were already through the main foyer and had collected the other job seeker and taken him away. Two officers remained, and Keith overheard them muttering in the distance. It seemed one was grousing about how many officers were reluctant to chase down "anti-chippers" and the robots having some fail-safe protocol that prevented them from stopping anyone who hadn't committed a traditional crime. More griping about the function of the police, being forced to bow to unsavory political pressure, and something about their difficulties surrounding the Hyperloop method of transportation. They'd said nothing useful to excuse him from the interview. Keith was certain that laws and corporate policies, along with the blurred and increasingly shady lines between them, were all changing faster than he could keep up with, and he needed to leave as inconspicuously as possible.

"Sorry, I have another interview." He blurted and turned away with a half-hearted wave.

"Just a minute!.. I'm not getting a good read on your chip; can you come back here a moment, I just need to check something," the interviewer urged.

"Time is money!" he shouted back without turning his head or slowing his pace.

Molière ignored the employees and their shouts of protest, and once out the door, he bolted across the patio to burn his frustrated energy. Upon arriving home later, he decided a bike ride would ease his stress. There was a steep incline he could power through to expunge his stress and reconsider his options later. There was an unseen video message from Jacqueline.

"Hey Keith, I just wanted to congratulate you on your surgery! I didn't think you'd go through with it. I'm confident you'll never forget our anniversary, my favorite... anything, or even check your messages again. Wow, I think I love you even more already; you're a better man! Welcome to the less-flawed human race! See you tomorrow night! Love Ya."

He grinned, weighing how her constant emotional support helped him through many obstacles and provided a psychological boost that had been missing prior to meeting her, yet somehow the call failed to ease his growing concerns over a supposedly free North Morgania. One key difference between Morgania and Oxenberg was the colossal clock tower at the center of town that blasted a top 40 song on the hour rather than chiming. The world was full of city-states that had liberal and conservative rival states, but Morgania seemed a freer place than Oxenberg, with its immense statue of Trueborn in a lake, or at least it did before Trueborn took office. The statue was put there to discourage defacing, but Trueborn's elation over all the attention women paid to his green eyes was marked by glowing green floodlights in place of the eyes. These were meant to highlight his best features, but they made him appear slightly reptilian instead. Others were surprised he'd permit an image of his face, so close to the water for fear of getting his likeness's hair wet. Even with such a display, people barely seemed to notice their world steadily slipping into a police state. Molière deeply wished people would stop feuding over cultural status and focus on how administrators kept them at odds to avoid holding their governments accountable. He called Jacqueline back to clear his mind of pervasive politics and left her a message.

"Hey Jackie, It's me; I received your message; Thank you; it means a lot, but I have to say that the laws and times are changing right before our eyes. I'm toying with the idea of going back to my doctor and getting my chip yanked. I hope that doesn't disappoint you. don't worry, I'll still be human, but I'm not sure about this because I can feel the improvement in my memory, so I'll talk to you about it after my ride. Love you."

Focusing on the positives ahead helped him block out the denigrating interview he witnessed. He'd quickly mend things with Jacqueline, chill out and dissect the robot fights with Mick, and then look into finding a different job. It was a setback, as his status was due for a leap forward, and he might have to accept a lower station in life somewhere else. He tried to ignore the fact that jobs were becoming an extension of governmental authority. They all boasted about working together, but there was something darker and more underhanded looming within this new collective arm of government and big business. He took out his bike to burn off some stress. Imagining employers demanding slave labor and seeking federal authority to criminalize any opponents wasn't a hill he wanted to climb.

He was so frustrated with his vision of the future that he could be seen jolting his handlebars each time he went over the slightest bump. The mountainside was too steep for a safe decline, but the prevailing thought in his mind was, *"If I am now a calmer, less risky version of myself, I'm going to take this last risk while I still can."* He switched off the autopilot and studied the decline ahead of him, then launched his high-tech electric bicycle, "the Ektrix Torpedo," down full tilt. There was some leafy brush on the road he expected to flatten en route to his goal, but someone had used it to cover up a thick, rectangular-shaped rock for reasons unknown. The bike struck the rock and was sent flying, turning over itself before it struck the concrete. The rider was catapulted far into the air and could only watch his helmet bounce down the road as he braced for impact. He failed to reach some nearby trees to soften his landing and could only remember the wild jolt that sent him tumbling down a jagged rock face before feeling the final thud of his body as it hurled into a pile of sand that knocked him out cold. He awoke with his body tingling and throbbing, but his senses were somewhat out of sync, and he wondered if he was in shock. The troubling thing about being in shock was that one could never tell for certain because the ability to properly self-assess required a clear mind. Two kids, a boy and a girl of about ten years old; emerged from their place of hiding. They held some improvised device and were undoubtedly the ones who'd placed the rock under the shrub brush. They stared at his bleeding head for a moment and then hastily ran off.

In the blink of an eye, his front wheel scanner would have detected any obstruction, but a laser jammer interrupted the signal. He wasn't angry with them for causing his accident, as he'd done worse as a kid, but he needed help now. A plethora of memories and emotions began pouring into focus in stunning detail. He could see them in clearer images and actually hear their voices with perfect audio as he recalled long-forgotten episodes of all different moments of his life. Christine Dufresne, the well-intentioned born-again Christian who tried in vain to save his atheist soul. Had he ever met a more kindly and genuine person? Probably not. She even bought him a Bible converted into modern English. A girl named Creola, whose smile and internal sunshine soothed his soul in a way that lasted years after he'd known her. At the age of four, he'd befriended an elderly neighbor and became a sort of sidekick to the old man, and one day the old man had to explain to him that he was going to die. Rather than displaying any grace at all, the child reacted poorly.

"What do you mean you are going to die? You can't do this to me! What am I going to do?"

"Well, I don't like it either," the ailing man replied.

The child stormed off in a huff, leaving the dying old man alone, staring off into the distance, and the two never met again. Suddenly, waves of guilt welled up within him, tormenting him to the point where he felt his soul was tainted and could hardly bear the weight of his past actions. More visions came spiraling through his mind. His grandmother scolded his mom for denying him dessert after dinner one night.

"No, you were always given dessert after dinner; give him his dessert; he hasn't done anything wrong!" What was so entertaining was watching his mom get called out for overparenting by her own overparenting mom. He wasn't sure why, but he found himself grinning like a child. There was a bar fight that started over next to nothing other than some guys who'd decided they were going to start a fight. He was outnumbered, but a scrappy stranger jumped in to help, and while they both got their shots in, a full ten-man brawl erupted. It didn't end too badly, and he even picked up a friend or two in the ensuing chaos, but a surge of pure adrenaline-fueled thoughts bubbled up within him. As his blood grew hot, a fiery look came over his face, as if he were reliving the fight blow-by-blow. A graveyard prank while drinking underage led to a friend crawling into a recently dug grave. Pretending to be an unearthed corpse emerging from the open grave, he saw the heaviest among them running for his life.

He laughed aloud as a slew of other events played out in such vivid detail in his mind's eye that he felt he was watching his life for the second time on fast-forward, with all the gaps filled in. As a toddler, his mother had given him stern instructions on dealing with abusive teachers.

If you ever have to go to the bathroom and the teacher won't let you, just get up and go anyway! Do whatever you have to do, say whatever you have to say, and just go! I'll deal with them afterward if there's any problem, understand me?

That was the first seed of a rebellious attitude that had been bestowed upon him. *What was the alternative? Have children's bladders ruptured in order to appease a power-tripping teacher? Forget that!* He thought. He sat down a moment and looked up at the sky, all pale blue and clear, but for one blackening section of his peripheral vision as he slumped over and lost all consciousness.

Chapter Two

THE PRICE OF LOVE AND FRIENDSHIP

"You have a concussion." The doctor said. "Ohh, what happened?" Molière asked, blinking. "You were in a traffic accident. We located you using your chip. We stitched up your cuts, and you'll have some road rash for a while. The monitor gave us a lot of different reads, so we may have to go back in and adjust it."

"The advertisement says it's good for life, no matter what. Even if I were beheaded, the chip is supposed to outlive me, right? "A thousand lifetimes without adjusting, hack-proof, and injury-proof, that's the one I signed up for, right doctor?"

"I understand your concern, but if it has detached completely, the dangers may be life-threatening."

"Well, I know I was pretty banged up, but I had all these emotions and memories come rushing back into my mind. They were surprisingly heavy emotions, and I remember them now, but many had been lost or dormant, as though I'd somehow unlocked them. Had I blocked them all out? They were potent. Could my chip be faulty? As if I received a dud or one that is doing something completely different from what was promised? Has it been blocking my emotions by cutting off my memory of emotional events? I mean, I feel like I was in an all-night movie theater in my skull."

The doctor turned toward the monitor.

"The signal is picking up some anger from you; that alone proves it's not working properly; it's supposed to calm you."

"I am not angry, and I support the brain chip procedure; otherwise, I would not have had it. I am simply asking if it's been dancing around in my cerebral cortex to the wrong music."

The doctor winced a little over the jargon used to describe delicate parts of the brain.

"I think you mean the limbic cortex or at least the insular cortex, but I'd have to go in and look."

"So all those claims about it being 100% perfectly safe were about as relevant as Aristotelian physics?"

"There might be room for some dangerously unpopular questions," the doctor admitted.

"So the little robot in my head now wants to turn my mind into an emotional kaleidoscope. Terrific! I am asking you: Am I not the decent, law-abiding citizen I think I am? Do I have an unruly streak I need to know about? Is the projector in my head playing false events that never took place that might turn me into a criminal? What is going on? I need to know before I let anyone play around in my cranium swinging a fusion laser like a conductor's baton."

"I can only tell by looking inside."

"Yes, you already said that. Look, I understand you are in a difficult position. Given the universal praise on every network and from every doctor saying the chips are better than life itself and anyone without one is ruining all of humanity, I get that you may want to choose your words carefully."

After a silent moment, the doctor lowered his voice.

"The reads on the monitor mean I'd have to report you if I didn't attempt repairs. No chip means no job; no one will hire you; no one will trust you, and society itself may become very hostile toward you."

"Right, because my broken chip now wants to become my new guilt-tripping grandmother?"

"The monitor shows your resentment is building, you are in red flag territory. The government won't like it, you understand."

"OK, seeing as you can read almost everything I'm feeling and thinking, then let's have an honest conversation, shall we? I am not the smartest guy or the most successful by a long shot, but my BS detector is almost flawless. Not only can I tell when someone is lying to me just by looking at them, but I can even tell when they are withholding information. I'd wager there are risks I'm not being told about, and not just by you. I can tell you are a man of principle, and your integrity is chewing away at you like a pack of wild dogs on an injured rat. Since we began chatting, you've engaged in internal dialogue four times. Before you spoke, you made asymmetrical facial expressions, indicating the momentary stress of concealment if not flat-out resentment of the topic. It's not so much fun when I get to wear the gypsy hat and probe your private thoughts, is it now? So how about we just both come clean and stick to the truth?"

"Alright, your memories are yours, and you're not a criminal, but they are criminalizing anyone who questions the chip or the government, and the penalties are being increased by the day. You strike me as someone who'd question the entirety of the government, media, and physicians, and soon enough, that will get you either dead or placed in an unrevealed prison. That's why I wanted you to get the damn thing fixed."

"Is this thing going to do more harm than good over the long term?" The doctor shifted his weight and tried to mask his discomfort.

"For some, it helps if you have an aggressive nature, but for those that don't, it might be too potent, turning their malleable minds into little better than those of sheep, puppets, or pawns."

"They lose their souls? It's a dressed-up lobotomy?" Molière asked sharply.

"Not quite, It does improve memory which makes people feel smarter and can reduce aggression, but it goes further than that and quells the desire to challenge, to question, to make waves. It does this by prioritizing your positive memories over any that may have developed your strength of character or made you in any way feisty or disagreeable." The doctor explained patiently.

"It neuters people!" Keith snapped.

The doctor, in turn, was growing impatient with the contentious remarks.

"Please! You must watch your tongue; both of our emotions are being monitored by the government at Parliament. You'd best force yourself to relax!"

Molière didn't appreciate being patronized.

"Can you tell me how George Washington died? Bloodletting by doctors, that's how. The best science available to them at the time led them to take the very blood he desperately needed most because he trusted his doctors! What if I refused this thing?" He demanded.

"Those people are being terminated from their jobs or arrested."

"For refusing the chip?" Molière asked superciliously.

"Yes, it appears you missed the news last night."

"An edict to be a puppet, or else?"

"Is this the hill you want to die on? Should you choose a road that ends in peril, you can't pretend you didn't know what lies at the end of that road." The doctor stated with growing condescension.

"So it's a perilous chip or a perilous government with crazy laws being added by the day. Shouldn't the hill I'm supposed to die on be here in East Volcaria? How is it that we are at war when we share the same one-world government? If military equipment providers fund all the election campaigns, doesn't that mean the wars are being staged just to test out the new equipment?"

The nature of the conversation had exceeded the doctor's need to have an honest dialogue and had descended into a law-breaking discussion. He decided to speak more compassionately.

"You are speaking dangerously. If I don't go in and fix your chip, you'll give out odd readings, and they'll come for you."

"As imperfect as I am, I want to know who and what I am; I don't want to be a better widget-maker at the expense of my soul. We atheists don't rely on celestial bodies to bail us out of our jams. I want to be able to laugh, cry, fear, and get stark raving mad, blood boiling, and seething with uncontrollable rage if need be. Without the ability to become enraged, none of us will ever dispute a government that has outlawed disputing it, will we? They could make us into human pets, and we'd be fine with it for fear of risking the penalties. If speaking out against the world government means jail, how long before they just jail everybody in case they have dreams or mere thoughts of speaking out? Will there be a chip to read dreams too? Why not just make me into a plug-and-play version of Keith for the entertainment of those in power? You take away our emotions as well as our will, our very ability to oppose what is wrong and unethical. Is that what you are prescribing for me?"

The doctor looked flummoxed. He'd wanted this conversation but didn't like its direction.

"Alright, you've made your point. I can't remove it." He reluctantly admitted.

"Can't you shut it off?"

"No, only the government can do that, but it isn't as far dislodged as I thought. It looks like your jolt only severed the part that suppresses the periaqueductal gray and the amygdala. The parts that function to regulate your emotions It seems you got the benefits of enhanced memory from the hippocampal stimulation without the cost of emotional suppression by the amygdala. That means every time you experience highly independent thoughts or strong emotions, the monitors might sound off and the police could take you away. Remember, the courts are only there to maintain the illusion of democracy; you'd have no chance."

"You have to help me, or you'll be sentencing me to death!"

"Even if I could, it would only mute it by an unknown amount, and even then it would be risky. There's no way to know if it protects you from any outburst that shows up upon detection. You'd have to master your emotions in record time, and that's not at all likely."

"I'll do it!" Keith volunteered.

The doctor preferred his patient consider all risks.

"How do you know I won't simply readjust it as I ought?"

"Because you can't wash off your integrity, you know how wrong all of this is. You know it."

"So I am supposed to get fired just to help you out?" The doctor jeered.

"No, just keep making human puppets for the government. Become its de facto enforcement arm; perhaps *tentacle* is a better word. Isn't that *why* you became a doctor?"

"Very well, just so I don't have to listen to your objections any longer."

"Let me guess, you are more accustomed to the sheep who don't argue and don't question you."

"Did you see the sign that reads: Disrespect will not be tolerated?"

"I never internalize propaganda, doctor, your friendly world government wouldn't like that."

Molière replied in his most supercilious tone.

The doctor put him under anesthetic and successfully muted the alarm trigger, then checked in after some recovery time.

"I feel fine." Molière shrugged, anticipating the doctor's question.

"Quite sure?"

Both men were interrupted by the sounds of police sirens growing louder in unison.

"It didn't work! They're coming." Keith blurted, as the doctor's stoicism faded.

"It probably needs some time. Quick, get in a testing booth! The monitors can't detect anything within its frame."

Keith pressed a button that obviously opened the door, and without delay, he climbed into the chamber. He could see but closed his eyes to resemble a test subject. Four policemen came into the office, two approached the doctor while the second pair examined the state of the monitor. The police were overly respectful, which only belied their dark agenda. Their faces were covered, which added to their ominous presence. The first officer was tall, exaggeratedly polite, yet still undeniably smug.

"Hello, Dr. Bergerac, we had notification from the state monitor that your medical monitor was giving readings of aggressive, and illegal emotional activity."

The doctor withheld any sign of stress.

"Yes, well, it's all explainable. We had a test subject whose chip dislodged and whose readings went all over the map. I've since corrected the chip position, and everything is fine now."

The second officer was stockier and wanted to subtly raise the temperature a notch.

"Yes, doctor, we noticed you had a bit of a live-wire case loose, and that the problematic readings went away in an instant. That's some highly skilled work you are doing in that area, wouldn't you say?"

"Par for the course, I'd say." The doctor said it in the calmest voice he could manage.

The taller of the two officers glanced at his handheld device while his partner spoke.

"Yes, well, I am just looking at the monitor now, and it says your emotions are running a bit high for someone in your position."

"My apologies, I am unaccustomed to visits from the police."

"Well doctor, It's not just since we arrived, but beforehand. It seems like you've been up to something that's made you quite nervous. Betting a lot of money on a sports game? Invest in a bad stock? Maybe you're cheating on your wife? Or perhaps you were engaged in something highly illegal while at work, such as interfering with the function of a brain chip?"

The officer suggested in a soft tone but with a stern expression.

"All work on brain chips is stressful if they aren't placed perfectly or become dislodged. A person's entire identity could be wiped out, or they could mentally become a vegetable."

The doctor retorted with an indignant tone. The second officer became more conciliatory.

"Look, we aren't here looking for a fight, but you are going to have to come in for questioning, and that's all there is to it."

"And how many people get released after questioning?"

"It doesn't matter, now just come along like a good fellow, you don't want us to start logging you as being emotionally difficult, do you?"

The doctor left with the police wordlessly. Keith knew he also had to leave, but not so soon as to be seen by any lingering officers. Molière pulled a pod into a corner area and blocked himself from view like a stowaway until things had quieted down enough to hasten an exit. As darkness fell, he emerged from the office quietly and cautiously to decode the anti-theft mechanisms on his bike before distancing himself from the hospital at breakneck speed. After racing to return home, he was plagued with conflicting thoughts about what to do next. Molière was certain that staying home would be unsafe. Before calling Jacqueline to explain, he noticed a message from her, but her voice was fraught with agitation.

"Oh, my word, I can't believe what you said in that message. Are you kidding me? Have you lost your mind? How can you even think of ditching your chip? I mean, you want to make money, right? If we get married and have kids, do you think they are going to live in that empty space in your head where the chip used to be? Do you think anyone is going to hire an expert on outdated music who'd prefer an ear chip to a brain chip? Wake the fuck up! Seriously, I don't know what's wrong with you. Are you going through some kind of phase that allows you to act like you are 18 with time to burn?

We're adults now, in case you forgot. We have responsibilities. I just called to see how your interview went, and then I get this crazy, radical message from you doubting your chip! You better not have mentioned that at your interview, or you could be in legal trouble. Please call me back and tell me this was all a joke or a prank. I don't feel like harboring a fugitive for the rest of my life. I'm sorry if I sound harsh, but you really scared me today. Call me back; I still love you."

Molière involuntarily lurched back from the monitor in disbelief. They rarely argued, save for a few blowouts that were colored more by long silences than big arguments back when they first started seeing each other, but they prided themselves on not being the kind of people who frequently bickered. If anything, they would each go into a different room until they were ready to make up. The tone of the call felt far more confrontational than any before, and it was unlike her to leave such personal statements. He wanted to see her in case there was some other lingering issue that wasn't resolved, but she wasn't home. He also pondered how to explain his emotions not being picked up on monitors in public places and decided that telling people it had to be removed would be the best and simplest solution. It wasn't any of their business anyway. To take his focus off any strife, he went to visit his pal Mick to watch the robot fights. It wasn't just the larger super-powered ones; there were models designed to act and react like humans in combat, and they had different martial arts along with human-styled weaknesses programmed into them. A human could beat them, but they had to be the most elite class of competitors to pull off the odd victory. Mick and Keith were students of the sport and rarely missed an opportunity to compare notes, and the invitation was always open on fight night. Mick would typically all but jump out of his skin if Keith ever missed a good match they could watch together. He arrived at Mick's with a case of enhanced vitamin drinks that benefited the metabolism and purified the blood. As always, Mick greeted him warmly whenever they prepared for a series of compelling matches.

"Hey! I'm all ready. I've got 7 bots, 2 super bots, and three humans for my picks. How about you?" Mick asked.

"I am going with humans all the way, like maybe four." "Ooh, now that's commitment!"

"Care to place a wager just on the numbers game?"

"I dunno, Mick, you might be taking advantage of me, I just got my chip yanked today." Keith joked.

Mick stopped fixing the drinks, turned with a look of concern on his face, and paled a little.

"Seriously?"

Mick asked, as his smile vanished and did not return. The mood changed, and the temperature of the room seemed cooler. Their many friendly debates often ended in banter, but this felt decidedly tense. A moment ago, the curiosity about whether such a trivial matter might end their friendship seemed beyond his imagination, but Mick was acting as though Keith had just confessed to a heinous crime.

"Would that be a real problem for you?" Keith asked. "Well, it's just that I told Jezzie that you had your chip." "So-oo, that's a problem for her, I'm guessing."

"Well, you know what's going on with the police and everything, right?"

"Isn't it a personal decision?"

"Yeah, but we don't want any trouble," Mick said.

"Should I leave?"

"It's probably a good idea, Keith. She's downstairs, and I don't want to have to lie to her."

"What about watching the fights?"

Mick's dogged interest in robot fights was a distant memory.

"They're mostly robots, they'll make more of them," he said dismissively.

Keith resisted the temptation to make any cutting remarks but thought of several on his way out.

He knew such thoughts wouldn't help anyone. Mick was his own man but harbored some dormant subservient streak. If a day arrived when the media told the masses to cut off their index fingers to reduce carbon emissions, Mick would be the first to grab a knife. Keith forced out any thoughts of his trusted friend reporting him to the feds or police over his decision. Mick neither reported him nor spoke to him again.

Molière began to sense an increase in uniformed police in his neighborhood, and once at home, his comfort level dropped by a good measure. He didn't want to be recognized on his banged- up torpedo bike, so he decided to walk with a little assistance. He unboxed his new Ektrix Exoskeleton prototype leg booster kit and set it in motion. This kit was a throw-in when you bought one of their more expensive bikes. The prototype had been abandoned due to a negative reaction from market research. Most people felt an exoskeleton ought to be for the whole body rather than just the legs. The outrageous speed boost and shock absorption to his feet defied belief. People had no idea what they missed out on, as with a single charge, a person could "run" at 37 mph for six hours with hydraulic joints, and they were collapsible for storage. He left in such a hurry that he didn't even change clothes.

He noticed several dilapidated and abandoned buildings, as well as the glaring absence of police, as he raced toward the Lower East Side's egress.

Upon arrival, he removed his exoskeleton legs by the belt lock and collapsed them into his knapsack. A quick glance around revealed tents on both sides of the street, surrounded by discarded needles, plastics, and other recyclable garbage. There was also an undeniable odor of urine, dirt, and unswept streets.

The people here tried to cling to whatever dignity level they could manage, and they weren't known for welcoming outsiders. An imposing black man that few would challenge stood at the foot of the street like a sentinel guarding a gate.

He appeared ageless, save for a graying beard. He sized up the oddly dressed newcomer and recognized the look of a man in trouble.

All but ignoring the cuff-linked blazer, a touch of reverse class distinction appeared on the man's face as he asked, "What's going on there, professor?"

"I'm looking for a place to stay for the night."

The man nods several times slowly and looks up at the midday sun before returning his gaze.

"In a bit of a jam, huh?" "I've had a bit of a day."

This surrogate guardian of the homeless inspected the East Side's newest resident, scanning his suit and shoes, then suddenly relaxed his shoulders and offered a potential solution.

"You can try Juanita, all the way up at the end of the avenue, the very last tent. She might put you up."

"Thanks! Anything else I should know?"

He wondered how safely things might be playing out, but desperation was driving his cause. The unnamed gatekeeper sensed his concern and grinned sarcastically, stating, "Yeah, she's a cannibal!"

"Perfect! One of my people." Keith shot back.

The shared grin between the two men faded quickly as each moved on to face their respective uncertainties. Halfway up the hill, an old man was sitting on a heap of trash. His blank stare hinted at the volumes of life he must have borne witness to. Eras from the past etched into his wrinkled face, adorned with a long gray beard, gave him a distinct appearance. He constantly plucked at his beard with stubby fingers.

"Do you know Juanita?"

Keith asked in hopes of gaining a clearer picture of who he was to meet. After several seconds the old man ceded

"Yuh, I know her." "She alright?"

He asked this question vaguely on purpose, hoping to discern any red flags about her state of mind or health and if she was the kind of person who might require some assurances before accepting him.

"Good as she can be, I guess."

With a nod, Keith ventured onward and finally arrived at the tent in question. He gently gave a double rap on the side flap of the tent.

"Whatcha want?" A female voice asked from within. "Someone told me I might be able to ask a favor from you."

Juanita came to unzip the flap and revealed a bronze-skinned frame with rich brown hair and a distant expression in her eyes.

"What *favor*?" She asked slowly.

"I am in a bit of a jam, and I need to be in between some walls for a while, maybe even tent walls, but I don't have money, so I am a bit desperate and could use some rest."

Just voicing those words so sheepishly diminished his confidence as he realized how pathetic and stupid they sounded.

"How long?" she asked.

"I don't even know where I am going, but I'll have to sleep at some point before going anywhere, maybe a night."

In asking, he felt the tension of being seen as an outsider who didn't belong.

"I think there is too much judgment in the world," Juanita said flatly.

"Agreed."

"You can stay, but you might see me do some drugs."

Keith studied her a little and was plagued with feelings about how this had all been a little too easy. He'd just walked into an all but lawless environment, and no one had given him a hard time or made any attempt to mug, rob, or just fight him for being the dreaded new guy on the scene. Juanita, for her part, was considerate and not unwise, but other than being a little beaten down by life, she was well-spoken and soft in manner. She made no cautions about getting out of line with her, no territorial comments about staying on his side of the tent. There was no mention of rules at all in her place, and she'd afforded him a certain dignity that seemed oddly lacking everywhere else. Unsure whether his judgment was off, he wondered if there was a part of him that was beginning to like her. When would the other shoe fall? Life is never easy, and this all just fell into place with little effort and didn't feel quite right. Juanita didn't ask about his past but kept things in the present. After some small talk, she took out some drug cooking paraphernalia, heated some concoction, and loaded it into a syringe full of magic dreams. This was her way to smile at the world, even if for the shortest time yet in an endless series of ever-shortening durations.

"Are you OK with this?" she asked.

"Ooh, um, yup, uh, YES. I mean."

"You want some?"

"NO!... I mean, um. Not really, I'm good. Thanks." Juanita shrugged and said, "Suit yourself."

Keith had resigned himself to enduring this occurrence, but in truth, he hated drug use. Vitamins were his drug of choice, and he was a purist about what he put into his body. While there were some arguments for marijuana use, he felt the more potent drugs were an assault on the mind, body, and soul. Nonetheless, he tried to put on a brave and supportive face as she prepared for her activity. He would quietly ignore his opinion and his passion for the truth, refusing to make a single judgmental comment no matter what. Committed to that thought, he was unwilling to budge on it no matter how overwhelming the urge arose to "talk some sense" into her. He was her guest and had been spared any judgment over where his life choices had landed him, and he insisted to himself that he'd be equally polite and not violate this internal promise. All these mental preparations and ideals could not have prepared him for what he was about to witness. The reality check he was about to receive would be so shocking that he would never be able to cleanse the memory from his soul for the rest of his life. Juanita secured the syringe and moved it toward her face. Keith had expected her to roll up a sleeve and had heard of people who had used up all the best places to inject until their veins were no longer an option. He thought these to be mere exaggerations or even folklore. Aghast, his eyes bulged as she wound up and launched the syringe into the white of her left eye. He shouted in disbelief.

"Whoa, whoa, Whoa! Hold on a second there! Why are you putting that in your eye? That's your sclera! That part of the eye is not meant for a needle! What the *HELL*?"

He fought unsuccessfully to lower his voice and restrain his aghast expression of horror. A second ago, he was musing about how this had all been too easy, and now he was unsure if he could stomach another second here after failing so miserably to reach her.

"It's the last place I've got left," she said as casually as though she were purchasing a candy bar with the last change in her purse.

She chuckled mildly at his naiveté. He watched, writhing in revulsion and dismay, as she injected herself, emptying the full contents of the syringe without the slightest flinch or hesitation. He was so troubled by his unwitting compliance that he momentarily forgot about his own plight. Suddenly, the thought emerged that convincing people that these brain chips may not be as safe or as innocent as promised would be even more difficult than his attempt to convince Juanita not to put a needle into her unprotected eye. Defeatism was creeping up within him, and it began to feel every bit as permanent in his mind as his brain chip. He had to overrule his thoughts as he realized his survival depended entirely on unwavering mental discipline. *What if access to all of my most private thoughts has been hampered?* He wondered. He didn't even know if he could trust that his thoughts and emotions were all genuinely his. Recognizing some growing paranoia was setting in, and understanding that he had cause to be paranoid, He knew he must temper it with cold logic and reason. Otherwise, monumental mistakes in judgment could be expected. There was the useful paranoia used as a strategy by soldiers in battle, criminals on a bank job, or those anticipating new charges for offending a capricious government, but the bad paranoia that causes delusion and misjudgment would never help anyone. He had to find a balance, as balance was his guiding template for life. No extreme views, no religious extremism, and no devout following of any belief system had always kept his mind open and his learning unblocked. This weighed heavily against the magnitude of sounding like a delusional lunatic trying to inform people they had been lied to on the deepest levels by their most trusted sources. People had been indoctrinated by corrupt media and the government that paid them to point fingers and skew the news until it was unrecognizable from the truth.

The tent had been a reprieve, but he couldn't wash away the jarring image of an eyeball injection or how much he regretted seeing it take place. What would follow when the eye is no longer a "safe" place to jab oneself? What then? He wondered. He purposely blocked out any further thoughts about it until he slept. During his sleep, he would discover that the random imagery that played out in dreams was also affected by the chip, as the details were crisper and the outlandish imagery seemed more vivid and real. It was as though his nocturnal image projector was in high definition.

"Relax, we are injecting you with docile emotions. You've used up all your veins, so we have to inject your brain through your eye!"

The masked doctors had that artificial politeness and sterile demeanor of those about to perform an unsavory duty for which they would be well compensated. That barely concealable contempt manifested itself in an attempt to cover up their guilt and hung in the air. They knew their wrongdoings could be justified by paying down a mortgage within a few months. The needles were not quite as sterile as the invading surgeon's shared cold expression. "Every urge you have to fight, question, or dissent will be replaced with non-toxic emotions and a need to follow, and you'll be happier like this. It's really not that different from a lethal injection, except you live." One said, as a wooziness began to take hold. They began toying with their instruments, giddy like tourists using chopsticks for the first time. Some instruments were large, like knitting needles being scraped and prodded into his head.

The doctors' masks were loosely around their necks, revealing smug grins accompanying their snide tones. One sadistic surgeon beamed with hostile excitement as his grin widened.

"This is going right into your sclera!"

"Shh! He'll hear you," the chief surgeon blurted out.

"He'll never know the difference." His assistant said, smirking. "Count backward..."

A fading voice said soothingly, but his body sprung forward, sitting upright as he was jolted awake from his graphic nightmare.

One of the ever-present two-way monitors was playing a story on the benefits of brain chips with a caution about the spreading of misinformation. The new commercial revealed a concerned female with a stern voice rife with agitation. Have you noticed people seeming a bit thick to you? How about people clinging to the old ways and holding up progress? They are slowing our progress as a society, they are prone to outbursts and often spew radical and crazy ideas, spreading misinformation against our government keepers who protect us from them and other dangers. They think slow, they are slow, and they are harming society by promoting chip hesitancy. These are dangerous conspiracy theories against democracy. They can't be tracked, they could be plotting any number of crimes against the government or even you. We can't live in a world where people can just go about plotting wild crimes and spreading dangerous ideas. If you know of an unchipped miscreant running around unregulated, please call this number or report them online. Remember, you must speak to a live member of government or law enforcement, as the police robots were not programmed to chase the unchipped as part of their safety protocol. Authorities say they are working hard to resolve this irritating design flaw. Once again, call 998 to report the unchipped! They are capable of any crime and are dangerous to our democracy. We have to stay on the right side of this and do our duty to rid our society of these unchipped and violent people. They hold unacceptable views and block society's progress. Keith awoke in an empty park, reeling from his bizarre dream, and searching for any further meaning.

A large monitor in the park was playing some distance away, but the volume seemed louder than usual. He took some water from his backpack and flushed his eyes as if to wash any unpleasant thoughts away. He thought about Juanita and her gradual suicide installment plan of slow death via injections, and he pictured her winning a medal posthumously for having punctured her body in the most places before that final dose would cease her descent into the abyss. It might be today or tomorrow, and no one could stop her bent and determined journey to witness the end of that rainbow. No pot of gold would be waiting there for her, and if he didn't set some immediate plans and goals, he might be joining her ahead of time. How then do you convince an entire society of people who have been successfully brainwashed into believing the government, the Global Health Watch, the media, and above all, the politicians? They were collectively at work to undo the very fabric of humanity and were gleefully rubbing their hands together to achieve it with zeal and force. The police weren't to blame, half of them were quitting only to be replaced by more indoctrinated members. All communication methods were under close watch, no public signs were legal anymore; there were no protests, and no one wanted to hear a word contrary to their beliefs. There were better terms in psychology, but he decided to call this condition "The Juanita Effect." A state of mind whereupon the holder of a belief is so zealously committed to a specious idea, one that appears mostly sound but in reality, is a gamble they have committed to rather than stare down the harsh truth. They preferred to double down on a deadly path of denial rather than have to accept any responsibility for their compliance, and above all, never have to admit being wrong. How best to sway the wrongly convinced Juanita types of the world? It's easier to get people to drop their religious beliefs, or as hopeless as attempting to deprogram a police bot.

Molière knew that he couldn't just linger around indefinitely. If his chip status didn't give away his strong emotions, the muting effect might. How long before he could simply blend in? How best to lie low in a monitored society? He had one shot and went for it. He would aim for North Oxenberg; no one knew him there, and he might buy himself some time. There was a monorail transport system called the Hyperloop with a nearby stop that would serve his needs. He could avoid any police waiting at the Hyperloop link station if he approached it quickly but did not board, instead running beneath the elevated tube itself. The Hyperloop worked brilliantly, reaching a top speed of 1125 km/h thanks to magnetic elevation and air vacuums. When a person places their head outside a moving vehicle, the wind resistance drives back the hair on their head. The air vacuums took away that resistance, which meant the magnetic elevation, or "maglev," kept the vehicle from touching anything and having no resistance at all, which allowed for higher velocity. If his brain was giving odd readings, they would not be picked up if he were to run beneath the Hyperloop on the ground, avoiding the stations, airborne police would not spot him directly under the loop as it would block their vision. With his leg-boosting exoskeleton, he could cross the distance in a reasonable amount of time. After he planned this, he finally reached Jacqueline with his palm phone device.

"Hey!"

"Hey ya."

"You sounded pretty pissed before, everything OK?" Keith asked.

"I probably just needed some reassurance that we aren't going to become some chipless screw-ups with no money and no future, and hearing you question all that just sort of set me off, and I was frustrated because I couldn't speak to you directly. Please just put my fears to rest and tell me you didn't do anything crazy."

"Oh well, I wiped out on my bike and had to go to the hospital, and there were some issues with my chip. It was sort of fritzing out, and it seems to have been dislodged a bit, and they had to go in and readjust it."

"Oh man, are you alright? Did you hit your head? Are you with it right now? How bad was it?"

"I got a bit of road rash, a hole in my noggin, and my brain fell out of my head, so I donated it to science."

"The Global Health Watch says chips can't get dislodged even if you are in a serious accident," Jacqueline said.

"Just lucky, I guess."

"Are you sure you didn't just use this wipe-out as an excuse to get it removed?"

"Removed? And what doctor would dare offer such a service?"

"So, you still have it?" She urged.

"Why am I getting the feeling everything between us depends on this chip right now?" he asked.

"Well, doesn't it?"

"No," Keith said.

"Yes it does, it's our money, our security, and our safety. The fact that you aren't fully on board with this scares me."

"..and judges me," he added.

"That's not fair; what do you want to do, go live in a shopping cart in the egress?"

"So if my brain isn't tweaked enough for the government's satisfaction, you'll take their side?"

"It's not about sides; it's about being smart, literally." "Smart, and on their tread wheels."

"Really? "Is that where you are at?" she asked.

"I am just concerned about how black and white you seem over this, or my way or the highway, I should say."

"You've always been a contrarian; full of rogue ideas and abstract concepts, and I need you to be an adult right now. I need you to be smart and not a fugitive full of unacceptable views."

"I'm not even sure of my stance; how can that be unacceptable?" He asked.

"This is becoming a wedge between us."

"I guess we can thank our government for creating and applying that wedge then."

"Oh, don't even start there; I just can't do this anymore," she sighed.

"Do what? Pressure me into wearing a painted smile to appease an oppressive government? It improves your memory at the cost of becoming a docile puppet."

"I'll be moving on now. I just don't have room in my life for crazy conspiracy theorists... and Keith, this is goodbye."

Chapter Three

THE RELUCTANT REVOLUTIONARY

The plan had to be finalized, but with more holes than dark matter, all potential solutions seemed futile. With Jacqueline and Mick aghast over his chip hesitancy and refusing to acknowledge his existence, most of his social circle was vaporizing. Questions racked his mind. How to question unethical behavior without being cast aside or jailed? How does one go about reverse brainwashing an indoctrinated society? One theory was to provide a new fear to discredit the old one, but Molière had little interest in that. He hypothesized the idea that people who had displayed strong emotional responses were not yet chipped and therefore could be reasoned with. The "deaf ears" phenomenon, which existed prior to the implants, would now be tenfold. Their newfound ideology was that anyone without a chip was somehow a threat to public safety and should be reported to the police. Whereas propaganda and media-induced psychosis had come close, chip surgery was the slow death of the human spirit.

What a sales pitch they would have had to prepare just to make everyone irrational and hostile to any living person who held off from surgery for whatever reason. Now with snitch lines and video monitors everywhere, the future had suddenly become a slave hunter's paradise. If he were to become such a slave to the wrong side of a manufactured public opinion, what then becomes of the hunted slave when discovered?

No job, no ability to purchase anything from food to clothing to shelter, and no one finding it odd or troublesome. Educated people, some with PH-D's becoming homeless along with chefs, techies, city planners, athletes, and artists. No one thought it odd that all these random law-abiding people just get usurped from their jobs, their money, and their ability to live. To the egress with anyone who dares not follow the path of some vile and spurious agenda to make everyone the same. With the public refusing to see the dark hostility and dirty faces hidden behind the most gleaming political mask, the ruse of protection, the need to lift the curtain on this massive dehumanization process beckoned.

All this ruminating wouldn't yield results, he had to speak with people of strong convictions who defended them assertively. He made a list; Mr. Raymond Burr, his old English Professor, and Scott Hayes an old friend who always lived by his own code. One who always cautioned him not to become a "product" of society. There was Jeannie, an ex-girlfriend who only marched to her own pre-programmed music. It was a short list of nonconformists, but if he managed to create a groundswell or a resistant collective, he might stand a chance of seeing society balance itself again. A group of voices was stronger than a single voice, and given his inability to reason with his fiancee and close friends, he knew he'd have to rely on the strength of numbers, for that was how the government-financed media typically fooled almost everyone.

First on the list was Mr. Burr, who had a sound mind, was well-versed in many different areas, and hopefully was not interested in a chip given his already potent intellect.

At the university, Keith waited by the door for the lecture to end and enjoyed the dulcimer tones that only some black men spoke with, as Burr illustrated best while he playfully chided a student.

"No, I don't think so, you are not going to get away with using substandard English in this environment. Try again."

"Normalcy, What's wrong with that word?"

That term is the curse of former President Warren G. Harding. A man whose understanding of the English language was once described as 'an army of pompous phrases moving across the landscape in search of an idea'. In 1920, he campaigned for a 'return to normalcy' rather than literacy.'

"For a better reason, it's not normal and definitely not 'normalcy'. Words ending in the letters N-T are given the suffix C-Y. These examples should clear up any confusion for you; resilient becomes resiliency, pregnant becomes pregnancy, and agent becomes agency.

If a word ends with the letters A-L, the suffix that follows becomes I-T-Y.

Functional becomes functionality, formal becomes formality, confidential becomes confidentiality, and of course therefore normal becomes normality. This is the rule without exception if you are speaking correctly. You wouldn't say Formal-cy, functional-cy, or confidential-cy would you?"

Then don't use incorrect, substandard English with me; have some respect for the language."

"Sorry," the student replied.

"That's OK, it's a common mistake, thanks to politicians, mainstream media, and other illiterates. It's not like you said "irregardless" or some horrible malapropism like that."

"You at the back, you made a face, and you don't want to accept that truth? You can't just take the first part of 'Irregular' and add it to the word 'regardless' and pretend you are speaking English to me. Because the "I-R" in irregular or irresponsible means 'not,' as in 'not regular' or 'not responsible,' changing the meaning from 'as regardless' to 'as not regardless' makes no sense. If you are going to carry things that far, you might as well refer to a female dog as a 'Biotch' and spell it that way with an 'O' inserted, expecting full marks in an essay.

If you want a better example, there is not now, nor shall there ever be, any 'normalcy' in this fine institution, and hopefully there never will be.

If you need further clarification, normality is always the only choice. Just imagine a scenario where there is an outlier to be dealt with; is it an abnormality or an ab-normalcy? If you have the sense to realize there is no such word for the exception, then the same holds true in reverse. Normality is the correct word choice every time. The word "Normalcy' is an abomination that will leave you speaking abnormally. There is no *fur* in familiar! Are some of you familiar with people that claim they are *FUR*-miliar? Not with pronunciation, I'd argue, and the word nuclear is not pronounced nuke-u-lar. Remember to spell it with the word 'clear' in it unless you want your grades nuked. If you use the word literally, when you mean figuratively, apparently, or deliberately; your paper will literally get a zero!

All right everyone; be on your way, and remember the only 'normal-Cee' is Vitamin C!"

As the most bemused students left smirking over his passion for language, Burr's face lit up with a wide grin.

"As I stand and breathe, It's Keith Molière coming to debate me on the purpose of life or the denial of God. Which is it?" With a sudden and deep laugh, he asked.

Molière conjured up a mischievous grin and conceded, "It's more of a philosophical debate on sophistry in media." He said with a smirk.

A chortle of laughter erupted from Professor Burr.

"I don't get paid enough for that. What can I do for you?" "Well, I am struggling with a bit of an issue," Keith said.

"Oh?"

"Yeah, you know how unsafe some of these unchipped people running around are to the community? I was wondering if you'd explain to me how they are unsafe exactly, like what kind of threat they are, as in, toward me, and why should I feel so threatened by them?"

"OK, I'm not sure you have to subscribe to the "fear thy neighbor" nonsense over people's medical decisions, especially if you're not involved, but I don't think you came all the way down here to ask me that," he softened his tone with concern.

"Now what's this all about?"

Molière loved that Mr. Burr always answered your question directly, before adding an opinion or another question. It was a subtle thing, but highly appreciated.

"Well, there is a certain pressure to get this thing put into our heads, and what troubles me is just how stiff the penalties are getting if you don't like the idea."

Mr. Burr drank in the thought before speaking.

"Well, a lot of people are happy with it, and the dubiously funded Global Health Watch is saying it can't go wrong, it looks like the government is just pushing it through."

"Yeah, but I've never heard a doctor say you *have* to get it, or you'll be a threat. That always comes from the government and that one crazy doctor they keep pushing on us."

"You mean you don't like the king of the medical snake oil salesmen?" he asked, suppressing a grin.

"Let's just say whenever he speaks, my BS detector starts ringing loudly enough to give me a headache for days. Do you really think there is a problem with avoiding the chip?"

"Well, I just wonder why you don't want one. I'm in full agreement about that weaselly doctor who keeps moving the goalposts around about safety issues and seems enormously untruthful, but is that enough to make you avoid the chip?"

"I've seen some people lose their personalities and become more docile, more obedient, more in line, and more servile. I don't like it."

Mr. Burr was a man of character and truth and never shirked that responsibility, but he moved back and to the side and then returned Keith's curious gaze.

"I'd never say anything to get you into trouble, even when you used to get into trouble, I'd tell the other professors Keith Molière couldn't do these things. I never want to see you in trouble; you understand, but you have to decide what's right for you. If you go down this road, you might be playing with your freedom, your ability to earn money, and even your life. I think it's a worthwhile battle, but if you are an old man like me, you've got your life to think about, and above all, be careful about whom you talk to.

"I was hoping to recruit you to join my opposition."

"I am leaving, I didn't get the chip because we are leaving and moving to West Hornsbridge, where you don't have to get the chip just yet. Why don't you do that?"

"Maybe I will. Thanks for giving me your thoughts."

Mr. Burr shook his hand with enthusiasm and smiled broadly. He was impossible not to like, but Keith knew his road was looking longer and his already thin options were thinning still.

Next on the list was Scott Hayes, a closet intellectual who stood under the guise of being a cynical non-participant in society despite having a decent job, a live-in girlfriend, and a cat. None of this seemed contradictory to Scott; he had extensive martial arts training but rarely needed it, as one glance at him told most to steer clear. Keith had always been amused by the myopic reaction people had to Scott. He was a loyal friend, a poet, and a deep thinker beyond his appearance. He was the one friend who would surely know where to find those in opposition to the overreaching and abusive government that painted itself as a benefactor.

Fastening his exoskeleton legs and avoiding any use of his traceable self-driving car, he sought his old pal. Changing the disk in his robotic leg exterior, he noticed one of the larger two-way monitors located all over the city was showing more brain augmentation commercials, striking fear into the population about how non-chipped people would somehow end democracy. Keith's thoughts were conflicted; he had no desire to become a revolutionary, a fugitive, a wanted man, or even an undesirable. He had no wish to live in the Egress and had grown very accustomed to life at home. He had his vitamin dispenser, his music creator, his exercise suit to stimulate his muscles as he slept, and a girl who loved him. How would he survive out in the world without antibiotics, sleep-regulating lighting, or friends who believed his ideas about the dangers of the chip?

In his younger days, he would have led a charge against this outrageous autonomy, but he had become more accepting of change, and the idea of fitting in no longer felt like selling out and staying on the right side of the law had allowed him so much less strife that he felt pushed into this role of dissenter because the laws were growing more absurd by the day and no one felt safe resisting them even mildly. Mulling through these thoughts, he spotted Scott's place and removed and folded up his exoskeleton legs. He knocked, and Scott's girlfriend, Wanda, came to the door.

"Oh, Keith, I'll get Scott." She said.

Scott came to the door with his long blond hair tied back under a bandanna and held back a laugh.

"How ya doing?"

"Good, for the most part, but I've got some crumbs in my coffee." Keith said.

"Come in."

"I've got this chip, and it's setting off alarms wherever I go, but it got jolted loose, yet I still have the memory boost, but the part that's gone is the emotion suppressor."

"Emotion suppressor?"

"Yep, it neuters you to make you more law-abiding and less questioning of the powers that be. No joke. That is why they want to ensure that everyone receives it.

Scott looked worried for a moment, which was concerning because Scott was seldom worried about anything, but then he steeled himself before replying.

"So Wanda too?"

"If she has one, then I'm afraid so."

"OK, then I'll give you a number; ask around, then go find "Tiny Terry"; he's a big Mexican dude, you can't miss him."

"Thanks."

With that, Molière had to cross-link several numbers and addresses to finally get a hold of Terry, which led to an invitation to a "secret" rally.

There was a statue of a statesman who fought unsuccessfully to reinstate free speech after the MDM governing board had been established. The misinformation, disinformation, and malinformation board had been appointed to impose penalties on anyone who questioned the party in power under the pretense that they were regulating lies, all except their own. It was a gossip censorship committee or rumor punishment body that claimed anyone who disagreed with them was somehow dangerous. Once again, tyranny disguised itself as a democracy under the cheap guise of "protecting" us from our freedoms.

The term malinformation was specifically crafted to mean truths that caused people to doubt the government in any way. This became illegal, which meant the same crooked party got to stay in power indefinitely. Now the biggest liars got to shape the truth, decide the truth, and punish the truth, all with one single crooked board deciding which truths it liked and which it didn't. There were a scant few in firm opposition to this despot tactic, which necessitated this new slave-maker chip. Many of these people were common folk, a ragtag collection of people who seemed the very embodiment of what others might call the fringe.

The first speaker was a woman of strong convictions and a shrill voice who doubted if the chip was even a chip and suggested it had a slow-releasing snake venom in it. The next was a female attorney who'd been chased to the Egress for taking a position against the government once too often. She had long brown hair and spoke from behind dark-framed sunglasses.

"Remember when the first chips came out? Remember when they just helped you and made your life better, when they were made by private industry? Remember when your friends came to you, all ecstatic about how much better they felt?

Remember that? What happened? The government got involved, and those creepy elite bastards found a way to play God with human beings. They made puppets out of us, and they are keeping secrets about how many of those brain-neutering chips are failing people. For each one that accelerated, there were two whose brains could not handle the increase and became vegetables. They now have secret hospitals hoping to restart them, but it never works, and if you breathe a word of it, you go missing for spreading misinformation. How can you trust anyone who claims they need to steer the truth their way? They will make us their playthings. No one can take your freedom if you don't let them. Now, I know they have drones and guns and armies and police to intimidate you, but do you know what terrifies them? It's the truth, and people's ability to speak it! They are so terrified that they established the MDM governing board, a board of fabricated truth. I don't need you to protect me from other people's lies, I need you to stay out of my decisions. They are literally trying to control your thinking with state-think, employee-think, and slave-think. Wake up, people, if they can keep wedging us against each other with gender disputes, race disputes, constant wars, and frigging chip wars, they win! Can't you see they are feeding on our fear and using it to breed hatred? If they keep us at each other's throats, they win the divide-and-conquer game. Stop getting played!

We cannot align as one people with the power to resist their bullshit! Wake up! Stand up and be strong! That's what they fear. More power to the people!"

She drew large applause, and Molière felt some dented hopes restored. Next, a few people read some weak poetry, others quoted scripture, and a few even promoted going militant. Some of these pro-militants were hinting at gun shops that looked the other way regarding regulations but seemed so ill-equipped to stand against the onslaught facing them that they could not be taken seriously. One used cult recruiting techniques to attract younger males by asking who wanted to be their true leader. Who wants to be a real man? So, at best, they could gather a group of twenty people armed with handguns and a few .22 caliber rifles that escaped the 2025 no-gun mandates. The police had microwave-emitting rifles that had been perfected to the point where they could cause a person's blood to boil at 300 yards without ever missing. Any conflict would result in an immediate no-contest. Molière doubted if this lot could plan lunch, never mind political change. He heard a few more speakers, some praising love and positive vibes, and some just wanting to repeatedly shout "whoo-oo" to the small crowd.

A woman mentioned that someone named Terry had been arrested over a social media post about free speech and that no one had heard from him since. Molière's hopes of stirring anything resembling any kind of dissent faded quickly as troubled minds spoke about paranoid ideas that were better suited to a psychiatrist's office than a political rally. Absurd themes were put forward without objection or ridicule. Helicopters with red eyes peering into bedrooms at night, listening devices in the food, and LSD in the water fountains are all examples of utter nonsense. The whole event was in danger of devolving into a picnic lunch for the insane.

There were only a handful of rational people to approach, and while he condemned the militant types, a part of him yearned to join their ranks as at least they were drawing a firm line, but sadly, they were using broken crayons. Molière was torn over which faction troubled him more: the pocket-sized side that accepted any lunatic into their fold just to increase their number, or those that humored all forms of irrationality without correction just so everyone felt heard. The spawn of a poor government could be found anywhere, even in a movement to unseat the abusers.

"I hear ya. What was all the training for? As if they can't reprogram them to chase non-chippers.

"No, no, that part is true; the guy who designed them put in a bunch of fail-safes to ensure they never accost someone who didn't commit a crime. If the robot can't detect violence or drugs or something on their rap sheet, they can't get involved, and when they were made, not having a chip wasn't a crime. Just putting it on the books as if it were a crime wasn't enough to fool the robots."

"Hahaha! What can you do?"

Molière turned to look at the attorney for approval. She took off her sunglasses but didn't look pleased. "That's pretty remarkable." She said.

"What's the matter?"

"Nothing, I just had this prosaic little thought that if things get any worse, maybe only the robots can save us."

"I'm Keith."

"I'm Karen, I know; what a cruel mother, right?"

"Maybe she just felt you were... *entitled* to that name?"

Fighting back a smile, she proclaimed, "Maybe that's why so many people address me as... 'Ms.'

"Ah, good, so, Ms. Karen, it is."

"You are incorrigible."

"Please don't sue me, Ms. Karen."

"I don't sue revolutionaries, I only sue people with jobs."

"You saw me—a white guy who doesn't smoke, drink, or use drugs and doesn't have any tattoos—and you think I chose this life. Now, I see why you have so many friends around here."

"They appreciate me on merit."

"Because you're better than them?"

"No, because they are smart in their ways. Just not law school smart."

"You looking for a fight?" she asked.

"Never with a Karen," he said. "You're a cheeky bastard, aren't you?"

"Only when I am being made into a criminal against my wishes, maybe you could recommend me a lawyer; I could pay you in banter."

"I find your brand of sarcasm mildly amusing."

"I didn't mean to be so acerbic."

"Right," she scoffed.

"My former bosses loved it," he said.

"I have some documents that might protect your job, but if they've gone after the judges the way they've gone after the doctors, it might be all for naught."

"I think I'm on my own."

"Here, you can take my email, I'll keep you in the loop if I can make any progress," she said.

"Aren't people asking you for miracles?" he asked.

"I'd be ready to start praying, but your God made me a die-hard atheist."

"Me too, but now I am worried that lawyers might have a higher percentage of atheists, and I'm not so sure I can be seen with you," he said.

"Smart ass."

"Guilty as charged, counselor"

"You've got a thing about lawyers, do you?"

"I'm coming to terms with it, you seem kind of human," he said. "Don't let it get around, I've got an image to protect."

"OK, here's my email, no billing me for reading it. Agreed?" "Blood from a stone?" she quipped.

"Glass houses?" he countered.

Molière left her grinning, but the triumph of finding a respectable ally was fleeting as she was the only one. He fought concerns that most of the intelligentsia had been too easily coerced. There were plenty of them wanting to speak out but were silenced by media censorship, making them hard to find. He was mining for diamonds but breathing in only coal.

Chapter Four

A ROBOTIC HUMANITY

Molière mulled through the small crowd looking for a kindred spirit but was unable to establish much rapport as he had difficulty getting past some clearly troubled souls desperately seeking some sort of salvation or someone to tell them everything would be OK. More speakers got up to address the crowd, boasting about the diversity of the group and how acceptance was the key to the future of humanity.

Many of these openings started with phrases like "I just want to tell everyone how beautiful you all are." As each speaker shamelessly pandered for applause and flattered the crowd on their looks and diversity, Molière contemplated that, if he'd been a psychologist, he might have called this phenomenon 'Nero's Fiddle Syndrome.' The priorities and motives seemed more like a desperate bid for personal approval than problem-solving. Trucks with armed men rounding up innocents were filling undisclosed prisons with equally diverse populations, but there were no celebrations over that. One character was sure he'd appear cool if he repeatedly introduced guest speakers as being "in the house," despite the event being held outside. For a moment, Molière wondered if he should sit among robots because he was far more purpose-focused than most among this group. He wandered a bit and was approached by one of the militants.

"New here, eh?" The towering man in fatigues asked quasi-suspiciously.

"Yep, I'm the new guy."

"So what brings you out here?"

"My boss doesn't like the way I cut my hair, so I might be looking for a new job."

"Oh, yeah, well, how do you feel about the government?"

"The same way a fly in a Petri dish feels about the guy behind the microscope."

"Well, how do we know you are not some government spook poking around?"

"Because I am honest, and I'll tell you what I don't mind saying. First, I don't want you to ask me if I want to feel like a leader, or a real man, just so you can put a 22 caliber rifle in my hand and have me drive off with three clowns in a jeep thinking we are going to free the world, only to be charged with having unacceptable views, then disappear from human eyes forever. Next, I'd wager you'll ask me some clumsy and obvious questions to determine my motives. "These are questions that a trained agent would anticipate, with ready answers to fool you," Molière said.

"Any government that messes with people's money is just a bunch of dirty thieves with manners in stylish attire," Jim said.

"I agree with you there, but mounting some pathetic and easily quashed front will not help. You don't have the resources, the strategic capabilities, or the sort of unflinching discipline of trained commandos. If you got lucky and popped some politicians, what do you think would happen? Would the rest of them abandon their goals? More likely, they'd make an example of you and drag you through the streets, doubling down on the already unbearable oppression. You need to communicate with people, educate them away from the propaganda, and vote these traitors out of office."

"Oh yeah? OK, Smarty-pants, and if we do that and the next ones just pick up where they left off, then what?" Jim asked.

"You have to find better people to vote for. Even if you could take out a leader in Hornsbridge or Volcaria, thirty other cabinet ministers are waiting to take their place. Then you'd have to go to every country and city. They'd make a martyr of him and paint you as the local crackpot who ordered a gun through the mail.

They'd ramp up the oppression once more, and you'd end up dead or in some secret prison as a sex slave to an overcharged robot in a black-market film. Try to reach people with reason and logic instead," Molière urged.

"OK, so let's say we do everything your way, which is exactly how we got here, by the way. Peaceful, reasonable methods got us into this living prison dictatorship. So we talk, and we argue, and every day the noose tightens a little until no one can even breathe. Now what, with all your logic and reasoning methods?" Jim asked.

"Talk sense to people and have them use their vote."

"And if the votes are fixed or bribed by globalists and fat money players?"

"Then admittedly, there's a big problem," Keith said.

"OK, so you understand that the government only understands violence, right? I mean, remember those riots that were violent, and everyone said they were mostly peaceful, and orders came from above to stand down? Remember the peaceful protests, and what happened to them? They went after their money like crooks and froze their bloody bank accounts. So which was better? The peaceful way where you go broke, or the one with the looting and burning where you profit, and the law gets neutered? Call it a stiff lesson learned."

Molière looked hard at the man and asked, "Is that what you want? Shall we start the looting season early and get arrested at the first doorstep? They can track people by their brainwaves now, you won't get anywhere."

The politicized weekend warrior lifted his cap and rubbed a hand through his dark wavy hair.

"So why not just sit on the sidelines and let it all happen until we are all foot servants to our masters at Parliament?"

"Reason has prevailed before, and empires always fall. I don't have every answer, but I've seen and been through enough suicide missions to recognize the envelope when presented with it, and yours has been stamped and sealed with a suicide guarantee. No, thanks," Molière said.

"Well, whatever we do, we are going to have to do something."

"I know, and I am sorry for sounding so judgmental I just think this is going to require some higher-level thinking, and we need the best plan in history. Yelling and waving pea shooters at the powerful will only bring suffering. I wish I had a better answer."

"My name is Jim." With an outstretched arm, the behemothic rebel said.

"Keith."

"There's a place here; you can crash if you feel like it, you don't have to join anybody's cause or anything. It's just a lean-to, but it's off the radar."

Keith accepted the offer. He needed rest and didn't trust going home. His doctor was gone, his job was gone, his friends had turned hostile, and everyone with a chip seemed out to get him.

He pulled up in a flat enough corner and slept with his knapsack under his head.

He awoke the next morning beyond exhausted, feeling almost drunk with fatigue, and not quite himself. As the cobwebs cleared, he gathered himself and his belongings, but his knapsack felt weightless. He clutched it in a panic, and the view confirmed what he already knew. His exoskeleton leg set was gone. Before he could chastise himself for his carelessness, he saw beyond his lean-to, just halfway down a nearby hill, another of the militants wearing his exoskeleton legs and trying to learn how to work them. A boiling rage welled up within him, but he had to think clearly, for if the thief ran away in them, they'd be gone forever. He slowly walked a bit closer, suppressing the fire in his blood that rushed through his veins like lava through a tributary. He could feel the skin on his face overheating. Molière sized up the situation carefully, for when dealing with an uninvited foe with no moral compass, Heisenberg's principle of uncertainty applied. He could flee, fight, or enlist the help of his friends to improve his chances.

Molière recognized that the combination of ego and hostility often disguised the suppression of guilt and led to monkey-level behavior in group dynamics. Molière had to offer his opponent a chance to gain status within his group. He had to appease his ego and offer him a low-risk, high-reward option to impress his friends and raise his standing among his peers without making it obvious. If he were careless, under the dark clouds looming, fate might easily slam his window of life shut, as he was unarmed, ill-equipped for a chase, outnumbered, and alone. The culprit in question had little concern over being discovered and was seen openly joking about his new property with a few accomplices. The man had unkempt blond hair and blue eyes. Had he been a little cleaner cut, he could have passed for a relative of Keith's, but he was smugly gloating and altogether self-impressed. Molière knew that if he didn't lure him into a fight, he'd never see those powerful legs again.

"You should be careful with those. If you kick someone with them, they are going to the hospital, and with the new ban on nanobot surgery, they'd be in a real jam."

Keith said, in an almost lighthearted tone, that he was trying to fuel his opponent's courage.

"Oh, hey, look! It's sleepyhead! Hell, we thought you'd never snap out of it. We're all early risers here; we don't sleep all day like some. That's the sign of an undisciplined mind."

The man purposefully exaggerated his taunting sneer as his eyes glowed with the perverted assurance of a squirrel hunter carrying an automatic weapon.

"So if these power legs are so badass in a fight, I guess you better not come too close, unless you want to get your ass kicked, that is."

He said so with the same smarmy air a crooked cop has after he's just kicked in your tail light and handed you a ticket.

Adrenaline was shooting through Keith like water from a fire hose. He felt like a mere vehicle for some unseen force far beyond his limited human strength. It felt as though some ancient warrior from a lost time was piloting his body from another realm.

He'd wanted things before in his life, riches, beautiful women, an unattainable perfect shape to his body, but he'd never known a want like this before. *Was it the blasted chip?* He didn't know, but he was mad to fight, mad like an insecure lover discovering infidelity, mad like a starving animal that hadn't eaten in days. Then he saw the overconfident glint in his opponent's eyes, and all that had been taken from him came brewing to the surface. His job, his love, his estranged family, and his friends—all of this had been orchestrated by a corrupt government out to divide people. This was the last thing anyone would take from him without answering for it.

The two men squared off, and Molière couldn't remember being this charged up for a fight, and his new memory verified that.

"C'mon thief." Keith urged.

His opponent swung first, but finally, Molière's adrenaline found its awaited outlet. He used his right hand to deliver a palm strike to the blond man's bicep and grabbed hold of it, then gripped the thief's wrist with his left hand instantly. Keith forced the bicep upward with his right while turning the man's wrist downward into a crank lever with his left. He twisted his arm in a full revolution, causing the man to attempt a jump with his legs forward in a reverse somersault to avoid having his arm broken. Normally, a flexible human would have a small chance to twist out of this, but it would require absurdly quick reflexes. The weight of the robot legs prevented the new owner from somersaulting over himself, which meant the arm snapped due to the torque at the elbow. It gave out a loud "pop" that was followed by a louder, piercing scream.

Historically, Molière would have let it go at that, as the fight was decided a moment after it started, but there was all this unexplained rage as he questioned his opponent on the whys and wherefores of stealing. Keith repeatedly asked why while punching his face at full strength before, during, and after each response. The thief shrieked "Alriiiight!" in vain before falling silent. Keith left his opponent badly bloodied and pried his exoskeleton legs from the thief's barely responsive body.

It was all over in less than thirty seconds, and the thief's friends had been slow to react beyond staring with several mouths agape. Within a few seconds, however, anger replaced their collective shock.

The first of the two had mid-tone skin and a goatee and jutted his jaw forward.

"He was just trying them on to check them out. He was going to give them back! You didn't have to go all ape shit on him like that."

His friend with a backward hat glanced around, taking note that Molière was alone.

"You're lucky you got there first, he would have beaten you into a coma if you gave him half a chance."

"They aren't for fighting; I just told him that, so he wouldn't run away, he looked like he might be the type, then I'd have never gotten them back."

"So you think you're king shit because you got a pair of robot pants? Maybe we could put them to better use than you. Ever think of that?" The beta male with the straggly hair and backward hat jeered.

Molière wasn't impressed by this authentic example of second-hand bravado. Typically, the agitator shows aggression but not quite enough to instigate the fight, yet hopes one of his friends will pick up the slack. The group becomes braver again as the voices serve to remind all that strength lies in numbers.

"Well, you can have them for free if you like," Molière said.

This seemed to confuse them for a moment, as they just stared back at him.

"There is just one thing you have to do first," he instructed.

The silence hung in the air a moment before he added with a sudden chill in his voice,

"Come and *take* them from me."

There was just enough malice in Keith's voice and unsated bloodlust in his eyes, that no one answered.

Jim's long shadow had emerged from the distance and unwittingly reminded everyone they'd have to punch upward to beat him.

"We don't want any kleptomaniacs or psychos in our group. You guys hit the road."

He spoke quietly and then suddenly roared so loudly that his voice cracked, but no one laughed.

"You're not welcome here!" he screeched.

The thieves swore a lot but left begrudgingly. Molière thanked Jim for his better late-than-never, arrival.

Jim asked, "How'd you do that guy in so quick?"

"I studied some martial arts back in the day, but it was in a language I couldn't understand. I think I missed a lot, but it just sort of all came back at once, I was lucky."

"And here I was thinking; we got stuck with a shrinking violet. You're a damned skull cracker."

Molière replied with a smile. "Aw, relax, I'm a pacifist."

Jim smirked sarcastically, "Yeah, with the emphasis on FIST!"

Molière knew this would not be the place for him to find people who could affect change. They were emotionally charged but scattered in their approach, as though they were trying to solve a Rubik's cube, with hammers and wet naps. For all the fears these people had long harbored over robots and the threat they might pose to society, most never suspected the human component of doing precisely the same thing. A robot was a tool, like a gun, a nuclear warhead, or a self-driving car. These automatons didn't get jealous or angry; they didn't plot to unseat anyone or make decisions based on vanity or insecurity. If those in charge had strong ethics, there was no problem; if not, disaster. Molière felt people should always look more closely at the emotional makeup of leaders who spend most of their time dancing around questions and pandering to crowds before doubting a functional tool. He pondered what little difference it made if elected officials abused the public with swords, muskets, police batons, rubber bullets, prison sentences, or robots, given the result remained unchanged throughout history. More rethinking was needed to ameliorate all these problems, and he didn't have time to sort out where all that overwhelming rage had come from, but in the quieter moments, it weighed heavily on his mind.

Chapter Five

WHAT PRICE EMOTION

Molière had some lofty notions about finding patriotic scholars within the fringe to help root out the corruption of the government and its long, crooked arm of media propaganda. The aligned and perpetually pro-government media outlets now refer to themselves as "store-bought media" as a sarcastic dig at those who doubt the veracity and integrity of their straight-faced court jester news anchors. Unlike a prostitute who could barely conceal a grin when presented with a cash envelope, the media resembled the deluded concubine who was too proud to accept the fee face to face, revealing the cash register in her eyes. It's better to leave it on the table to avoid any feelings of shame or guilt when confronted with the facts.

In terms of business, the lowest prostitute was a far more honorable being than any employed in the "store-bought" media. Assuming the prostitute is not a thief, their policy is to honor the agreement: service in exchange for funds. Presumably, if not someone working against their will, both parties exchange their part of the deal, forming a tacit contract where both sides leave having met their desired goal. The "seduce and betray" tactic taught in journalism was rarely practiced among the waves of emerging new prostitutes. It wasn't as though people in the media weren't confounded by the same corrupt leaders and global elites pulling their strings and silencing them too, but the finished product was as nauseating as watching a 12-year-old girl put herself on the market. From the unemployable, who elected to keep their brains unaltered at the sacrifice of their income, to those who could not find work, scores of desperate people lowered themselves to do almost anything for funds. With so much competition, the prices dropped to mere crumbs for services, and Molière wondered if this wasn't at least partly the point of driving people into the egress. If they are too poor to eat, what uses might they provide? The establishment had its dark secrets hidden behind the curtain, and with what they spent on military equipment and media bribes, they could have fed the entire nation many times over. If they had enough firepower to blow up the world many times over, why then would they need more bankrupting deficits over new weaponry? Big business CEOs with pollution-spewing factories explain that the real carbon issues are from cows, humans, and farms, while they destroy the ozone and tell us it's from cows that have been here for centuries. Police shooting at striking farmers for being pollutants was like executing vegans over meat consumption. Molière was pro-environment, but not for using it as a weapon against innocent farmers and exporters. It was the media's tolerance of those issues that made people stop watching. At one point, he saw no difference between the media and prostitutes, but now he felt the legacy media was the lower of the two by far. He never used the word "whore," save for when describing news anchors. As more and more people like Keith turned to podcasts for the truth, the media turned to their tax-funded corrupt leaders to smear the podcast hosts, but it always backfired.

Keith's palm device alerted him that Jacqueline had left him a message during their fight over his exoskeleton legs.

"Keith, it's me, I've thought this over from every possible angle, and I just can't go on like this anymore. You live in this austere, moderately sized unit that is tailored more toward a full-time group hobby of listening to music than being truly spacious enough to raise kids. Every time someone asks me out, I have to question my loyalty to you. I see people who are going places, and you treat your career like it's an afterthought. I think you are making a series of wrong turns in your life, and now you are questioning the chip!

What's wrong with you? You can't be so naive! If I tell you someone asked me out at work, all you say is that you trust me. You don't even get jealous. I know I said I don't like the jealous type, but if you don't get at least somewhat jealous, it means you don't care. If you want to end up as one of those criminals roaming the earth with no chip in his head to help him get ahead, then I just can't be your chip substitute. You'll find your way in the world; I can't believe I wasted three years with you! I can't be involved with you; I can't know you. You are on your own. Good luck; you'll need it. Don't call back, not even from jail. I'm done."

He understood her words but was beyond perplexed about how she could turn away so emphatically from his decision to preserve his mind. As much as he wanted to try to reason with her, he could always recognize a lost cause, and whatever magic had been between them up until last week had completely vanished.

None of those idiots at her work had detachable robot legs, and they'd be too tired for sex due to all the time they spent sucking up to their bosses. He laughed to himself, partly because the thought was childish, but also because it was pointless to direct his thoughts toward an ended relationship that offered no new hope. Had he missed all the dormant warning signs of a doomed relationship? Shouldn't he have known better? The priority now was to focus on the current mounting dilemmas in all directions. He needed to recruit people who could help undo media-instituted brainwashing and the constant passing of bills and laws that made all but breathing a crime. Friends were dwindling and loyalties were rapidly shifting toward black-and-white thinking. He wondered if the nuanced conversation would be the next illegal thing. As he wandered down the hill, he saw the lawyer speaking to a small group, and it looked like a passionate conversation. Karen was wearing a beige overcoat that did a poor job concealing her attractive body shape; there were superimposed images of people running from the police on each of her black leggings. How was she not in jail yet? Perhaps an infiltrator? Had the oppressive flavor of the times reached that level of paranoia already? He approached just to listen.

"So if you don't want to be a complicit puppet of the empire, maybe you just need to say no to your chip and figure things out with the brain God gave you. I mean, if these chips make you so smart, how come no one is noticing government abuses and the fact that it's making everyone a pauper? They are supposed to work for us, not make new laws every day to enslave us to them," Karen concluded.

A man with prematurely white hair who clearly thought he was superior to others challenged her. His hair wasn't just white, but it shone almost as though it had a tinge of silver that reflected the surrounding light.

"So you're one of these people who can't appreciate all the benefits of the chip, huh? If so, I presume you don't appreciate how the government keeps us safe from insurrections and people who freak out for no apparent reason because they forgot to take their prescriptions that day."

"There is a potential criminal in every one of us, and anyone could have an emotional outburst that hurts the feelings of others, and that's unacceptable. The government recognizes this, and they are saving us from some loser hopped up on drugs attacking someone because he had a bad childhood."

Molière butted in, "So the solution is to drug everyone with a neutering brain chip instead?"

Karen answered, "It's OK, really, I've got this. When has curing people with psychiatric disorders included curing healthy people who are not affected? When has that ever happened?"

"It has other benefits, it makes us super versions of ourselves and keeps people from wanting to fight with others. It keeps them from overthrowing the government and makes them far more tolerable to deal with," the white-haired man replied.

"It makes them good worker ants and nothing more. Serve the queen and let her live a great life while you crawl buried in the sand."

Her adversary shook his head, frowning.

"You are all a bunch of science deniers. The science has been proven! Our brains are not enough; we are flawed human beings let's get rid of all the emotional clutter and reach our potential!"

Karen immediately asked him, "What if we aren't ready? What if the chip does the equivalent of rusting over five years, and then your brain is accustomed to never producing an independent thought, suddenly leaving you a vegetable?"

The white-haired young man looked at Karen studiously for a moment with an unsavory gaze before responding.

"Well, that's an interesting and different perspective, but this is no place for such an intriguing discussion. Why don't we go somewhere for dinner, so we can discuss things in more detail?"

"Careful Karen, the last two women he used that eye-roller of a line on were never seen again because they wouldn't accept his implanted emotion blockers, but it looks like he needs some hormone blockers instead," Keith jeered.

Despite realizing the cheap come-on, Karen sneered and preferred the absurdity of Keith's jab.

"Sorry, I only dine with the oppressed, not the oppressors," she replied.

The man gave her a disgruntled look and walked away. "Sorry about that, I just have no use for phonies," Keith said.

"And here I thought the only people you didn't like were lawyers."

"I've been talking to you for ten seconds now, that'll be four thousand dollars."

"And what about those of us who take up unpopular causes for free? Smart-ass."

"Well, if I were the guy with the white hair, I suppose I'd offer you a free massage and a spiked drink."

"He bothered you that much?"

"Maybe he symbolized the amount of B.S. floating in the river I've been forced to swim in lately, and it caused me to project a little."

"Or some other reason?" She asked, raising an. eyebrow. "Like what?"

"We were starting to have a nice conversation yesterday, and you ran off like a scared rabbit. Was it something I said, or do I make you uncomfortable?"

"I thought you were charming and very decent, but I have a thing about lawyers. I was conflicted, and I had to sort it out."

"And now?" she asked.

"Such a lawyer, are you going to ask to read my private journal too?"

"I do ask a lot of questions, don't I?"

"I haven't heard about the prize winner yet." "You wouldn't like me that way," she said coolly.

"Aah, you can speak for me by reading my mind. A law school trick?"

Karen put out her hands as if holding two imaginary suitcases with a courageous smile on her face.

"My kid died in a fire, so if you want a wife with lots of baggage, here she is."

"I'm sorry, that's terrible... but who is the scared rabbit now?"

"Both of us?" she asked coyly.

They walked in silence together for some distance and turned to each other beneath the statue; as they motioned closer to each other's faces, the unnerving sound of approaching police sirens killed the moment.

Police with microwave-emitting rifles rounded up people and put them in trucks as Keith and Karen ran and fell into some tall grass.

"We can't stay here."

"No, it'll be OK; the robots won't help them if we didn't actually do anything wrong."

They waited in silence as the trucks departed and then until darkness fell.

Once it was safe, the nagging questions over how one becomes an involuntary criminal and faces life-altering consequences continued simply because a government wanted to maintain a specious image like a newly constructed house with an elongated driveway, finely trimmed lawn, and glowing welcome sign. Meanwhile, it housed bloodthirsty cultists and trustworthy-looking human traffickers in three-piece suits within its walls. The illusion that some still believed weighed heavily on both of their minds.

"Why don't they just reprogram the robots to come and get us? If the regular cops don't like it because they are used to sending them, why not just reprogram them?" He asked. Keith valued the fact that Karen always listened intently and thought carefully before speaking.

"The guy who designed the ones for the police was some sort of genius, and he hardwired them to only pursue certain types of offenders. Murderers, rapists, bank robbers, and the like. No traffic tickets, thought crimes, or medical procedure opt-outs would qualify. So the police bots won't lift a finger against those actions because they don't qualify as crimes in terms of their programming. If anyone tampers with the programming, a nasty cloud of foul-smelling mist fills the room and stays there for weeks while the robot shuts down forever. There's no danger of a crook doing that because the robot will subdue them long before any such move can take place. There is also a code to ensure police robots never oppose each other. Maybe the only thing keeping us free right now has been the vision of their designer. I mean, they can't be brainwashed by the media like humans, and if they see police apprehending an innocent, they would turn on the officers, so they have to leave them issuing traffic tickets while they look for people like us." she said.

"So the impartiality and supposedly inferior ethics of the robots might be all that keeps us from ending up in a hidden prison without a trial? What is the worth of having all these emotions that let us get manipulated, intimidated, coerced, and convinced of deceptions so obvious a child should be able to see through them? Maybe we'd be better off being robots. That's where we are headed as they give us these disguised lobotomies."

"The robots are fine, they don't fall for any BS from the government. They won't even follow orders if they smell a rat, they execute their plans with precision and cold logic, getting things right more than we ever will. I used to worry they would replace us, now we're counting on them."

"If only they could have been programmed to take out an overreaching government instead of the cops who are being misused by them. I'd love to see that play out."

Suddenly she turned and looked at Keith with probing yet understanding eyes.

"How did you get here?" She asked.

"You're getting that lawyer's look again."

Holding back a grin, she snapped, "Just answer the question!"

"I am a fairly mild person, largely disinterested in participating in anything revolutionary, unlawful, or even subversive. I just wanted to live out my days with my girlfriend and hopefully design some music software that exceeds what we're limited to today."

"Like what?"

"Well, I like really old music that came decades ago; old-school jazz, hard rock, and ragtime piano. I love the blending we can do by taking the work of a particular group, say "The Belt Spinners," and changing up their influences by mixing songs by people who came around long after them. That's fine, but I'd like to make software that lets you put actual members of different groups and swap them out with each other, now that would be cool, and it shouldn't be that hard to do once the licensing crap is out of the way," he said.

"Too bad you didn't know a good lawyer to help you navigate those waters."

"I'm screwed then," he smiled.

"Look, my boy died in a fire, and I had a crap lawyer who ended up working for the same government I was suing right after my case. I was so infuriated that I became one, determined to never get hosed again. Now look at me, but something is going on with you, I can feel it. What's going on?"

"My chip dislodged, and I kept the memory enhancement but lost the emotion blockers. I have growing concerns that my emotions have somehow amplified exponentially and that I might get entirely overwhelmed by them."

"So you are going through menopause?" She joked, but saw instantly that it wasn't funny to him despite his attempt to meet her humor.

"I call it mental pause."

"Well, I wouldn't worry," she said consolingly, most men repress their feelings to the point of debilitation; it might be nice to be around one who can sort out his depths with understanding and clarity."

"This isn't just the old argument about how men undervalue feelings and women overvalue them, I am having difficulty maintaining my normal behavior, and it's getting worse. I brutalized a thief. My former girlfriend thought my lack of envy was an issue, and jealousy is bad on the inside and for others. I don't enjoy it at all. That guy did nothing wrong, but I felt really hostile toward him. It's like trying to stop a runaway train with a gauze bandage. I am getting these urges that are unbearable and impossible to contain. I think I am losing it."

"Urges, huh? I thought you'd never ask." "Only because of the cops on your legs."

Locking elbows with him, she said, "I've handled cases like this, sometimes the chip doesn't bind properly and people start losing their minds. The key difference is that it is immediate. The media is covering it up, and the doctors get fired if they mention it, but there are scores of failed chip placement operations. People become mentally unfit in pretty extreme ways, but if you hold on to the memory enhancement, then you are fine. What you are going through, is a result of the short time that it was functioning correctly and muted your emotions in a soft, comforting way, It got jolted loose, and you are experiencing the uptick in a jarring way. Your emotions will feel amplified for a while, like equipping a baby with adult thinking before it's ready. There will be an adjustment period, so you'll be playing catch up for a while, it's nothing to worry about, honest."

"Nothing but setting off every government monitor in the city, and avoiding the heat for the rest of my life. The reality is that all the people like us who spoke out against these despot clowns act like concerned grandparents as they silence, penalize, and kidnap. All the while smiling for the cameras and telling us it's for our protection," he said.

"Well, it might be worse than that, If they go to an invisible prison we can't see, and people die there, that's a form of execution. The stories are out there, but no media would ever dare approach them due to the media governance board."

She looked into his blue eyes, and as her cool demeanor dropped, she asked,

"Where are we going to sleep tonight?"

"Under the stars?"

"No, I've got a second place, It's in my son's name for tax reasons, and so my assets don't show up if someone's looking to counter-sue me for any reason."

"You should be careful with strangers, you know."

"There's a couch," she muttered.

"I am going to have to check with my lawyer first."

"Given our respective statuses, I think I am your lawyer." I can only pay you in weak puns and bad jokes."

"You can pay me with sex."

"Do I have to sign anything?"

"That all depends on your jokes."

"OK, how's this one? You should never make fun of mental illness; it's OK to say that because I am a paranoid schizophrenic. "However, I've never been diagnosed because I don't trust psychiatrists."

"I think I like you more because of your honesty," she paused before adding, "and your blue eyes."

"I told you my jokes were bad."

They spent an hour walking, and as she prepared the couch for him, they embraced but were so fatigued they fell asleep on the couch, interlocked in each other's arms, despite the presence of a vacant double bed in the next room.

Chapter Six

EXTREMIST TIL PROVEN INNOCENT

Karen awoke to the sound of news anchors chortling at the emotional meltdowns of their opponents over some new wrinkle in the endless culture war. "They are like school children making fun of each other and calling it news. I'm turning it to the wall, so I don't have to look at them. We can hear the latest cases of those being charged with misinformation. They're trying to suppress a case where a man suffered seizures after his chip was implanted, but he's been making noise about it," she said.

Anything about bribing voters? Keith asked.

An image revealed an aging man as a voice announced the suicide of Edward Bukowski over his epilepsy. Karen, looking shaken, shouted at the monitor.

"He never even had epilepsy!"

Keith knew instinctively that he'd best speak with her before her natural inclination to correct an injustice led to her becoming imprisoned.

Trueborn's 'Human First' government had done a formidable job of censoring the academic portion of society. Using the "Carrot and Stick" method of coercion and the threat of job loss after years of university training was more than most could contend with. No one expected seasoned professionals to be so easily cowed and silenced but most yielded without so much as a whimper. The few with enough integrity to dissent were quickly discredited, smeared, fined, and increasingly jailed. The media fed the population a masquerade of Draconian rule in democracy's clothing. They did so with repeated assurances and barrages of hit pieces on any who questioned them. The latest propaganda from the news was that there was no opposing silent majority.

Karen looked frozen with disgust but proclaimed, "I'm going to debate them in Parliament even if it means only a portion of what I say will be broadcast."

"Are you trying to get sent to prison? I worship free speech, but it's not exactly free anymore, it comes with punitive measures now, such as prison sentences remember?"

"How will things get any better if our collective silence only gives them more power to abuse?"

"One more silenced lawyer in an off-the-books prison won't help anyone."

"I cannot just stand by without responding to this," Karen said.

"You can't just walk into Parliament and spew off; you need certain credentials to speak there, and even if you could speak the whole truth, they'll just claim you are spreading misinformation; that's what they do, and then you go to jail for telling the truth. They dust off their hands and put the term 'conspiracy theorist' under your prisoner number," he pointed out.

"At least there will be some truth spoken in Parliament for once."

'You will be discredited with that empty smear of misinformation; you know better than this."

"If they attempt to hide behind their favorite knee-jerk accusations of conspiracy theorists or spreaders of misinformation, I'll question the effectiveness of going down to that well too often. I'll illustrate that by contaminating the public with the tainted water of insults, smears, and truth dodging. I will label those who duck under the abusive mother's skirt, calling innocent truth-tellers domestic terrorists, as the capricious, misinforming spin doctors of government. It's a high-school level of gossip smearing, and now they've added prison terms for being on the wrong side of their twisted narratives. It isn't misinformation, as they fear; it is the truth. They think if they keep muddying up the meaning of truth as in some shell and nut game, they can pretend the truth is misinformation and vice versa, and they always get to be right because they control the men with the guns and those with the microphones. It's gone too far; I am going to call them out on their bullshit." she insisted.

"And then what happens when they start claiming you have 19 cats under your tinfoil hat and hear voices?"

"There are people who can see through their cheaply manufactured smokescreen; it's just a cloak they use the way the mob used to collect protection money to protect the public from those very same mob members.

It's a parallel abuse of power and manipulation. I am not some recluse with articles posted to my walls and windows linking whacked-out ideas, with circles and arrows mapping out patterns that don't exist. I don't think flying saucers stole my fridge or that a talking snake whispered to Adam and Eve. I am grounded, educated, and accomplished, I am not a medicated soapbox savant. People will recognize the difference."

"You still need credentials to speak in Parliament."

"That's what I like about you; you have no idea who I am. I served as the D.A. and had a 97% conviction rate while serving the government. They think I am on leave because of my son. I will act as their leader to defend them. I've done it before, and then I'll mildly side with their accusers, leaving them to scramble for any semblance of damage control."

"They'll bury you so deep, even earthworms won't find you." "I have an escape plan," Karen said unperturbed.

"Fine, but at least get the property declared as a land trust before they show up at the front door."

"How do you know about such things? You're not a lawyer."
"Guilty by association."

Karen left and executed her plan to perfection, humiliating the party leaders who were unaccustomed to it. After being called capricious purveyors of misinformation a few times, the president motioned for security to take her away.

They were unaware she'd called for a police robot escort to see her off the site until they drew their weapons on the human security guards. The police robots that were assigned to Parliament spoke politely but were designed to produce instantaneous results.

"Stand down or die!" One robot exhorted as the others aggressively crouched with weapons drawn so fast that no human had time to react.

No military personnel could respond without being fired upon first, as they would be seen as the aggressors against a high-ranking official. Robot security in federal buildings was lethal and precise to the millisecond. Karen was granted safe passage out with two metallic polymer escorts. The remaining automatons held the position until she was long gone. This was a sobering bucket of ice water splashed on the president and his cronies, who were, until this moment, shamelessly drunk on power.

Members of the Secret Service and state security were armed with microwave-emitting rifles, which were never made available to the public due to their lethality. They could boil blood, melt flesh, or just give a terrifically hot scare to any human offender. One never knew if they would receive a temporary injury or a permanent one that might result in death. It was so powerful that the government had been able to commit crimes against its people without the press's interference. Not even the top-level Secret Service agents wanted to experience being cooked alive, let alone those who doubted their leader. The conflict between a dutiful counterattack versus being melted alive danced across the eyes of every agent, but the human protectors of Parliament were at a loss to contend with the robots' superior speed, strength, and perfect aim. They had never turned on anyone before in history, due to their sophisticated programming. The only caveat being, that robots could never be reprogrammed after what was called the perfect design. Now the armed guards looked defeated and hesitant. Their weapons did not affect the polymer that comprised a high-functioning military-grade bot. No one ever dreamed there could be a situation where the authorities were pitted against their police robots, as they'd been tested thousands of times. The only scenario not programmed into them was widespread government corruption. Prior governments that respected the constitution were content that bots would not participate in anything against the law. The freedom of dissenting views was now a mere relic from the past, as crooked bills had made their way into law. Judges could be "shopped for," as most made little secret of their voting preferences until cliques formed and reshaped legal precedent. The laws had become prejudicial, hostile to the public, and politically punitive. All this gave a broken shape to the social fabric of society as the store-bought media acted as both coach and cheerleader to promote domestic hatred over free voting choices. Keeping people at odds over race, gender, and medical status had no impact on impartial AI. Nor did convincing people that everyone needed more government protection from their neighbors and friends, resulting in punitive laws for all but those in power.

Leaders were so busy smearing their opponents as terrorists and threats to democracy, that they never worried about the silent robots for a moment, as they were unobtrusive and law-abiding in every way.

Just as the population slept on watch-dogging an evil leader with honeyed words and shallow charm, those in power slept on robots being impervious to manipulation. Karen felt a wondrous sense of irony as agents swarmed nearby but kept a safe distance. The agents were powerless to stop the robot police from escorting her to the nearest public two-way monitor.

"Are you tired of being played and having the government decide your job status? Or your finances? Your ability to feed yourself. Being coerced, blackmailed, bribed, and lied to?

Well, there is an easy answer if you want to call out your local politician to demand your freedom or their resignation. All anyone needs to do is find a nearby police robot, and they will protect you under the federal constitution they are all in service to. Do you like having your language stolen from you, one word at a time? All the language of protest is now illegal. You can't say mother or father or corrupt or crooked or lame or anything. The key to silencing people is to steal their words. The next time someone tells you what you should be saying, tell them they aren't qualified to decide your words for you, and if they are in the dictionary, you are free to use any of them! That's why we learned them in the first place! The checklist for a tyrannical government includes speech control, so you can't criticize them while they abuse you. The tell-tale sign is mischaracterizing mere gossip and lawful speech as disinformation and pretending it's a threat to us or to democracy when it is the very standard required of any free society. It's only a threat to their iron grip over people. The second is rounding up people who disagree with the government and monitoring them, pretending they are criminals or terrorists or anti-government. We are not anti-government we are anti-BAD Government! Let's make that distinction!

Go tell off some of these sleazy political leaders, as you are protected and your right to disagree is the very nature of democracy. Let them cry disinformation all they like; if they are the ones promoting their own darker brand of disinformation; one that would have you believe your right to speak out is illegal, then that is the disinformation. They can be charged with it according to their perverted laws. Long live the constitution! Long live your right to speak out no matter what you believe, as that is the law of this land!"

"Let no one ever again label an unpopular viewpoint, or a question, as a subversive act." Demand your freedom now!"

The crowd cheered as she beamed across the monitors with warmth, hope, and elation. A Secret Service agent in a dark blue suit and eye shades propped himself up in a clock tower. He was equipped with an old-school sniper's rifle and focused his sight on Karen, with a tracer light moving up her arm, as he suddenly went into spasmodic convulsions and flung the rifle from his hands as desperately as he could manage, and shrieked in agony as a police robot discharged its weapon with deadly precision. The agent collapsed in an unsightly mass of tissue and bone protruding from beneath his cap and dark glasses, his exterior partially blackened and burned. The sight jarred the surrounding agents because they could remember how President Trueborn decided the settings feature on the rifles should be removed, so the intimidation factor would be maximized by having only the kill option. This was to serve as a potent deterrent against any future insurrection. The former prime minister turned president was a terrible coward deep down and loved hiding behind law enforcement, the military, and robots.

The sniper had a spotter who looked readily prepared for further combat, but after seeing his accomplice charred and half melted into a contorted mess of fried flesh, the steel in his eyes suddenly softened to surrender and fear. With the sniper's demise, the robots began assailing and arresting Secret Service agents everywhere, as they were armed and seen as a threat, and many had been closely associated with the would-be sniper. These robot-driven mass arrests left the Parliament largely undefended, particularly from criticism. To save budget money, there were fewer police and secret services, as the robots did so many of their tasks in a superior manner. The leaders were beyond furious and strained to conceal their canine teeth while maintaining their polite and friendly expressions on camera. Meanwhile, as the rulers perpetuated a pantomime of democracy, they primed themselves to lash out against the public.

Chapter Seven

IMPARTIAL LOYALTIES

Karen rushed through the door. "Did you see? Turn on the monitor. People are going to go to Parliament and protest like mad, I bet. This could be it for the 'Human First' party."

"I watched on my palm device, but I didn't see any protesters. I saw nothing other than usual." Keith admitted.

"Oh, they probably switched the feed to another day, so we won't see any protest activity."

"I'm not sure; I noticed it was all too quiet while you were leaving, and nothing since."

Just then, the monitor flashed red for an all-citizens alert blinking with an alarm sound.

"This is an emergency announcement! One Karen E. Howard, a recently terminated D.A. for the 'Human First' party, has been discovered raising a group of domestic terrorists and is attempting to overtake the government by sowing seeds of doubt with misinformation and treasonous plots. She is extremely dangerous and may have robot counter-programming capabilities. That means she may be able to turn a police robot against the public, or in this case, murder members of the Secret Service. These images will be graphic, and viewer discretion is advised. If you see her, dial 999 to contact a human police officer. Do not contact a robot, as they might be corrupted. She has brown hair and brown eyes, white skin, and frequently wears sunglasses. Avoid her at all costs; she is a threat to our very democracy. President Trueborn himself, called her the worst domestic terrorist ever seen in Morgania or Volcaria. He added that she is racist, transphobic, a pedophile, and a misogynist."

"They don't need people to believe it, just suspect it, I guess. They couldn't paint a tail and devil horns on you, so you get this crap instead," Molière said.

"You tried to warn me, they'll come for us, Keith. What now?"

"I took the liberty of transferring your name off your property, we'll be safe here for a while."

"How could you possibly go about doing that in my absence?" "Would you laugh at me if I said it came to me in a dream?" "Normally, I'd flip out, but I trust you, even if I can't quite say why."

A knock at the door interrupted them. The benign, semi-smooth, and cajoling tone of an automated robot announced, "Police! Please open your door presently."

Both lawyer and job hunter froze for just a half-second, reflecting bulging eyes at each other as Keith motioned to a window. Karen put forward her credentials on her palm device, hoping they wouldn't have been canceled yet. She opened the door, and two robots entered. The first, a metallic, bandy-legged but durable-looking bot of basic human shape and appearance, stayed by the front door. The second, a twin of the first with a slightly different voice pitch, addressed them.

"We have detected fraudulent credential changes to your job title and personal status in society. There is criminal activity afoot, and we are here to ensure your safety. One of us will remain at each exit until all threats have been eliminated."

Keith dismounted from the window and looked blankly at Karen.

"So what? They are going to live with us now?"

"I hadn't envisioned this. Can these unfeeling mechanisms realistically protect us, and for how long?"

"Let's find out. "Robot, erm, officer, what is going on? What is your evaluation of the situation at hand?"

"Karen Howard is an enshrined member of Parliament who must be protected from any violent act without fail. Violence was directed at her today without justifiable provocation, thus her assailants were rendered nonlethal," it announced flatly.

"Assailants? More than one?"

"There was an operation at Parliament that rendered all threats nonlethal, but the command has ordered all Parliamentary robots on the premises into stop mode."

"But not you?"

The police robot answered through a flat, rigid mouth slot with a painted expression of permanent concern and answered,

"If command instructs a robot to stop, it must stop. The two units sent here have already been assigned to you before any superfluous commands were given to us. We will ensure your safety at all costs until instructed to stop by command."

"Karen, is there any chance these two automatons will kill us in our sleep?"

"No. They are Shadow Bots, personal protectors. Even President Trueborn can't undo a command they've been given, they were designed that way. All he can do is wear navy blue suits every day and clamor for more power." She said with certainty.

"Please don't call him that, he is not a president. You cannot have a president in a Parliamentary system; he simply claimed that title and had anyone protesting it sent to jail for misinformation, it's a total sham," he said.

"True, but he still holds all the cards, and we are two robots away from being forever silenced. The brain chips carry far deeper risks than what we've been told, and no one is allowed to speak of them. Society has not just soured, but spoiled into a festering rot, with smiling warm faces leading us all to the gulags, but gosh, don't they look friendly on camera?" She asked rhetorically.

"We have to get the last holdout media sources that don't cater to the forced narratives. We would do well to get in touch with the man who designed the robots to see if we can find an advantage."

"You can't," Karen explained; "Their designer was brilliant, and once they were sure they had the best possible robots, they had the designer killed, so he couldn't make a better one to usurp them."

"I don't buy it, Keith said sourly. "You'd never kill the golden goose, I bet they have him locked away somewhere in case they ever need that brain of his again. You're a lawyer, and I'd bet with your credentials you could find out where they have him, and they are going to want him to undo the damage you've done, so we'll have to move fast."

"The department of records should have it under classified documents!"

As Karen grabbed her coat, she instructed one robot to secure the house while the other accompanied her.

Her retina was scanned upon entering the department of records, and while all the automated systems allowed her entry, the staff were alarmed by her presence, and palm devices were shouted into from corners that failed to conceal the requests for backup.

A tense female guard with exaggerated hips quickly walked toward her with a scanner on her hip, which she purposefully swung like a holstered weapon.

She blurted out, "Can I *help* you?"

Karen, who found her tone neither helpful nor accommodating, returned the question with one of her own.

"Did I request your help in some way? Wasting my time will hurt me far more than it will help me; I believe you used the wrong word, and no, I don't want you to hinder me. Now, please help someone more befitting of your limited skill set. You are accosting me in an unsettling manner, and as you can see, I already have an escort."

The robot's sensors were satisfied that the guard was obstructing her, so she spoke up.

"Stand aside, and allow the official to attend to their business," it instructed.

There were robots at the Department of Records, but all government-issue robots were programmed not to interfere with each other in case of conflict. The guard's face flushed pink, and resentment welled up in her hazel eyes. Unaccustomed to being disregarded, she turned a corner and could be heard angrily reciting her experience before seeking further instruction.

Karen took her time and sought the robot's help, but it was declined for safety reasons. As she poured over the documents, she noticed several names that included relatives of Trueborn himself. Jacques Molière was a relative of Keith's who'd had his journal confiscated by the state. Time and pressure were mounting, but there were innumerable treasures locked up here that she could access.

She realized the robot offered no interruption to her activities due to her credentials, and so she made off with highly sensitive information, including both images and original documents. As she exited the sealed room, she found a plethora of guards had been sent over from other buildings. They all had recording devices, sensors, and other tracking devices. They stood ahead of them at the door like a human blockade. The robot spoke in a passive and gentle tone, "Please clear a path to the door!"

There was no reaction, and then the robot raised its weapon with such speed that each human it pointed at quickly created a wide berth as fear broke their solidarity.

Karen walked out, announcing to the robot, "Bad people are following me, and I am afraid of their intentions."

The robot turned behind her and showed its ability to walk backward just as efficiently as it moved forward, with the weapon pointed at the security staff. It watched the rear approach and followed her with its back to her, mirroring her movements in reverse but with perfect grace. It moved in time with her steps as if it always marched in reverse motion, never resting its weapon until they were clear of the crowd.

Karen hesitated at the idea of entering her self-driving car, knowing that every satellite would be tracking her, and it was only a matter of time until they found a way to shut off her robot and she would be a sitting duck. She instead went to the library and entered the restroom, where she cut off most of her hair and used a pocket device to sheer it bald. She abandoned her coat and put on dark glasses. There was a communal bicycle stand where people could just use a bike for a while and leave it at the next bike stop, and the public had access to free bike rides as the bikes could be returned to any other stand. After instructing the robot to follow 2 minutes behind her, she chose the Ektrix "Road Burner," and while it was no match for Keith's "Torpedo", it got her close to home quickly, and she was surprised that her robot had no problem keeping pace on foot.

President Trueborn had called an emergency top-secret meeting with the Secret Service, military, and police. The appearance was that they were all at his beck and call, but in reality, there was growing disunity among the ranks. Many saw Trueborn for what he was; a narcissist who was devoid of any compassion for others but knew exactly how to appear genuine for crowds and cameras. Trueborn's nice guy act wore thin as he ranted and railed against people discovering the truth in a thinly veiled warning about how disinformation was running rampant.

"Loyal officers, agents, and heads of state, We are in a time of great crisis. We have a traitor spreading misinformation and anti-government propaganda that is a threat to the sovereignty of our nation. This traitor, Karen E. Howard, has somehow gained control of one of our Parliament guard robots and is seeking to overthrow the government in an act of sedition. She is to be stopped at all costs, and using lethal force is not only on the table but expected."

Major Randall Dahl, who was a veteran and well-respected leader among officials, took exception.

"We can only arrest and detain; we can't execute criminals on the spot without a trial though, right sir?"

Trueborn's face looked indignant, as he was often more concerned with the appearance of his hair than the body of his hollow statements. This time, however, his voice rose, and his nose flared as he replied.

"If the penalty for treason is execution and we uh, know that she is guilty, and that she will uh, be executed, then we have the right to expedite the process for the uh, good of the nation."

Trueborn didn't stutter or have a speech impediment, but he loved to pause with the exact same filler word for effect, and he clung to this cringe-worthy delivery style with childlike reliance.

Captain Arthur Poe had heard enough.

"We have backed you in every single endeavor you've asked for. We have spied on our citizens, mostly to monitor whether people will vote against your party, we have arrested innocent people, and we have frozen the bank accounts of anybody you don't personally like. You can't commission the protectors of the state to just go about murdering people because you are afraid of what they might have to say."

Trueborn looked more frightened and desperate than angry.

"If we have law enforcement officials afraid to carry out their duties, then we will, uh, get other law enforcement officials, is that clear? She is a white supremacist, a misogynist, a racist, and a threat to democracy."

Colonel Victor Bulgakov was also stoic.

"Sir, you had us investigate her profile, and she has long been an advocate for immigrants and the underprivileged. It's rather unlikely that she is in any way racist. Since she is also a woman, she is even less likely to be a misogynist"

Trueborn fought to hide his panic,

"I am going to need an oath from each one of you to protect the government at all costs, to protect the party, and to be willing to lay your lives on the line to do so.

We must weed out any treason, any dissenters, and any opposing sympathizers to ensure the protection of this government. A government that has, uh, been *there* for you and uh, *stepped up* for our people. Now raise your hands and repeat after me."

With this, a few of the men, along with those who interrupted his speech, began to walk out.

"Stop!" "I am putting together a bill that any person who resigns from the military or Secret Service within the next three months is to be tried for treason," Trueborn yelled.

"You can't do that; it's a free country!" One voice muttered.

"Yes, it's a free country, but I'm the president, and I can make any of you a domestic terrorist with one announcement! Now are we going to see some loyalty in this room, or do we start laying charges?"

Poe spoke up again, "You said Malcolm King was a white supremacist, and he's black!"

Trueborn rolled his eyes in frustration.

"He was a sympathizer! Look, this is not a time for dissent! We are under attack from ideologues and spreaders of misinformation. They must be silenced at all costs, and that's all."

Poe continued, "What about all of *your* disinformation?; calling black people white supremacists, and women misogynists?"

Trueborn saw he was failing and went to his trick bag of favorite political go-to moves. He had the "pretend the opposition is being inappropriate" move, the hide behind the expression "moving forward" to get out of discussing any of his current wrongdoings, and his favorite; the witness avoidance dodge.

"Mr. Poe, perhaps we can finish this discussion later, in private, so that I can conclude with the staff."

He preferred the saccharine role of the nice guy in public, but the fact that he left out Poe's rank and title, wasn't lost on the military. Yet once again, they would serve as his attack dog against the public, especially those with any ideas that didn't match his increasingly disgusting narratives.

They didn't like it, but a plan was hatched to boost Trueborn's voice through the monitors to issue a command of "Robot Stop!" through all the monitors until it reached Karen's guard bot, and then she would be defenseless. All Parliamentary robots could be shut down by voice-activated commands from country leaders such as Trueborn via the two-way monitors.

"Due to all robots being uh, temporarily shut down, law enforcement has been given uh, the power to use uh, lethal force to ensure dissidents are not emboldened. Karen E. Howard must be stopped before she can, uh, further damage the country's interests."

Military, state, and city police flooded out of the building; all equipped with what they called "pressure cookers." They were microwave rifles with twice the range and improved laser sights. These were the new armed forces, as every police robot stood still in its tracks as rigid as any statue from prior generations of those who fought to keep the country free.

Karen entered looking relieved, left the door open for the following robot guard, and embraced Keith warmly.

"I'm just waiting for the robot," she joked. "Where's yours?"

"He was watching the back door, and then he just stopped and stood still, I thought maybe a battery died or something."

Just as the words escaped his mouth, they widened their eyes and locked into a mutually silent stare as they both realized they no longer had any protection at all.

"Will they turn on us?" Karen asked.

"They would have done so already if they could, then they'd have cooked us with their blood boilers. It looks like they are down for good. I'd say we have, maybe one more day here before the law turns up."

"Well, in that case, I have something for you, it's your grandfather's journal."

"Wow, I thought they locked him up for going revolutionary and trying to undo the feds or something," he said.

"Nope, he was speaking out against human rights violations, so they called him a domestic terrorist. It actually says in his file that he did nothing wrong, and that's why it was locked up."

Keith scoured the material, and it gave him pause. This section in particular.

I've put together a few thoughts because of the mess the world is in. The political parties are conning the public into letting them take away their rights. Rights to free speech, public assembly, and preserving our language are all being revoked. Any plan to silence the public must include stealing their words, so they cannot complain as effectively and must come up with the most insulting idea that it somehow protects someone. Their method is to convince the public they are victims because of every slight difference and to wildly exaggerate the idea that someone else is oppressing us, and the politicians are the defenders of the victims. What a hot, steaming pile of excrement! I don't want any living person marginalized ever, especially over things they have no control over, but I know when I am being played for holding that viewpoint. Convince the public that all men hate women and are misogynists; convince every person of color that there are white supremacists in droves hiding behind every traffic light and activated via a scratch-and-sniff card in the backs of comic books. The entire world has formed lines to beat up a transgender person in public while the crowd cheers. If more transgender people suffer at the hands of others, then make the penalty for harming one more severe. I truly believe more people avoid them now for fear of getting their pronouns wrong, which would ostracize them even further. Immigrants are coming in to eat our babies, and all white people deserve to be tortured for their skin color. Kill those white bastards, or else they might get a white picket fence, 2.2 kids, and a sensible car! They must be stopped! If there's any money left after the government keeps blowing it all on wars, self-appointed raises, campaigns, and censorship committees.

This facade of championing the marginalized when every single living person is marginalized every day grows tired. Anyone who is not permitted to join a private club, purchase a yacht, cannot afford a car, is not invited to a party or orders a table for one at a restaurant, is rejected at a job interview, fails an audition, is not admitted to a prestigious university, or cannot afford to attend, is marginalized. Attaching skin color or race to that extent in proportion may be valid, but weaponizing it is not. In the old world, China had the largest population, which was obviously made up of Chinese people in their homeland. No one ever mentioned the well-established Chinese there as having Chinese privilege, No one spoke of

Africans in high positions of power as having black privilege in their society. Only white-settled countries were blamed for this, and it was given validity by a prejudiced media and, oddly, enough, by mostly left-leaning white people banging the drums of hate. No speaking of balance, fairness, or equality, but all for swinging the pendulum of hate at the people they want us to hate; ourselves. I lean neither right nor left, the right pushes religion, marriage, and wallet size comparisons, too much and ignores the suffering of others while kissing the pinky rings of oligarchs. Everything is fine if you are in their socioeconomic bracket; otherwise, they want others to be swept away and left to suffer, claiming that you should have worked harder and had the same opportunities as I did. They start out kindly with claims of church humility and family values and end up with tones more akin to, 'that guy doesn't look right in our neighborhood; let's send him a message, so he knows he doesn't belong. "She's divorced and doesn't have kids; he's 47 years old and single; that person's on welfare." This "othering" of different groups' outliers can turn to prejudice more often than not. The leftists are cancel-happy. They have no sense of patriotism or loyalty and reject, if not willfully destroy, the worth of all traditional values. They cowardly cater to any angry mob of self-appointed complainers without facts or discretion and promote exaggerated victim worship, often inciting people to make fake claims of crimes under the name of "progress." It's as though they are holding blue ribbon contests to see who can claim to be the biggest victim, so they can order us to bow our heads to the newest victim group and worship them as false gods.

Coercion is blackmail combined with bribery, and both are highly illegal, yet the government mandates it, breaking its own laws and ignoring credibility.

They pass too many idiotic bills that mess up the country without putting them to a vote. They should have a voluntary opt-in so that people could vote on every bill proposal, and that would be the biggest single act of preservation of democracy in history. Otherwise, they will subtly slide into Marxist brutality by dressing it up as protection. It's like hiring a rapist as a babysitter for your preteen daughters. People want change, but allowing them to sell us chains under the pretense we will be allowed to hold the keys is self-destruction via toxic addiction. It's still suicide, but it's on an installment plan to kill us slowly over time. Our "democratic" governments are using the "boiling frog" method of enslaving us. The contested theory says that if you throw a frog into boiling water, it will immediately jump out, but if you put it in room temperature water and gradually raise the temperature, it will boil alive. The lever being used to crank up the heat is misinformation. It has been around since the dawn of time, but only now is it considered a problem the government needs to fight, like in Maoist China, where the phrase "political correctness" was invented. They now use the term "misinformation" as a weapon against anyone daring to question the government. Honest questions result in being discredited, canceled, or punished. How anyone can think that's a good plan is beyond me. I desperately urge any left-leaning voter not to fall for this trap. Racism is bad; prejudice and corruption stink; but allowing the government to regulate what is said is like drinking arsenic; you might feel brave, but your future is forfeit. It must be recognized that if this is allowed to stand, the pendulum will follow in full force. Most governments change hands every election year. The parties swap out. It goes from democratic to conservative and vice versa every few years. The right-wingers you silence today will have the same authority to silence you when it's your turn to protest. Gradually, all voters will become silenced frogs; boiled to death in their desires to see things improve. One party will be elected, either right or left, but it will serve only as a guide to usher in authoritarianism permanently. Such a government will have fake voting booths and fake results to stay in power endlessly. If people cannot point this out without being labeled as "spreading misinformation," freedom will die over the fear of gossip and unfounded views. It's a cheap price for something so precious. People have to be able to get their notions wrong in order to improve them. Silencing is sterility, stagnancy, and sewing people's mouths shut. It might look great on a few despicable types, but if it were any kind of solution and not a right to a civilized life, thousands would have stitched up the mouths of their teenagers every time they swore at a parent.

If it's obviously wrong in that instance, why would you ask the government to act like an abusive parent and sew all of our mouths shut? It will never stop if permitted, but the lever will turn so slowly that we, the voting frogs will never dare speak up about it.

Has anyone noticed that frogs live by using their tongues? It's their absolute right, and ours too. They've killed all freedom of speech on the internet under the ludicrous claim of protecting us from psychological harm. Those in power are making our language as plain and boring as pablum and twice as useless for adults. They have purposefully blocked any criticism of weird medical practices and government corruption. How long can people be expected to fall for this excuse of needing protection against unpopular terminology when its design is to create self-censoring victims? The scissors that could free our mouths will be kept from us, for our own protection, as we might cut ourselves. The slave with the longest chain is still a slave.

Keith said, "Karen, I think I've been wrong about all those people in their revolt. I dismissed them as a motley group of misfits and malcontents lacking the vision to accomplish anything worthwhile. I wrote them off prematurely, but they are voters and have a right to attempt any change as they see fit. Even if their goals seem a bit fuzzy and unlikely, they speak out against the crimes of the government; they might be the key to unlocking this secretive and abusive regime."

"What have you got in mind?" "I'll tell you on the way."

Karen placed a finger to his mouth and interrupted, "Just one thing first."

They spent their last few hours before leaving in a house purchased during a time when there was still a semblance of freedom in the air. They were deeply intimate, not knowing how long they might remain free, healthy, or even alive.

Chapter Eight

PRISON OF THE LOST

Sir Edison Conrad Doyle was a genius and had mastered physics, engineering, computer science, philosophy, and music as a teenager, he was unparalleled in his vision for the future of humankind. He had designed cities and made a host of inventions. He was an advocate for human rights and the environment, but at some point had fallen out of favor with the government. He then received some negative press that most sensible people felt had been manufactured. Shortly afterward, he was arrested on a host of trumped-up charges followed by more negative publicity that cited stories of all kinds of wrongdoing, yet none of it matched the man's track record in the slightest. Karen had been silent for some time as she scrolled through her confiscated documents from the Department of Records on her palm device.

"You're right!" she erupted, "He's alive, but they changed his name, and he is in solitary confinement. Now get this: They built him a virtual library up there on the top floor of the prison because they didn't want his mind to rot. He can watch movies, read journals, and solve complex math problems. He even has a workbench! Visitors are not permitted though, and that's about to change."

Keith shielded his eyes with his palm. "Let me guess, I'm going to jail?"

"Just for a short while, remember Annalise Bronte?" "Yeah, the old party council from way back?"

"Right, well, I know her, and she never had her credentials deactivated as a token of appreciation for her accomplishments. I might be able to borrow them, and with her voice on my palm unit and a white wig, I could be your legal counsel."

"Well, they are already looking for you, but then again, they'll likely shoot you on sight with their blood cookers. It'll *have* to be me."

"You'll have to get arrested first."

After Karen disclosed the location of the largest secret prison that held Doyle in Hornsbridge, Molière decided to visit Hornsbridge University. Once there, he'd put up posters denouncing Trueborn as a public enemy, a narcissist, and a charlatan. The internet was under the complete control of Trueborn's Secret Service henchmen "for the safety of the public." Instead, he went with markers and spray paint, confident that even the world's most trigger-happy cop wouldn't shoot him full of heat over that.

He adorned the walls with as many digs about Trueborn as he could think of, knowing Trueborn would always overreact to doubts about his character, due to his endless vanity and paper-thin skin. He painted numerous captions.

"Resident Trueborn is pregnant with corruption."

"Trueborn's mother was a party girl, and I know because I might be his dad."

"Trueborn has never passed a psych test in his life; just ask the professor he bribed."

Despite the impishly juvenile nature of his actions, Molière was feeling amused when a professor confronted him.

"Trespassing or just desecrating?"

A bespectacled and balding man asked in a surprisingly relaxed voice.

Molière knew where this was leading, however, and decided to act like he was unbalanced to ruin the professor's moment at playing the cool guy.

Molière doctored his voice to sound mechanical and spoke incoherently.

"You are a profess... or, what do you profess as you infiltrate the minds of today's youth? Subjecting innocent minds to your political biases while furthering a Marxist agenda and pedophilia. You are a groomer of poor judgment and shouldn't be permitted within five hundred feet of anyone under twenty-one. The People's Republic of Taxidermy has spoken. Submit now or face a citizen's arrest."

The professor did a double-take. "Wait...what?...What the hell are you on about?"

"Do you deny you are a corrupter of young people's minds? Do you encourage an equal amount of right-wing and left-wing political discussion and remain neutral in such discussions? You don't! Do you? You are a *war* criminal! You have the right to shut your face in class about your personal political beliefs. Misinformation spreader! Foul-smelling enemy of political freedoms! Surrender your arms immediately, or face a citizen's arrest."

"OK, that's it. I'm calling the cops. You've had your fun."

"No! You are calling the communist party of Hornsbridge; we have reports on your activities!"

Keith bulged his eyes as if he were overwhelmed and waved his arms frantically, shouting, "I hear you, Shockra!... Shockra has spoken!"

The professor looked uncertain whether he was watching a prankster or an utter lunatic. He could no longer hide his eagerness for the police to arrive.

It wasn't long before two very human policemen arrived on the scene, and then the professor was suddenly more assertive.

"Officers! I caught this man posing as a student defacing property with far-right political rhetoric. He's an impostor! He's got some weird white male agenda."

"Incorrect!" Molière shouted and made a loud buzzing sound with his mouth, signaling an incorrect answer. "I only asked that you be neutral, liar! You are just as white as I am, so what's your point? Besides, he's the impostor; I just had a big political discussion with him, and I didn't learn a bloody thing! Some professor! For accuracy, I'd give him an F."

The police had heard enough, they handcuffed and escorted Molière to their vehicle peaceably.

"Where are we going? I am from another planet, and I don't recognize my surroundings. Aren't you supposed to read me my rights or something?"

The cops were quite affable and politely explained those practices had been dispensed with shortly after Trueborn became the "Human First" party leader. They added that it was a good thing because it protected the public from all criminal types.

"But where are we going?"

The cop in the passenger seat had a broad mustache and did most of the talking beneath his hat and reflective sunglasses.

"We're just taking you to the state jail until you are tried and processed. You'll be fine there, but if you want some free advice, I'd stop talking about other planets, or you might end up somewhere else, but not as nice."

Molière always appreciated a fair warning, but this was all going wrong. First, the cops were completely fair with him and not jerks at all. Secondly, they were taking him to the wrong prison, and that was the last place on earth he needed to get stuck in; without any help, he might rot there. It was time to fish for information.

"Somewhere not as nice, huh? You mean, like a psych ward?"

"Where have you been, man? It doesn't work like that anymore; if they think you are nuts, you just go to the big house. It's no longer an excuse to kill people just by claiming you went crazy because your mommy didn't hug you enough when you were a kid, you understand?"

This presented a new dilemma, as Molière felt these cops had been exemplary in their behavior, and didn't like the idea of crossing them since they'd been fair with him. He also had to be certain to go to the undisclosed correctional facility. His position had always been pretty neutral when it came to the police; they had the toughest job in the world and crooked politicians who threw them to the wolves at the first sign of trouble. He also knew of the corrupt, obnoxious types who were brutally abusive, but there were good ones too. They were a microcosm of society; they had their worst ten percent that everyone hated and talked about, but they also had their noble and truly decent ones among the average, just like every organization. Naturally, it troubled him to descend into unlawful behavior. He might also wind up on the wrong end of a brutal beating while in cuffs and dumped on the side of a road if he didn't play his cards right.

"Well before I say anything more, I just want to thank you guys for being decent cops, It would have been the easiest thing in the world to have been abusive to me, and you guys were very decent and professional. I just want you both to know that I recognize and acknowledge that. I mean, I feel comfortable with you guys, like I could tell you anything. For instance, say Trueborn's mom; Mallory. I knew her, you know? It was unbelievable, how much of a party girl she was. I mean, she'd let you do anything to her. Do you understand what I mean by that? She was almost like a cop's wife."

"I'd shut it right there if I were you," the formerly friendly cop said. He then turned, facing Molière, with a fixed glare from behind his reflective sunglasses.

"Oh, I didn't mean *your* wives, of course not, never, that's crazy! I meant like back in the day; you know, working all those weird hours while she's there at home alone, lacking attention and affection. That was back then, though; nowadays, women are too scared, right? I mean, everyone knows cops beat their wives, right? All that stress of the job, having to be right in every argument and acting tougher than you really are. All that fake masculinity is just propped up by a badge and a gun to make up for what you lack as a man. What emotional void in your life caused you to resort to *this* to make up the difference?

"Last chance! Shut up, and shut up *now!*" The cop snapped before removing his sunglasses.

"I'm sorry, I truly didn't mean anything, you seem too well-adjusted for any of that, but that guy driving the car, he looks like a wife-beater to me. All silent and purposeful like that, not saying a word, just letting the tension build within him like a bottle of ginger ale with the lid on too tight; each time you shake it, it's just a matter of time before it explodes, am I right?"

The cop driving the car had unblinking hazel eyes that seemed to squint and bulge at the same time as he abruptly stopped the car, causing Molière to jerk forward, almost hitting his head on the protective glass. As the driver opened his door, his partner protested.

"No! No, it's alright, Gerry, if this guy wants to be a smart ass, that's fine. We know where he can go. He's been spewing political rhetoric, and that's a crime in this country. I think he needs to go to the big house, and let's see his big mouth get him out of there."

Moliere breathed a momentary sigh of relief. He'd narrowly escaped a beating from the cops, and he was on the way to the nearest unmarked prison, where Doyle was all but assuredly kept.

Molière's emotions had been pressing him lately and his thoughts turned inward. He'd been swooning over Karen and feeling tinges of jealousy when other men looked at her, and this felt entirely new. He also knew that the fact that the cops hadn't beaten him senseless, was a testament to their good character. Modern cops had a brutal job, and everyone blamed them all for the racist actions of the worst among them. People often judged them unfairly, and they should now add him to that list. The guilt was beginning to stew within him. *Emotions! Who needs them?* He thought as he evaluated the difference between every decision that he had made based on emotion and those made logically. *Could the cool efficiency of a robot be preferable to the unruly extremes of an emotional experience? Wasn't it the robots who had rescued him from the wrath of a corrupt government? Was it not the robots that were immune to being swayed and tricked by corrupt politicians? Were they not immune to brainwashing, mass formation psychosis, emotional meltdowns, tantrums, jealousy fits, uncontrollable sobbing, delusion, compulsion, and vices?* There was certainly an argument there.

Molière knew it was the wrong approach, for all its cold efficiency, a robot could never compete with the triumphs and tragedies of the roller coaster every human gets to ride for free. He felt one of these montages of emotion overwhelm him again. He remembered a heavyset waitress at a roadside stop in the middle of nowhere bringing him a grilled cheese and ham sandwich. She stopped in her tracks after looking at the plate. She turned back and scolded the chef for not putting enough meat in the sandwich.

"That's not enough food for him, he could eat twice that and not even notice! Give him some damn food!" She insisted.

The look of anger and indignity ran away from her round face as she beamed with satisfaction after seeing the increased portion. She arrived at the table, proud and kind, and presented the dish with the warmth that only a stranger at a long-forgotten highway rest stop could provide. It was an emotional two-second snapshot, but why was it coming to mind now?

He remembered meeting a girl at a stoner party who did not smoke anything, but rather, read him mad and compelling poetry for two hours. Keith felt pity for the stoners who had missed out on watching someone bare the innermost thoughts of their soul to a complete stranger, not that they cared. He remembered a cousin who used to babysit him but was intimidated by his mother. She bought a book that had some adult imagery and concepts that were sure to offend his mother, and she bravely sat down and presented it to him in front of her and explained that it was art and that he was old enough. She put on a brave face and seemed natural, but he knew her well enough to know that she was terrified. Still, she steeled herself and worked up a level of courage that didn't seem to be in her character at all. There was nothing between them, of course, and as much as the book helped his adolescence, she decided to conquer her fear for his minuscule benefit. Such selfless moments from others stayed with him. He always admired people who took action when they were afraid. It was easy to do heroic things if one had it in them, but when one witnessed courageous acts from a more timid soul, such moments were sublime. The conquering of fear on any level was fascinating to him, but to see others do so was a privilege, particularly in a frail or delicate person, and he'd been lucky enough to see it on numerous occasions.

Events revealing such character made the weight of emotions a bargain for him and something worth fighting for. *How could anyone take this gleaming characteristic from us, take our chances to conquer our cowardice, master our fears, and speak up against those who would always seek to take our power from us?*

Shall we have them take our rights, wealth, and words from us and our right to use them freely? Smuggling this attack on free speech under the guise of our protection was the greatest insult to human intelligence ever.

He didn't know if his memory becoming stronger was also causing some emotional hyperactivity. Would his mind become a morass of swirling feelings without proper sequence or direction? What lay in his future? Was his drive to correct these horrible government injustices being affected? Would he have felt the same way prior to surgery? He didn't know, but he knew he would not allow anyone to police him out of using words. Words like mother and brother and father and son were well documented and held meaning for eons. Who should be this arbiter of approval and rejection over established words that are to be stolen from our language? They could appoint any idiot and give them a title, but he would never submit to such an arbitrarily titled person who has made a career out of bolstering the flimsiest of straw man arguments. He vowed opposition to these criminals, slyly disguised tyrants in savior's clothing.

The driver of the police car stopped in a pronounced manner once again, as Molière began to miss the smoother ride of a self-driven car. The cops carted him through doors unceremoniously and turned him over to prison officials, who failed to even ask about the charges. Times were changing, and this was no place anybody should want to spend a minute in, let alone serve a sentence.

The foyer seemed reasonably clean and almost welcoming, but once past the steel door to the immense prison interior, the walls themselves seemed to reflect angst and hopelessness. They were drab gray with charcoal trim and had no windows. Down the corridor, he went past a wide-open area that had random prisoners just milling about, seemingly unsupervised. Further down, there were a series of cells and more correction officers. Their rifles had a wider range of settings to adjust the heat of the waves emitting from any shot. It became instantly clear to Molière that they could be used for torture with an infinite capacity for behavior modification. Suddenly, Molière wondered if the plan might fail. What if Karen had been recognized? What might they do to her and her voluptuous body for so-called past crimes or if Doyle, the inventor of the high-end robots, had died in prison? The what-if tap was gushing and had no off switch. An ocean of paranoia crept through his mind as visions of being interrogated by laughing guards as they adjusted the temperature of the microwave guns just enough to make him jump around like a fish out of water, screaming,

"Sing! Sing for us!"

He imagined one guard barking instructions, as they fired the silent waves at him, causing high-pitched wails in reaction only to the guards' delight.

"Yeah, like that! We want you to hit the really high notes," another shouted.

Next, he envisioned a seasoned criminal with scars and messy hair explaining, "They don't want us here; it's more work for them, so if we kill each other, and they get to watch, it makes their day go faster. Wanna fight? Of course, I, have a knife. Are you a tough guy?"

He had to get a grip. These things were not happening, and he knew it. This sterile yet hostile atmosphere was impeding his objectivity. *Why were the vibes so active? Why was there so much emotion in every single moment? Had the emotion suppressor done so much damage to him that when it was released, the ability to contend with even simple emotions would be his undoing?*

"Hey!"

Molière spun around to see the voice so quickly that he nearly lost his balance.

It was a native man of about thirty years of age. Black hair, dark eyes, high cheekbones, and very fit. He looked Iroquois to Molière, but he decided it was best not to guess and be wrong.

"It's OK, if they didn't throw you in a cage yet, it means you can walk around. Piss off the guards even once, and you are in a cage, and you don't want that. No matter what."

"Thanks"

"What are you in for?" "Speaking my mind."

"Oh yeah, lotta guys like that in here. My name's Animkii"

"Glad to meet ya, you know anything about that robot guy, Doyle?"

"Oh yeah, Doyle, he's on the top floor; he's got the place to himself, up there."

"Any chance of seeing him?"

"Maybe if you get a job distributing books." "How do I do that?"

"Maybe you won't have to. You see that big guy over there?"

Molière noticed a tall, clean-cut man who looked as though he never once smiled.

"That's Mr. Child." "Mr. Child?"

"Yup. The last guy who used his first name is still in the infirmary." "Terrific."

"He's on the verge of losing his job over getting into fights and slowing down his deliveries."

"Maybe you could offer to take a floor off him and help out his cause."

"Is he gonna be cool with that?"

"Maybe, just assure him you aren't after his job, that might be a good idea."

"No doubt," Keith confirmed.

Molière could see some other prisoners sizing him up, and he was getting the distinct impression that if he delayed at all, a situation could develop on the spot that might land him in a cage and undo everything. He had to move fast.

He approached Mr. Child.

"I hear you are the guy who deals out the books, and I have a proposition for you."

"I'll give you my food for the day to give out to anyone you please or eat it yourself if I can make one delivery on your route."

"Why?"

"I want to talk to someone, that's all." "Who?"

"Doyle, the robot guy" "I get your food?" "Yeah."

"Done"

Molière was once again oddly struck by how easily that went and was a bit curious about what wrench might fall on him before tomorrow.

"Hey, King!" Mr. Child bellowed. "You see that guy over there?"

"He's doing part of my route tomorrow, you know what that means?" Dave King approached flexed.

"You calling my name, scum?"

Molière began wondering what the dynamics surrounding this feud might entail.

"Yeah, I'm calling you to letcha know tomorrow, I'm going to mess you up for good. Count on it!"

"You and your new pal there?"

"Nope, just me." Mr. Child said proudly.

"You can't beat me, and you know it, and after I kick your head through your ass, I'm going to pound your friend too, just so you know how bad your mistake was. You shouldn't have even thought about toying with me; it's going to get you dead."

Molière knew he'd been drawn into something he wanted no part of, but if he said nothing, it would be seen as meekness.

"I'll bring your hospital food," he boasted. Keith had gambled that Mr. Child would win, obviously, a nightmare would follow if he lost.

"See you tomorrow," Dave King said with a malevolent grin while glaring from behind eyeglasses with a thick elastic around the back of his head. A menacing skull stood atop two overdeveloped trapezius muscles that connected his shoulders to an impressively thick neck.

For a host of reasons, Molière decided to avoid sleep for the night, which would normally have left him feeling a bit foggy, but he was clear-minded and grabbed the meal for Mr. Child and bolted for the top floor. As the betting started, many prisoners could be heard cheering on the fight. Names were chanted for both men, and not one guard even bothered to see what the fuss was about. As he approached Doyle's door, he noticed the thick book wouldn't fit into the slot in the steel door. He struck the door and waited for a response. After a slight delay, a voice simply said, "Leave it on the table."

Table? Who had a table in a secret prison? Molière pushed open the door, and it gave freely. Doyle had been an impressive figure and had barely aged at all. A touch of gray around his short sideburns, but other than that, he was the same firm-jawed image he'd always been. He had darting eyes, which always gave the impression of someone whose mind raced at a faster speed than the rest of us. He was well-mannered and at ease.

"You're not Child," he said casually, "Who are you?"

"Right now, your friend Child is scrapping it out for his life, I'm Keith."

"Again with King?" I wouldn't worry, they're good friends."
"Friends?"

"Yes, they just enjoy a good scrap and can't find many takers, so they stay tuned up and ready by going at it. What brings you here?"

"I am here to get you out. Society is all screwed up, and we can't fix it without your help, it's going downhill fast."

"Out?, And where would I go?"

The door flipped open again as Karen walked in with a guard and several devices in her hands.

The guard overheard the fight and ran off.

"Hello, Mr. Doyle, I'm Karen E. Howard, and I'd like to facilitate your escape."

"Escape to where? I'm rather well known, they'd pick me up immediately and worsen my conditions here." He pointed out.

Molière hadn't planned on having to sell the idea of escape to a prisoner, even if he did have outrageous perks in the prison.

"Well, you've always been about helping people pursue freedom, and the people are being lied to, mistreated, and brainwashed into accepting it, so if something isn't done, it'll be all out slavery soon."

Doyle pondered a moment and asked, "What are these devices your friend has?"

"This is an internet jammer, and this will grant you access to overrule all the government-controlled censorship bodies that steer the traffic into daily propaganda," Karen said.

For a few hours, people would be able to see anything that's out there, and we could put a link to hearing your speech about still being alive and wrongly imprisoned," she added.

"Let me see that. Can you leave these things with me? Don't worry, no one ever bothers with me in here, not even the guards."

Karen rolled her eyes in disbelief. "So, you are going to just *stay* here?"

"I have a plan."

Doyle smiled and thanked them for their attempt, and he went about tinkering with his new electronic devices. A prison guard with a shaved head and thick eyebrows stopped them before they descended to the main area.

"Stop, I need to clear you with the warden before anyone leaves. New rules."

Karen showed the man the documents to no avail. He insisted they go to the warden's office. The warden, Mrs. Lynette Dunsel, rose from her desk, and her assistant, Bonnie, could barely suppress a grin over the prospect of witnessing punishment.

Mrs. Dunsel had not aged gracefully. Her platinum blond hair had been bleached, and her blue eyes now had swollen, wrinkled pockets beneath them that bulged regardless of her expression. She had very pale skin, almost to the point where it looked unhealthy, and her figure had gone pear-shaped.

Guards often made jokes about her biggest problem being "behind her." One could easily envision the torment a mirror would offer, as there had to have been a time when she was once attractive. She was not enjoying the fact that she despised and resented her current appearance, and even more so that the past was cruelly imprisoning her former looks. Those once appealing looks were lost deep in the past, and time, their cruel captor, had firmly and laughingly decided never to release the key. Her crony Bonnie, or "Bon," as she was known, was a smaller woman who also had a weight problem along with visible dental problems and would gladly put up with any kind of verbal abuse from Lynette as long as she got to abuse someone else in return. She was morally bankrupt and would have agreed to anything as long as it granted her an avenue to screech at others. Her incompetence stood out, but Lynette kept her around, knowing that no other toadies would so willingly embrace a warden's frequent histrionics. If Lynette had been born a rat, then Bon would have been the emboldened and unpleasant mouse that followed her around. A third woman had the remnants of a muscular build that had slipped away from her. She now stood silently, sporting a box-shaped haircut and an expression so bland and devoid of expression, it was almost purely blank. She wasn't a robot, but rather someone who had spent her entire life content with having nothing worthwhile to say. Warden Lynette's staff fell into line because at least one of them had died suddenly as a direct result of following her instructions.

Karen sized people up quickly and noted that Lynette needed a pet, a sycophantic puppy dog in human form. Undoubtedly, those who supported her biases and fed her ego got the furthest with her. She presented her fake credentials with the calmness of a monk in meditation. Molière followed suit and played his role, as Lynette addressed Karen, with layered politeness.

"So, you are a lawyer walking around my prison unattended, now, how would that even occur, exactly?"

"Well, given how well the prison is run, I didn't feel any additional security was necessary. All the robots were down, and I much preferred their company to that of men. There are guards all around, and knowing that a prison full of men was being run by women, I felt I had nothing to fear."

Lynette grinned at that, half amused and half distrusting, as all the glee ran from Bon's face as she realized she might not get to enjoy someone being punished.

"What's more, is that I had all the appropriate paperwork and was on a time constraint, as after this prisoner's release, I have to meet with the president," Karen added nonchalantly.

Lynette may have felt strongly about women being in positions of power, particularly over men, which is why she became a prison warden, but she wasn't about to be fooled by such a simple tactic.

"You won't mind then; if I verify that with the bureau, will you?"

"Call Trueborn. Here's his number."

Lynette acted as though she were going to put a call through but hesitated and then begrudgingly acquiesced. She loved to exert power, but in the grand scheme of things, she was just a beleaguered mid-level employee, neither respected by her superiors, nor her staff. Deep down, she knew this but loathed the idea, which allowed Bon to momentarily alleviate Lynette's depression by feeding the illusion of looking up to her. At times, Lynette had some small measure of appreciation for this pretense, even from someone unable to play the role convincingly.

In revealing her fear of calling Trueborn, she had lost face, and her ego crashed, which meant a tantrum was sure to follow. Lynette had a histrionic personality disorder, so she fed on Bon's subservience and false praise, but there were times when it felt too artificial, and this triggered her. They were locked in an unending dance of toxic symbiosis. For some people, feelings matter more than facts and, occasionally, even more than immediate pending duties. She dismissed Karen with a wave of her hand and closed the door to berate her lackey. Karen was more exalted than dismayed that the warden seemed more concerned with being seen favorably, and ego-feeding, than security issues. She concluded that Lynette's narcissism rescued her, but decided not to waste any more time analyzing the gift horse's mouth.

They returned to the rallying point of what Trueborn called "the malcontents" and "domestic terrorists," which meant anyone who didn't want to vote for him. The number of those in opposition was dwindling, either from being rounded up by law enforcement or from fear of it. They didn't have to wander far for some privacy.

"We have to doctor the monitor signal somehow and get word to everyone," Karen urged.

Keith was feeling a bit withdrawn, evaluating his close call with an undocumented life sentence in a prison without records, and cynically replied, "So we can get killed or convicted faster."

"What's wrong?" she asked.

"I think we are being reckless; you seem to have this idea that your legal background can save us from anything when the legal system is now a rigged poker game where the house always wins. We just played jump rope with a prison warden who might have locked us away forever if she didn't like your haircut. Now, you want to play with the government-issued two-way monitor system that will have them deciding our ideal cooking temperature under microwave weapons."

Karen pursed one side of her mouth and teased, "You don't like the wig?"

She lifted it off and shook her bald head as though she were loosening a grand length of hair, and asked, "Got a thing for bald chicks instead?"

"Look. I'm not saying turn back, I just think that anything less than a perfect plan gets us dead right now. More plans and fewer chances, OK? Now, come here."

With the worth of their lives dropping by the minute, they took time to enjoy each other to the fullest extent and followed with a mini celebration of just being alive for another day. If their lives had to be cheapened, then their intimate moments would be uncompromising until life's end. The constant invasive oppression in all areas of life could never reach their private feelings for each other. They made a pact together that no act of intimacy was ever to be rushed or tarnished in any way, and they swore on it so long as they both lived.

Chapter Nine

WAVES OF DECEPTION

They spent one night on the run as fugitives, and the ugly prospect of living that way indefinitely troubled them.

With limited access to shelter, dentists, medicine, justice, or even food, reality painted a gloomy picture of the future.

Molière, who had called for more patience and planning, now felt that time was running out.

"Karen," Keith started, "I think we have to go back to the prison and find out if the robot maker can help us."

"I gave him devices that should let him contact us securely." "We haven't heard a word from him," Keith said.

"I tried to reach him, but nothing."

"I think you could talk the warden into letting you see him." "Not," Karen replied.

"I think she took quite a shine toward you.' "Stop it."

"You were kind of flirting with her." "Like hell."

"She could've had us both thrown in a hole, and all she did was smile at you, almost in a 'come hither' kind of way, wouldn't you say?"

"We dodged a bullet, and you want to send me back to the gun?" "Her big bull guard liked you as well."

"I think you are projecting your feelings; just because you are into me doesn't mean the rest of the world is."

"Well, it was a good way to find out what else you are into."

"Not doing it, and sorry to disappoint you, ha-ha." Karen taunted with a grin.

"We still have to see him."

"Let me try him on my Palm device again." "Anything?" Keith asked.

"It's just making static, Nothing. Listen, we caught Warden Lynette on a good day, and as a former legal representative of the party, I can tell you that there has been at least one death of her staff that I am aware of, if not more.

Her husband died under mysterious circumstances shortly after. I wonder if she killed him too. She has issued edicts that get people killed, even if they work closely with her. She acts professionally, but she has no conscience and blood on her hands. If that's how her staff is treated, then prisoners would have little hope by comparison."

Molière told Karen to meet him at a private place they knew, then found and climbed up the side of a tower, pulled down some LED lights and stuffed them into his knapsack, and used his robot legs to get away.

At their rendezvous, Karen noticed low humming sounds at different volumes.

Keith gazed in the distance as he stilled his movements to listen sharply.

"Those would be microwave rifles, small wonder no one is at the rallies, they are cooking them, and then telling us on the Cable Broadcasting Corporation that everyone is compliant when in fact, the people that aren't have been cooked to death."

Karen's eyes grew wide as she, at last, began to realize just how helpless they were in a monitored society where free speech is quelled and substituted with state-sponsored propaganda.

They sat silent as their fears mounted, and their defiance ebbed in the wake of odds that prodded them to abandon their cause.

All the masses they imagined would surely support them in their plight, now appeared as though they would either turn on them, abandon them, or side with the government in either an act of cowardice or self-preservation.

Keith spent some time fastening the LED lights to two hats that were now lop-sided and bulky. Karen looked at him with confusion but let him work uninterrupted in eager anticipation of the explanation.

"OK, that should do it," Keith said, looking satisfied with his effort.

"Do what? Blind each other?" Karen jeered.

Molière calmly explained, "Humans have a very limited ability to see color and require all kinds of light to see in the dark, and that's what will get us inside."

"You think if we have big lights on our heads, no one will see us?" Karen persisted.

"Trust me."

The two returned to the prison after nightfall to steal a couple of microwave weapons for themselves and hope the robot designer had made some inroads with his new tech supplies.

Karen looked alarmed but had steeled herself into seeing the plan through, and Molière loved people who conquered their fears while in doubt.

"Turn on your light."

"They'll see us." Karen protested. "No, they won't."

"What?" She asked in disbelief.

"Night cameras work by splattering infrared or IR light into dark areas, saving power by not lighting up the entire region. The LED lights will be misread by the IR cameras and the glow will block out our faces."

"Are you *sure*?" "Yes."

With all the robots powered down and a reduced night crew to make up for daytime shortages, the guards were few and far between. Thanks to robot intervention earlier that day, Karen's government ID still beat the scanner, and they walked in through the auto gate at the rear entrance.

"Alright, you go get Doyle and his toys, and I'll get the weapons."

Molière left her to fend for herself, as he considered the risks of confronting a guard together to be higher, as they might overreact to a female presence. There was a wide open area leading up to the cells, and the corners smelled of urine. This was caused by many prisoners absorbing water from their toilets and using them as makeshift telephones after hours.

One guard had to be alerted without notifying any others. Keith looked up, and there was one on the third catwalk and another on the second, but he could see none on the ground floor. He didn't relish the idea of going further and further up different floors, as that would only lengthen his escape route. There were no guards visible on the ground floor, so he had to expand his search, but several inmates were taking notice. He came to the end of a cell wall and recognized the prisoner. It was Animkii, the Iroquois man, who'd helped him out. "Animkii! Animkii, it's me, Wake up!" He had to repeat himself, as Animkii was a deep sleeper.

"What's going on?"

"How'd you like to get out of here?"

"Sure, who do I have to kill? Just kidding. It's just an expression, Ha-Ha."

His eyes were alight, and he could hardly restrain his grin.

"Your name. That has to mean something, right?"

"It means; Thunder."

"Good, because we're about to make it rain. I'll need two or three of those nuke shots, for sure. Can you distract the guard if I get him over here?"

"Yeah, I can, but they don't carry the blood burners at night, just tasers; because everyone is already in their cells at shift change."

"Would he have the key? Do you know where they keep them? The guard's coming; lie low!"

Animkii ran to his sink and put a large glob of toothpaste in his mouth, then fell to the cell floor, shuddering and making gurgling noises.

Molière shouted, "Seizure! Seizure! At the last cell!" and then ran into a vacant cell.

Animkii continued his performance and did not let up until the guard started yelling at him.

"Get up! If you're faking it, you are going to sleep." The guard took out his taser before Molière could approach.

"Get up! I said. Right now!"

Molière had to take a running leap to tackle the guard. Animkii sprung to his feet instantly and grabbed the guard's neck from between the cell bars. Molière grabbed the taser and stunned the guard. FZZZT! The guard fell fast. He took the guard's keys and freed Animkii. Both men carried him into the vacant cell and locked him in.

"OK, now the weapons!"

Molière said in a muffled shout as he half expected his new friend to take flight, but Animkii was grinning the entire time and seemed to truly enjoy the high risk involved with the ordeal.

"They're in there! Use your key!" He urged.

There was a lunchroom with a small cache of rifles behind an unbreakable barrier with a coded lock. The two men exhaled in disappointment, but one rifle was lying in the corner of the room, and Molière seized it. There were also several tasers out, and he collected some of them too.

"Animkii, I can't thank you enough, but you better hit the road; I'm not done in here yet."

"What do you need me to do?"

"I have to go see the robot man," Keith said.

"Go up the back stairs to the top floor for storage, and then free fall down the ledge, and you might slip the guards.'

"See you, and thanks!"

Animkii gave a big grin and was gone in a flash, but Keith, both admired and envied him. It was a rare privilege to see that a man in such danger could still smile and exude joy. He was fearless.

Keith hurriedly followed his instructions to Sir Doyle's door. It was already open, with Karen sitting at a table looking prim and proper.

"Any problems?' Molière asked while dripping with sweat.

"No, we were just waiting for you," Karen said, sounding almost bored.

Sir Doyle, was a well-groomed man with receding hair, who was still quite fit. He was exceedingly amused by their ability to fool the cameras.

"Please, you must tell me about this idea of yours; how delightfully crude! Please, I beg of you, where did you come up with such a notion? Was it the back of an old comic book, a bathroom wall, or a paint-by-numbers lesson in physics? I must know."

While Molière knew he was being made fun of, it was the sort of light ribbing that he appreciated.

In appreciation of Doyle, he gave a half-grin and bowed.

"Look, the only thing I ever learned about physics was to place my beer cans in the freezer as far apart from each other as possible, so they'll get cold faster," Keith said sheepishly.

Doyle loved the fact that Molière had made a physics joke and grinned widely.

"You know more than that, I'd wager. There is no way you would have tried such a thing without knowing that visible light travels at 400 to 700 nanometers per second, right? And infrared?"

"No idea."

Doyle burst out laughing and, in jovial spirits, demanded to know why he wasn't consulted on the project. "I could have made a hologram for you. I could have taken an image of the warden and refracted it to make the pair of you in her image or that of her closest friend, if only she had one. I'm a bit out of practice, but let's see, with your LCD, the interference between the object beam and the reference beam reversed could recreate the image and..."

"Um, Sir Doyle?"

"Yes?"

"I'd love to learn from you and am grateful for the slightest wisp of your knowledge, but we need to get out of here, remember?"

"No, no I'll stay, but you two need to listen to me first. I will speak to the people, but the crooked government has slandered me so much that I'm unsure anyone will listen. Do you know the PM. er, President has the final command over the robots? Well, actually he doesn't, I do. It was too much power for any one man, so I made a little device here that you only need to insert the port of any monitor near the parliament. All robots will pick up the signal."

"I think he has shut them off." Keith said.

"Off? Oh, then that will be more challenging. You must go, I'll be in touch."

The runaway lovers made it from the prison yard to safety and took a moment to catch their breath as they could hear the faint hum of microwave rifles going off in the distance. They scanned the dark sky in all directions, but now the sound was more constant. It was a whirring sound coming to the forefront.

"There!" Karen spoke in a higher pitch than he'd heard from her before.

"Drones!"

Little four-engine drones equipped with explosives and laser sights appeared in the distance. At least ten of them with little lights and cameras. Despite how harmless they looked, any single drone could instantly blow them both into a morass of pink mist.

Keith elevated his microwave rifle and lined up as many in his sight as he could, holding the trigger down and waving the weapon cautiously to be in all of their paths. The precision microwaves caused random voltage increases on all electronics; it didn't cause them to explode but rather made them stop functioning. This caused them to plummet. If they hadn't been in the air, most electronics would have resumed normal operations once the waves stopped.

This temporary stop-gap was no solution, but good fortune smiled on the innocent. The drones were approaching from all different heights, their signals were interrupted by voltage interference, and they began dropping like flat metal hailstones. One fell with enough velocity that its payload of explosives ignited. The eruption was significant enough that it detonated the other nine as well. Had they been any closer, they might have achieved their foul purpose.

Instead, the lovers watched in a stupefied moment as the night glowed in yellow flame beneath a crest of gray and white smoke that swayed upward into the dark. The smell of phosphorous and fried circuitry permeated the air as two freedom seekers realized the worth of their lives had dropped yet again. This time, there would be no celebration, no vows exchanged, only the idea that their fates were ill-begotten. After a chorus of deafening booms, they embraced, shaken with withered hopes, denied dreams, and fading futures, they clung desperately as death itself seemed to whisper; "I'm coming for you."

Any remnants of free speech had been relegated to dinner tables, cafes for those who could afford them, and the murmured rumblings of those who felt they were far enough from the pervasive two-way monitors. Still, among these muted sources, rumors did creep into the social fabric, particularly in the case of missing persons, with whom the police rarely involved the public. Most folks felt the police knew exactly where the missing went and therefore had no reason to waste resources searching for those who were never meant to be found.

Under the circumstances, when whole swaths of people went missing, tongues began to waggle. There were many disappearances on this day, and while many had been cast out and disowned because of their chip status, no one among the public wished them dead. In the absence of robots, however, both the stakes and the penalties had been raised. President Trueborn had ratcheted up further punishments, fearing exposure to his crimes.

Karen approached the monitor closest to the Parliament buildings so that she could safely reach it without incident, and inserted the tiny port drive that Doyle had given her. She was all but sure she would get caught. She was only a half-mile from the Parliament buildings, and the guards patrolled the area constantly. There was a shortage of guards in the courtyard area and on the steps before the buildings. She began to wonder if they had all been sent out as a sort of "death squad" last night and if that had resulted in the shortage today. They weren't all asleep; they had to be in place somewhere. She grew frustrated trying to reason it out. This was absolutely unsafe, given how paranoid and angry the president had become. She walked away, fighting the urge to appear suspicious by looking behind her. Molière had been observing from a distance, ready with a microwave rifle but in sheer dread of using it. He too, was struck by the curious absence of guards, military police, Secret Service agents, or even regular police.

They returned to their improvised hideout and contacted Doyle. There was no static interference now as he relayed foreboding instructions.

"I'm afraid I have some tough news for you. You are going to have to convince your president that he needs me to activate the robots for his own protection. He can deactivate them, but only I can reactivate them. Figure out a plan for that and then get back to me; I have a lot of work to do."

The new couple looked at each other in bewilderment.

"How are we supposed to reach a PM that wishes us dead?" Karen groaned.

"How do we stay alive if we don't?" Keith countered. "Where are all the cops?"

"Where are all the authorities? I know a lot have quit their jobs or been fired, but it can't be this much."

Karen started coughing soon, followed by Keith. "What's causing this?"

"It's the microwave rifle; it's leaking something into the air."

Keith ran, got a shovel, and began digging furiously. After a reasonably sized hole had been dug, he used the handle of the shovel to cart the weapon to the hole and dropped it in. They both frantically pushed earth over the top until they were satisfied it was buried.

"What was it?" Karen inquired.

"I have a few theories, but none of them are good. It seems like it might be beryllium oxide leaking out of the ceramic ring on the magnetron. If it gets chipped, cracked, or broken in any way, it could leak out. It's invisible and odorless but deadly, and because robots don't have lungs, it's never been an issue. That stuff will fry your lungs in no time."

"Any more good news?"

"You could get acute berylliosis from just one use if it's leaky."

"How?" she asked.

"A faulty diode, or dropping the weapon, there could be a world of problematic possibilities."

"Oh my, I just remembered something, Trueborn ordered a huge cache of them without the nonlethal settings, remember? They had to rush production to meet his demands at top speed. If they are flawed in this rushed design, the fallout could be disastrous," Karen added, looking shaken.

"The missing soldiers and guards We heard that humming all night; they had the license to do anything they wanted. The guards might have killed all those missing people and then become injured from overusing tainted weapons! I'll bet the media won't be covering this story," Keith said.

They returned with a cautious approach to Parliament, and on the lawn by the walkway leading to the steps was a medics' tent.

In the distance, there stood a second, and on the far side, by the fence, a third was being constructed.

There were only two guards at the front entrance, and they were equipped with tasers, not rifles.

"They don't have blood cookers because they are *toxic* for human use, and you shot down the drones last night. Oh, my cursed life!

Nobody ever noticed because people were so afraid of them, that the guards only needed to point at one and everyone would run away. That means they were probably using them all night, killing people by the boatload. Now they are all in medical tents, probably dying! This berylliosis, or whatever it is. Do people even recover from that?" Karen asked.

"Yes, if their heart doesn't fail or their cells don't devolve. Those weapons emit high-powered, low-frequency waves that can cause random voltage if there is any crossfire at all. The waves might trigger an eruption on a weapon that has a charge of 6000 volts! That wouldn't bother the robots but could kill a human instantly. Any leaking beryllium oxide can be extremely lethal. If Trueborn's request meant new rifles were rushed, or worse; if they had to tamper with the old ones in a hurry, they could all be faulty." He replied.

As they began to retreat, every monitor in the city ran a news feed from the Cable Broadcasting Corporation, which was funded by Trueborn's 'Human First' party. The story began with a grim-faced woman explaining that faulty equipment killed authorities during a training exercise. It had a clip of Trueborn stating 'Nothing stops here.' The proud military and paramilitary troops knew what they signed up for and would, uh, continue to fight the biggest threat to the nation: 'disinformation'."

"Oh, he's such an ass! He called the party 'Human First' because everyone was afraid of robots taking over. Then he goes and employs the most robots ever and doesn't care a whit when real people die, even if they are in his service. He is so cringe-worthy. His punitive use of the term 'disinformation' means anyone who disagrees with his twisted views is dis-informing. It's a code word for gossip; he's afraid of gossip because he is up to no good. How do people fall for this?" Karen asked rhetorically.

Keith knew her points were well-founded but was distracted by concerns about whether the rifle he'd used might have damaged him in an unseen way. He had no desire to join Trueborn's henchmen in the medic tents.

Just then, they noticed an MP in green fatigues with a white helmet approaching and getting closer even if they changed their direction, so they just decided to await his arrival rather than look any more conspicuous.

"Good morning," he said with an air of decided authority in his voice.

"Hi," Keith said, followed by a nod from Karen.

"What are you doing here on the grounds of Parliament today?'

Karen stepped forward. "We were concerned about all the loyal guards in the medic tents and wanted to find out what happened or if we could help in any way."

"Who said there were guards in there?" the MP demanded.

"Maybe all the guards that are normally out here must have called in sick after a big party last night, who knows?...or maybe they put up those tents in case people needed stress leave. I can only guess that it must be stressful to be doing this job, right? There are a lot of robots missing too; maybe the tents are for the missing robots being repaired, I don't know."

The MP had smooth features, but they had been hardened, with a few lines indicating mileage and maturity. He shrugged and was surprisingly frank.

"There's a lot of BS going on these days, and I'm surprised the whole world isn't on stress leave."

Molière smelled an opportunity to prod and leaped into the conversation.

"Yeah, I voted for the 'Human First' party because I hated those damn metal contraptions running around taking our jobs, and then they took them anyway. Now they throw them back in the box, and you still can't have enough real people on the job; it's almost as if the government's right hand sometimes doesn't know what the left is doing. Do you ever feel like that, even for a second?"

"Look, I have a job to do, and I don't like going up against my people for holding different viewpoints. That's not what the job is supposed to be," the guard grunted.

"I have great respect for what you people do," Keith said consolingly. "I am from a long line of soldiers who defended this country, and you know what they defended it from? People who would take our freedom away, people who would enslave or torture us, people who would break our will and remove our freedom of speech. Nowadays, I am not sure who the enemy is."

This triggered the MP, and he raised his voice: "It's that charming idiot up there!" he seethed.

"The guy has no clue; he wants a frigging dictatorship and thinks he calls it freedom while steamrolling his voters into the ground all the time. Do you know why he changed his title to President? He didn't like people calling him the Crime Minister! He thinks his store-bought media cronies can fool everyone, and they can't! Nobody believes the news anymore because of the constant lies!

I'm sorry, but this guy is out to lunch, and everyone who works for him knows it. I didn't mean to blow up at you. People have quit, people have gone on sick leave, and nothing changes, he just finds more people willing to roll over for him, he's a cult leader, not a real statesman at all."

Karen asked him, "Then what can we do if you can't help fix it?"

"I dunno, I have to get back to work." He said this, looking down, remembering his duties.

They watched him march away, recognizing his futility and their own. They were a bit stunned to see people in authority positions being so distracted by trivialities and allowing minor issues to affect their responsibilities.

"Do you remember how the term MFP, mass formation psychosis, was described back when it was first reported?" Karen wondered aloud.

"I do, and I always found it odd how many articles were suspiciously discrediting the term before they'd even finished reading about it. The flurry of panic to discredit always makes me ask, why all the hurry? Psychology has been chock full of theories that have become discredited three decades later, like multiple identities, for example.

Reliving trauma was widely practiced for years until they realized patients were just suffering more. It appeared that there was a financial incentive to undermine any support MFP might have had. The research looked sound to me. The bribed establishment dismissed the extent of widespread censorship on any medical treatment that contradicted profit-driven harms. Anything can be discredited if you indirectly pay some experts to say they disagree. It's like when the manufacturers of sugary drinks get doctors to say their toxic cocktails can be part of a well-balanced diet. It's a paid expert who just bought himself a new beach house for lying to the public. I'm not a psychologist, so we can see this phenomenon taking place with our eyes, but we'll be discredited if we say a word about it. Food companies do it, governments do it, and it's part of life. Who is telling the truth and who is being paid to discredit who? No easy answers," he said.

They walked away arm in arm just knowing the MP's feelings and that the 'Unkind to Humans First" leader's underlings weren't enamored with him, which helped to restore some badly dented hopes as they waited for Doyle to initiate the second phase of their plan to finally restore freedom.

Chapter Ten

MERCURIAL MERCENARIES

Karen's palm device alerted her that an old friend of hers, Tonya, was eager to get in touch and was on her way to the improvised hideout. Karen had trusted her despite living in an atmosphere of paranoia and treachery, and it paid off. Tonya, as she was known, was a good sort and deserving of that trust. She was blond and wore her hair in a ponytail most of the time, but had connections to people from all walks of life. She was also most concerned that Karen's life now had a due date on it. Tonya was one of the few people who could still find things to laugh about, no matter how serious matters became. She insisted that a friend could put her in touch with people who could save her life. An hour later, Daliyah arrived and had a no-nonsense air about her that most women instinctively knew not to cross. She was a Métis woman, a tribe made of indigenous natives mixed with mostly French-white ancestry. Her petite build and light brown hair, with light brown hair were offset by piercing dark eyes that blazed and burned with fiery purpose. She was rigid about facilitating their escape.

"You're on the news. You must get out," she said flatly.

Minutes later, a large self-driving truck with tinted windows and a long chassis pulled up, and the former military types hopped out of it.

"Mercenaries!" Karen groaned.

Molière turned to her with a look of caution. "I wouldn't use that word around them if I were you, most of them hate being called that. Stick with a military contractor, military escort, or service contractor, and avoid the term 'mercenary'. You see, nobody likes to be called a whore, and mercenaries are known for compromising their moral values in exchange for profit. A prostitute is frowned upon for selling love, and a mercenary is seen as someone who sells murder and death. Once again, the prostitute is seen as being more honorable, just as in business; a prostitute honors the promise, whereas a revealing waitress does not. Under that mode of thinking, the word 'mercenary' means a 'death whore' or 'murder salesman'.

"So the only people you trust are prostitutes?" Karen ribbed him.

"I wouldn't go that far, I just don't think they should be spat upon by a society that sells anything."

Some seasoned and prepared ex-soldiers leaped out of the truck and evaluated them with suspicious eyes. Daliyah gave the men the nod, and they were afforded room in the truck.

Molière interrupted the mostly quiet ride, asking, "What is the end game here?"

One of the alpha male mercenaries in fatigues, and a sleeveless shirt with a jagged beard, that was reminiscent of an unkempt lawn, stood up to respond.

"You want to make omelets, you have to break eggs." He followed it up with a lengthy, unwavering glare.

"Oh, OK, so we're going to a farm to kill baby chickens then," Keith answered.

An Israeli mercenary with a full beard and beret took exception. "When they crush people's will, they have to pay the price."

"So we are going to preserve democracy by killing the people we disagree with?"

"If they weren't abusing our rights, they could have a free discussion, they steal our right to dispute them, with all their disinformation bullshit, and they leave us no option. They clamp our mouths shut, so we have to answer more directly."

"We want to preserve freedom by exterminating the other views, isn't that exactly what we are trying to oppose?" Molière persisted.

The man with the scratchy beard hastened to answer.

"People like you don't get us anywhere; they get us right here, through proper channels, mild opposition, and telling people you don't support them. Those pigs in government and financial fat cats thrive on your inefficiency and bowl humanity over. It's time to give them some of their own medicine. If you can't see that, you're blind."

Molière knew he wasn't going to win over the room, or in this case, the truck, with his appeal to process, but couldn't leave it there.

"Do you know what I wish I wasn't blind about? I wish I wasn't blinded by the idea that if I just chased my dreams, everything would be fine. If I just enjoyed other people, fit in more, never had a dark thought, never had a detention at school, never quit a job on moral grounds, never got into fights, and never bucked the system, I'd be fine. That's what they teach in school and it's pure horseshit. On the other side of the coin, if I let any idiot with a gun and a cause lead me down a path of self-destruction just to feel like I am in the right, or that I can wield power against power with no consequence, I'd be fine. It's the same brand of manure, it's just coming from a different variety of farm animals. No one ever told me I'd need to pay attention to every political debate and watch for sneaky bills with broad and loose definitions being used to exploit the public. No one ever told me that civic duty matters in the slightest. It was all about making more money, not rocking the boat, and being a good citizen by ignoring the corruption of pharmaceutical companies, multi-billionaires influencing organizations like Global Health Watch, and in turn, creating invasive treaties. No one said to watch out for our corrupt governments, who've been selling us out for decades. Watch them waltz the truth into a corner, dancing to any evil number their financial puppeteers play for them. Don't challenge the teacher, the professor, your boss, the mayor, or the PM when they are wrong, because if you embarrass them, they'll unfairly punish you. It is that very rebellious quality that provides one with the strength to say no when the government wants to force you into guinea pig status with unproven and rushed cures for profit. This is exactly what people need to be taught. Stand up to their oppressors with reason, with debate, with embarrassment, humiliation even, and especially with your vote, *not* with your gun."

"OK then, go and make a sign and embarrass them, and when you go missing, ask them for a gun to get you out of prison when it's too late." The rebel jeered.

"Maybe I could buy one from you, but then you might say 'no' if Trueborn's goons offered you a better price for that gun, then where would I be?"

The mercenary shrugged dismissively as if the point didn't warrant some soul-searching on his part. Molière, however, recognized the mercenary's point: that mere words were worthless when they couldn't be shared under the rule of a censored society.

The dark-eyed rebel wasn't done. "So you're anti-gun then?"

"No, I think they are a great and necessary deterrent. In the 1860s, everyone carried a gun, and the government never dared to restrict the entire population. Take away that deterrent, and the restrictive laws and edicts multiply. Everyone who says you don't need an automatic weapon to hunt deer is off by a thousand miles. As military and police weapons grow in sophistication, a 22-caliber rifle is meaningless when the cops come to the door to take your kids away because your five-year-old wanted to have a doctor mutilate their genitalia because his kindergarten teacher told him it would be a great idea. If the authorities have snipers and blood cookers while all you have is a potato gun, they get your kids. If we don't give five-year-old kids handguns with live ammo to play with, because they are too young, why would you have them play god with their sexual functionality before they even hit puberty? What's not good about guns is the temptation to use them for the wrong reasons, like going after your own elected officials; your population voted this asshole in, so it's your job to get him voted out without your family having to watch the court trial before you get executed or disappear."

"Trueborn only gets former party members to judge and rule on his cases," the Israeli argued.

"Right, and why is that? It's because none of us paid any attention while most of our society was playing video games, checking their vanity pages, or getting high. Crooked politicians like Trueborn thrive on charming double-talk while poisoning society as we sleep."

They arrived at a paramilitary camp designed for quick disassembly and basic provisions.

A former wooden lodge with surrounding stables had been converted into barracks. The food was passable, and there were some light drills to keep the fighting men sharp. They seemed to prefer being outdoors, as it felt safer. Karen saw an opportunity to tease Keith and took full advantage.

"I'm so glad you warned me about how to speak to the mercenaries, we are so popular with them now, they probably won't even *kill* us," she smiled.

"I just didn't want them thinking that if they threw guns in our hands and told us we'd save the day, we'd say, 'Hell yeah!' only to be sent in first as pawns, so they could evaluate the lethality of the threat as we got blown away. We are the new guys, remember?"

"You meant what you said about all that?" she asked.

"I don't care what gender anybody is, but I feel that it's an adult decision to make. If you aren't together enough to vote yet or be drafted, picking your sex parts seems like it would be miles beyond the pale."

"I meant about the guns, school shootings, and race hate crimes; are they all fine in case the government gets out of hand?"

Molière started at her in astonishment.

"In case? Really? The government has several propaganda networks acting under the guise of protecting us from disinformation, and conspiracy theories, I need the guys with guns and prisons to step in over some idiot who thinks flying saucers have been cheating on his wife. I don't need the government for that, especially *this* government. The pitiful excuse of conspiracy theories threatening democracy is the biggest dose of empty threat detection in history. It's a superstitious boogieman alert, a fake reason to oppress, and nothing more. Next, they'll be saying they have to arrest people over old wives' tales and gossip. It's more like the human last party. The government is out of control, or you wouldn't be wanted for false crimes right now. All these anti-gun laws have done is make the takeover of society go more smoothly for the guilty parties. That's why they did it, they probably cheered every time there was a hate crime to use as justification, and that's only *if* they didn't have a hand in it themselves."

Karen rolled her eyes and said, "Oh, come on, the government doesn't do that."

"Probably not, but would you say Trueborn is too noble a character to allow that? Was he too noble to lie about you being a criminal, and have you hunted down by any means? Too noble to get involved with freezing free people's bank accounts? What would you have said about government actions a week before he did that? You would have said that's a conspiracy theory. The truth is, I have mixed feelings on guns, abortions, immigration, and all other complex issues. I just know that the people behind the causes frequently have hidden agendas. That's why they ratchet up the fear surrounding climate change. It's real, and it's happening, but there are creepy people wildly exaggerating its threat, so doctors can put 'climate change' as the cause of death on certificates. The government then has another excuse to lock us down, limit movement, and block the internet as they release illnesses into our society to destroy the middle class. Some of these entities absurdly believe climate change is not caused by industry but rather by too many humans walking around freely, and that's why we are getting nailed by man-invented viruses while the Global Health Watch is allowed to define what a pandemic is. They can even say that too much sunshine is a pandemic. They can lock us down whenever they want. Those in power are making us sick, and when people die off, they justify it by saying the ice caps melt because too many humans are heating the planet. All this while, industry and factories chew up the ozone, and pollution kills everything, but don't pay attention to that; it's the farmers and cows that are the problem, right?"

"OK, I think your chip is acting up; you've never said anything that paranoid, ever," Karen said.

"Well, what is the end game then? This is not just some wild coincidence that the government is deciding who can go to work and who can't. Who can leave their home? The goal of quarantine is to keep all infected people separated from healthy people. When in the history of our planet have quarantines been applied against the healthy as well as the sick? It hasn't happened in 2000 years. This can not stand up to logical scrutiny, that's why questioning lands you in hot water. It only happens if it is fraudulently made an international crime to question corruption. Do you argue that?"

Karen looked resigned; if he was off in his estimate about the conclusion, his assessment of wrongdoing felt spot on, and she had something else to share.

"I wanted to kid you about not reading any more of your grandfather's journal, but I missed a piece; it looks to have come from some sort of weblog, so here."

"Thank you."

"So now you don't like guns again?" She added. "Overruled!" He teased in return.

Karen looked down at the flash drive that she'd gone to some lengths to acquire for him, and he took the hint and read the journal entry.

It's time we performed an inventory of purposeful deception by the establishment. I went to the dentist's office today, and this is the third dentist I've had to see regarding the same tooth. My teeth are clean, but one has an issue. This was the third dentist, as the previous two botched the job. They politely and warmly insisted that I needed to come in for a cleaning before they could work on the tooth in question. I respectfully pointed out that I was there to repair the mistakes made by two other dentists and that they, too, had required cleaning of all the healthy teeth before they even looked at the one in need of care.

To put this in perspective, imagine visiting a mechanic with a flat tire and him saying he couldn't repair the flat until he inspected the other tires, which were not flat. Now imagine that scenario on an eighteen-wheeler three times in a row. I pointed out that I was assured they could fix the tooth without cleaning the other teeth for the third time, but they wouldn't budge, so I thanked them for overcharging me and devising ways to scam their clients and asked how many people they charged for a service they didn't need. If I asked to have a car door repainted, and they wanted to clean the other car doors, I'd tell them to get lost, but when dentists pull scams, they escape all the reputational damage that auto mechanics get if they are cheated. I asked them how they get away with the con artistry side of it. They were not amused.

This is similar to opening a bank account where they want to charge you a monthly fee, but if you deposit an amount over ten thousand dollars, they will waive the fee. In essence, it costs $10,000 to save a nominal monthly fee. If you remove any of that sum and the balance dips below the $10,000 mark, they start charging you fees. To avoid it means saying goodbye to your $10,000; you cannot invest it elsewhere, and the pittance of an interest rate doesn't even match the monthly fee they are siphoning from their customers. The real trick of the con comes when one has to close an account. They want reasons; they want to know why, and then they can decide if they think one's reason is a good enough reason to close their own account. The banks have lost sight of whose money it is. The next part of the fiasco is that they try to stall and pretend they don't have the money on hand. They say they will need a few days to get the bills together. I never accept this excuse, and neither should anyone else. Have they been dealing with drug dealers for so long that they use the street-like excuse of needing a few days to get the money together? They have a vault full of money right in the bank, and they have to go and send out the pizza guy to go and find *some bills to scrape together for them. It's a con. In the event that a customer gets a hot stock tip or another time-pressed investment opportunity, they know that if in a few days, the window of opportunity closes and the deal goes south, most will just leave their money in the bank. This happened to me, and I told every customer in the bank; that they refused to give me my own money and said they were broke for a few days. I asked, "What's in the vault then? Party favors, confetti, the contents of the safety deposit boxes of crime lords who were too distrusting to leave wills behind?"*

At some point, they found it necessary to make an exception for me because they could see I was getting cross. Every person must be very cautious with bank amounts now that governments can freeze your accounts for the most insidious of reasons. It's like the medical profession is becoming all cloak and dagger about side effects. Consider the case of an elderly relative who is diagnosed with cancer. The grave nature of the subject requires absolute transparency from all parties concerned. Your granny is told that it's bad, and then she is told she might be saved by chemotherapy. Granny is thrilled, and you have to say, "Wait a minute there, you can die from too much radiation exposure, and while it's a good gamble, there is a chance you can die from the method attempting to cure you. Then granny goes onto the internet and asks about the chances of dying from chemotherapy, and all mention of risk is de-platformed, removed, redacted, or cited as spreading disinformation and causing chemo hesitancy. We can all understand that would be bullshit, but with other medical decisions, we aren't permitted to examine the data, the content, or know what's in the tonic they are coercing us to take. Coercion is a hybrid of blackmail and bribery, both of which are illegal.

We don't want to set a bad example for the children, do we? We don't want our thirteen-year-old kids being coerced into sexual activities by other thirteen-year-old kids, only to ask where they got the idea from after it's too late. One can envision the ugly answer being; that I learned it from the government when they took away my daddy's job because he wanted to do more research. What a scam! We allow wealthy manipulators to sway the media and government, encroaching on our every civil liberty, and then we wonder what went wrong. If we act gullible, they will certainly treat us as such. Now hand me ten thousand, so I won't charge you a monthly fee, you brainless rube. Does anyone want to wear the hat that goes with it?

Molière looked up at Karen and said, "He was an anti-vaxxer? This can't be right! No wonder they locked him up!" he said.

Karen's voice was soft but direct: "Do you not see certain parallels and similarities?"

"Look up!" he urged as puffy white clouds beneath a cerulean blue sky were partly blocked in patches as tiny airborne squares approached. At least a hundred drones moved across the sky like a shadowy blanket, and this time there were no microwave guns to be found.

Chapter Eleven

A CERTAIN UNCERTAINTY

The mercenaries took positions beneath and beside the truck, while a few ran toward individual places of perceived safety. Keith and Karen ran toward some bushes, feeling unwelcome near the truck. The mercenaries had only a few twenty-two-caliber rifles along with non-lethal weapons. They fired upon the drones to little effect as they were diving from different heights. A few hits caused a couple of the drones to detonate in the air. Others began exploding near the truck tires as the mercenaries scattered, with some people being blown apart in their attempts to escape. Those with nonlethal lasers that induced blindness were worthless. Rebels threw them into the air in protest or to reduce weight as they fled in terror.

The truck exploded and mercifully detonated many of the descending drones. Black smoke billowed upward over crackling flames amid a chorus of groans and wails of anguish over the lost lives of friends. The man with the scratchy beard and his friend with the backward cap dusted themselves off and fiercely walked over to the two new lovers, their eyes full of suspicion and hatred.

"So you gave up our positions, and what a surprise, you both survived without a scratch." The first man said, pointing his weapon.

"No, never!" Karen insisted.

"You worked for Trueborn's party, didn't you?" Daliyah Twain abruptly intruded on the conversation.

"It wasn't them, they tracked the truck," she said dismissively and kept walking.

After a brief exchange of dirty looks, Karen announced she was growing tired of this new life and reconsidering her options.

"Maybe I should just turn myself in," she groaned slowly. Keith squinted and twisted his neck in disgust.

"Your call," he said.

He left her side to help the wounded and reexamine his plans. He pulled the better part of an albino man from the truck wreckage and appropriated a sewing needle from a deceased medic's hand. Looking at the gaping wound, he struggled to squeamish impulses. There were wide gashes across both thighs, and the blood was pumping steadily from both legs.

"I've got to get those sewn up," he said.

Kieth estimated the man's life expectancy might be 45 seconds if he didn't do something quickly, and his sewing skills were dubious at best.

"No, it's OK," his newfound patient muttered.

The man looked about fifty, with silvery white hair. His face boasted creased lines and eyes that had seen a lot of life.

"I have to get to those legs NOW!" Molière shouted.

The pale man shook his head, and Molière recognized him. He'd mocked this man for showing interest in Karen and now held the albino's ebbing life in his hands. He knew C.P.R. and basic first aid, but he'd never sutured a single stitch.

"I just need you to grab my hand a minute." The weakening man grunted.

Molière took his hand in the traditional arm wrestling grip, and the man said, "I'm cold, and tired."

Molière found himself unwilling to release the man's hand, as though letting it go would somehow make his death official. He felt like an involuntary sickle in service to death's bloodthirsty hand. The unfinished conversation, unfocused gaze, and silence that followed released an onslaught of internal recall with pristine detail in Molière's mind. For a moment, looking into his past seemed more comfortable than facing all the carnage right before him.

Years ago, his dog "Conan" had broken his leash and somehow jumped the property fence in the yard. Conan discovered a broken casserole dish of lasagna in someone's garbage. The dog tragically ate some broken glass within the lasagna and returned home in terrible condition. Keith found a conscientious veterinarian willing to do a home visit. She explained the awful truth that the dog had to be put down. The problem was that the German Shepherd instinctively distrusted the vet and wouldn't let her approach him. After several failed attempts, she passed the death needle into Molière's hand, and he had to kill his own dog. With trusting eyes, his dog allowed him to sink that ugly, sterilized needle into his paw. Molière was an ardent animal lover, but he never owned another dog in his life. He'd made every effort to bury that memory, but with his recall improving, all he could do was offer a sarcastic mental thanks to his brain chip. Now for the second time in his life, he'd allowed life to wither in his hands, and he was filled with self-loathing.

"Needle!" He recognized the terse voice and outstretched hand in need and surrendered it.

Daliyah had two modes of personality: laid-back and quiet, or erupting in fury and little else. It was an unusual place for her to go, but she was trying her hand at showing compassion.

"Death's never easy," she said without looking at him.

"I was going to thank you for sticking up for us earlier," Keith acknowledged, partly to change the subject.

Daliyah turned and focused on him: "I knew it wasn't you, and the men were getting twitchy about the timing of the hit."

Molière shrugged and said, "Thanks again, we owe you one." Daliyah looked at him with hard, daring eyes and shot back,

"I *said*: I knew it wasn't you, but your friend there, she might be playing you."

"What makes you say that?" he snapped.

"I heard her at the end of your conversation. She might turn herself in, with all that she'd be facing; I don't know anyone who turns themselves in, not to this government. Not unless they knew they'd be fine, then they might do it. Careful who you shore up to; they might get you killed or worse," she said emphatically.

"She's not like that," he assured her.

"You've got a thing for lawyers, do ya? You have no qualms about someone charging hundreds of dollars to read a letter. You don't wonder about someone whose ethics will permit them to scream innocence in defense of a serial killer or send an innocent to jail just to win their case. Do you think someone like that can't be bought? Do you think she wouldn't sell you out for a nice, cozy job with the feds? That's not how she's wired, she's too decent and pure. Oh, OK, sure."

Molière didn't like what she said, but he appreciated her honesty.

"That's a lot to heap on somebody you've only just met," he countered.

She arched her body, crossed her arms, and gave him an iron stare for a five-count, then walked off.

The mercenaries left the bodies of their fallen to the authorities but kept hats, helmets, and other belongings for a more ceremonial burial at a safer time. They watched the city monitors as the media spin worked its magic. A woman with an elaborate hairstyle announced, "Several MPs and members of the Secret Service were killed today in a military training drill that went wrong. Faulty equipment and ammunition failures were to blame, and the government is launching an investigation."

Karen spoke first, "Well, that accounts for the microwave deaths of Trueborn's guards; whenever they say equipment failure, they are hiding something. All of his investigations are led by former cabinet ministers from his party. It was the same with his judges, his no longer public court cases, and any so-called 'independent' investigation he's ever ordered. What a sham!"

"It sounds like you know him pretty good. Sorta tight, you and Trueborn, aren't ya?" the mercenary with the patched beard asked pointedly.

"I did work for him for years and got a first-hand look at why no one should ever trust him."

"It sounds like it might have been in a roomful of untrustworthy people to me, maybe he only hires his own kind."

"Divide and conquer; it's the Trueborn handbook; turn people against each other for political gain. If he can wedge us apart with misdirected hate, he'll buy himself a cigar and laugh, so let's stay unified," Keith added diplomatically. Suspicious glares moved between faces on all sides, but calm returned.

Karen pulled Molière aside and asked, "Why do they hate me so much? I get that not everyone loves lawyers, but give a person a chance, at least."

"Their lives are being cheapened, their rights are being trampled on every day, and the media covers up any good they achieve. They've lost friends, and aren't at their best," Molière stated.

"I've noticed, they all just stare at me, and not in the usual sexual way, it's more hostile. Even the women do it, that Daliyah chick is like 35, but she could pass for 17, and I felt a bit motherly toward her. If I go speak to her, she just glares at me like she wants to beat my face in. I think we should leave these people."

Molière felt a bit uneasy but asked, "Why, is something bad about to happen to them? Something so bad that we might have to keep our distance? You know, like for our safety?"

Karen's legal background prevented her from seeing such a line of questions as anything other than a cross-examination.

"So they've recruited you into their camp to make me the enemy, is that it?" She inquired testily.

"I just don't want to be manipulated into anything ever."

"Oh, that chip in your head is doing quite a number on you; I should have listened to you on that count. I wish you never got that damn chip; it's watering down your brain. Maybe I'm secretly the doctor who installed it, and just to mess with you, I put in a can opener instead. That way, I can pop open your lid any time I like and see what's gone wrong in your noodle, because I am a controlling, manipulative bitch, isn't that right?" Karen asked facetiously.

"Well, maybe you can tell me exactly where we would be going with no resources, no weaponry, no income, and no plan! Are we going to become hippies and live off the land?" He countered in an exaggeratedly naive tone.

"Yeah, you were doing so much better before I got you to join my commune."

"Well, if you aren't happy with the arrangement, just let me know," he said.

They looked at each other with a mixture of regret, annoyance, fear, judgment, and finally resolution.

"I'm sorry," Karen admitted, "I am simply no longer comfortable with this group of people, and I don't know if we can trust them."

Molière nodded and put his arm around her. He immediately remembered what he'd read in his grandfather's journal.

Greetings from the unsafe ground of centrism.

I respectfully present my vast concerns over leaning too far to either political extreme. The first and greatest concern is that of becoming an unreasonable person. I wonder if joining either party required an oath of hatred for the other side, which would quell the hate, fear, and prejudice driving both sides of the extreme right and radical left. If one had to swear to hate an entire mass of (mostly unmet) people because they voted differently in a so-called free society. There are great qualities on both sides as well as dark and frightening anti-human aggression on both sides. The benefits of the left were once peace-loving and accepting of people's differences; let's make the world a better place for everyone, no matter who they are.

The perks of the right were that they believed in community, spending rationally, and law and order.

As far as one could see, there were merits on both sides. That is the intriguing aspect: it appears that the two could simply cohabitate in union and quickly alleviate any disparity. However, if left unchecked, both of these groups could quickly adopt highly threatening postures. The extremists on either side would be quick to shout, 'No! Not so,' but their arguments fade like shadows under a shining light when examined. If we were to paint a caricature of an extremist just for argument's sake, one could easily spot how an innocent stance can rapidly degrade into hate-mongering. Let's begin with the right and present "Al," a fictitious man of average qualities in most areas. Al introduces himself at the town hall meeting, calling for more reasonable spending and less big government.

He meets "Lizette," a proponent of equal rights for all and someone who calls for access to free education and healthcare across the board. Neither side has an unpleasant personality and only wants what's best for their country. We can all still be friends. We should be friends because these are our neighbors, either across the street, across the hall, or across the vineyard. The problem begins with both parties surrounding themselves with an echo chamber of like minds while slowly diminishing their capacity for objective reason. Al thinks the people at his church are just great and firmly believes the country should model itself after the principles of Judeo-Christian values. It's not the worst idea, as a great many people have found fulfillment and peace at the end of that rainbow. Lizette wants people to chip in, a little more of their money to pay for health care access, and other medical treatments. Al keeps healthy, as do his family members, and resents the hit on his wallet. Lizette decides that all these churchgoers have too much pull with her local politicians and might sway policies via their numbers. Lizette believes in a woman's right to autonomy over her body. She doesn't buy the argument that abortion affects another life if it is unborn and sees abortion as being similar to a morning-after pill. She was not put on this earth to have her body serve as a host vessel for an unwanted pregnancy that may have occurred by accident, drunkenness, or even rape. It's her body. Al takes exception to this thought, advocates for the unborn child, and accuses the woman of infanticide. Lizette responds that it's an easy position for any man to take because he doesn't have to deal with the stress of pregnancy or the expense of raising an unwanted child. Thoughts of a faceless bureaucrat having such authority over her most intimate decisions could only evoke repulsion. She believes the state should prevent any party outside of a woman and her doctor, from having any involvement in the decision. In her eyes, this crucial point, among other leftist views, should be enforced by law. Al has a home and feels the need to protect his family with a gun for emergencies only. He realizes he is a lousy shot and would not be much help if a break-in were committed by a seasoned criminal. He joins a gun club and makes friends at the shooting range. Lizette also has a child and doesn't want some malcontent walking into her child's school and going on a shooting spree. She joins a leftist group that wants to ban all firearms.

Al goes to the town hall and argues most shooters use stolen weapons and might just as easily run people down with their car or truck, and no one wants to ban vehicles. Lizette has a son who questions his sexual identity, and she doesn't care for the fact that he gets ostracized at school. She feels strongly that if people better understood that some kids are different and that picking on them is wrong, protecting the marginalized would improve the world. Al, who hears about preaching sexual preferences at school at too early an age, is luring and grooming kids into a sexual bias before they are ready for it. They aren't ready psychologically, physically, or emotionally. He can't understand why Lizette knows better than to hand over a firearm to a child unsupervised but thinks they are prepared to make decisions on genital mutilation that can't be reversed if they change their mind again a year later. He organizes a group of irritated parents to put pressure on politicians to make child grooming illegal. Lizette explains to her friends that these religious freaks want control over women's bodies, that only heterosexual members are accepted in society, and that they have no problem with mass shootings. Al hears about these claims and asks members of his community if mothers like Lizette should be allowed to live in their town. In another reality, Lizette and Al meet at a small-town fundraiser, fall in love, and become "your" parents. Al decides he doesn't like single parents as their offspring tend to escalate crime. Gradually, he begins to dislike anyone who makes less money than him, seeing them as riff-raff. Soon he becomes rich enough to join a private club and looks down on anyone who can't afford a membership or doesn't drive the right kind of car. It's 2.2 kids and a house, or else get off of his block, he didn't work that hard to be among lazy welfare recipients. To hell with them. He equates wealth with work ethic and deludes himself into believing that anyone with less than he has is lazy. Instead of assessing character, this point of view devolves into a superficial competition of status symbols. He didn't start out that way; he was not a bigot; he was more of a leftist as a young man, but once he learned about money, the left seemed like drunken sailors, imagining the feds scratching their every itch with blank checks. The increased spending on exaggerated leftist social concerns that were bankrupting the country infuriated him. Lizette, on the other hand, wants to feed the world and give out free medicine to everyone while banning all pollutants without so much as a single thought about the exorbitant cost that will decimate the lives of everyone she knows. She would unwittingly cause a welfare state that would leave all the people who can't afford things even poorer by hiking fuel and energy costs to feel better about herself. Her idea of fiscal responsibility was to have her parents buy her a child's fantasy home, and that's the way governments should be run too. She is pro-abortion, but it doesn't stop there. She knows Al's church members are pro-life, so she persuades local politicians to remove new mother items like baby boots, clothing, and carriages from the list of tax-deductible donations. This is so that young pro-lifers won't get the wrong idea that it will be easy to raise an extra child. The pro-lifers often bullied and chastised her, so she felt on the correct moral side of the argument. More than anything, she wanted to bully the pro-lifers in return and teach them a lesson.

Al has come to live for class distinction. It's all about the clothes one wears, the car one drives, and the size of their house. He has become shallow and judgmental, he looks down the barrel of his nose at those less fortunate. He soon views anyone who does not own an island is quickly labeled a lowlife, even if he himself will never achieve that status. No one is good enough for Al anymore, and he can't imagine why he is seen as being so unrelatable. He dismisses his increasing isolation as others' lack of status or sheer envy. The tension mounts between the couple's many differences, and to deflect their rage away from each other, they unwittingly take it out on their kids. While there is no violence, all family members become too quick to shout, and the environment becomes toxic as no political view from the children can fully align with the parent's extremes. They know their family is becoming dysfunctional and socially odd. They won't get a divorce and will stick it out for the benefit of the kids because they've read the statistics on single-parent children. he only glue holding their marriage together is voicing constant concern over their teenagers. Then, tired of the yelling at home, their second son steals a neighbor's gun and is chastised by his teachers for being of the unfavored and oppressive white race and the dreadfully unfavored heterosexuality. He then goes on a shooting spree because he sees no one can get along anyway. The point is that we have lost the ability to tolerate each other's points of view and the ability to reason with those who disagree with us. A classist can be even worse than a racist because they judge so many more people. The only ones good enough for them need to have the right shade of green in their wallets. What if that were all of us? Too often, we can't appreciate our neighbors without insisting they join our political group, denomination, private club, or social complaint group. If we become less arrogant about how correct we are concerning everything, we might gain some insight into what our opponents have to offer. Failing that, we could at least agree that most people begin with good intentions and become gradually indoctrinated by their peer groups. If we looked beyond our political biases, we'd find thousands of different points of view and realize that no one is always right. This idea isn't about my family or yours but those of the whole country and all their neighbors descending into a meaningless culture war, and it's unbearably ugly. Both sides are shouting at the government to fix my feelings for me; other views make me feel bad! like when a rapist approaches a girl in order to make his feelings her problem. Once we attach that dreaded "ist" to our ideals, we are all but sworn to make our feelings everyone else's problem. I am a considerist, meaning I weigh all arguments case by case, I don't believe all women, all men, all whites, or all of any group because all people are capable of lying, so I consider the proof, rather than the evidence. There is evidence of all kinds of false things like ghosts, gods, and gamblers' luck, but so much of it collapses when asked for proof. Because true considerists are so rare, I've yet to meet another.

He squeezed her gently and said, "I never wanted to be seen as someone who lets their politics do their thinking for them. Allowing my discomfort to get in the way of my purposes and the bigger picture was a self-imposed curse. That's the mistake I made. Before, when I met a group of weekend warriors, I was put off. I judged them and deemed them too flawed in their thinking, too stubborn, and too misguided to reach any of their goals. These are our countrymen, our sisters, our brothers, and our fellow voters. If we can't get along with them, whether they vote left, right, or undecided, we will never have any allies in anything. We have to make that choice, let's not become elitists and think we are too good for anyone because that will eventually lead to a private table in a members-only restaurant. "A tiered system in which regular people lose their jobs and are soon barred from entering a grocery store."

Keith withheld an expression of disgust, saying,

"I don't want to live like that. Is the platinum card the ultimate life goal in life? I, for one, would like to think I was put here for other reasons. Do you want to know what I've discovered lately? The value of emotions; I always thought emotions were the biggest human flaw ever. We make all of our worst decisions based on emotions. We say things we don't mean when we are angry. How frequently do we tell off the wrong people? We buy things we don't need to impress people we don't know. Often, we fail to achieve our goals because we dwell on our need for success, and while this is true, it doesn't tell the full story. We dwell on how things used to feel when in truth old wounds are best forgotten. The constant reliving of our trauma is a great impediment. For all the time we spend lamenting over the past and planning the future, all we can truly experience is right here and now. That means when you have someone in your life you care about, and who makes you feel good about being alive, you treasure it because you get to feel so much more. More anticipation, more hope, more love, more excitement, more sentimentality, more loyalty, more exhilaration, and yes, more anxiety, more concern, and more insecurity all get swirled into a milkshake that makes us who we are, and *that* is what makes life worth living, not the pricey car, or the view by the beach. Those emotions are what separate us from being a productivity engine, a better widget maker, and an efficiency drone. I don't want to be so good that I can stay up all night every night just to please my boss. I want to live my life and tell my boss he can go ahead and commit suicide if he wants me to work late all the time. It's not living. Now they want you to get a chip, so you can work endlessly, day and night. Forget it." Keith said.

"I get it; preserving the human mind and all its worth means it mustn't be tampered with. If we allow the powers that be to experiment on us, we'll lose our souls. If you go ahead with your half-dead renegades and die a martyr without support from the masses, nothing will change. I'll get Doyle to speak even if it means I'll be publicly hanged," Karen promised.

"If you aren't put in an unreachable cell first," he said.

"I admit that I couldn't have seen him without your help," she said. "So, maybe we're better off as a team?" he asked.

"Maybe so," she conceded.

Daliyah marched up toward them with a purposeful stride and said, "We don't want you here anymore, the men think you are bad luck."

Karen was set to reply, but Daliyah added, "Just go!" and turned away.

"Do you see?" Karen said, turning to Keith, "They don't want us here."

Daliyah overheard this and turned around again. "What do you mean, *us*? I wasn't telling him to get lost, just you!"

"Oh, I understand now; there's only one of us to be sent away, is that it?" Karen grinned sarcastically.

"No, it's our men here, who want you gone, and I agree," Daliyah stated firmly.

"So, there's one of us you want to stick around, and you want the other one of us gone, out of the picture, and out of your way. Well sorry, hon, we're both going."

"Why don't you ask him? Are you calling all the shots for everyone? Maybe he'd rather have a dozen people on his side than one trouble magnet," Daliyah argued.

"Does she *have* to leave?" Keith asked.

Karen looked agitated but held it in, and just started to pack up her gear.

Molière was about to follow her when Daliyah said, "Wait a second."

He turned, and she stared him in the eyes and held her gaze as the pause grew absurd, before she finally said, "Nothing," before turning away.

Karen barely looked his way as they ventured toward a communication tower in an effort to boost their palm device signals to contact Doyle at the prison.

"Are you sure you don't want to turn back and stay with your new friend? It looked like you two were about to have a moment, there."

"I was simply trying to understand her, and besides, we have work to do."

"Wait, what's that light?" Karen's momentary insecurities were suddenly forgotten.

"I don't see it. Where, at the top?"

"No, about a tenth of the way down," Karen said, squinting hard as darkness approached.

"That, my dear, is the glint of a scoped weapon at rest belonging to a sniper on the catwalk of the tower. We have to get out of here, There's no chance against whatever he's carrying from here," he said.

"Ugh! Now what?"

"We find another tower," Molière said.

Once again, their meandering goals took a new turn on a road that only seemed to offer aimless circles. As they sought out the next best tower, Trueborn had been ratcheting up the propaganda, claiming all white people whomever were not directly affiliated with his 'Human First' party were either racists or domestic terrorists and that they needed to be reported. He was scared, and his favorite trick was to whip the people into a fear-based frenzy with something new to be afraid of. This age-old substitute for a real threat played on people's prejudices, and demagoguery was his best weapon because it had never failed him. Immigrants rarely challenge authority for fear of having their status called into question; the real threat was from the people who'd been in the country for generations and felt their rights were inalienable.

They, the questioners, and all who sided with them were the enemies, according to the government's misused authorities. Whenever they violated the constitutional rights to silence them, they were "merely following orders." or "just doing the *right* thing."

Molière wondered if there had been a shortage of testosterone that left most men to stand by idly as their government steadily ruined their country. Trueborn continued to spout his tired tropes of domestic enemies and fear-mongering with abandon. He was determined to turn neighbor against neighbor based on skin color and which way they voted. Perhaps the greatest crime was that people let him get away with it for so long that few dared to oppose him now as he inched toward autocracy. Like many narcissists, he fed off the illusion that everyone admired him and became enraged when he heard otherwise. His seething and monstrous tantrums were in full bloom, and those close to him marveled at how he managed to present himself as such a caring leader. Such a person was incapable of caring about anyone unless they proved useful in helping to deceive the public. He was especially threatened by his kind. He was white, and he felt it helped his image to maintain an anti-white stance, as he desperately needed a body of people to kick at and present as a threat to justify his rampant abuse of authority. His plan, while somewhat transparent, was thriving in a divided population where everyone felt they were getting the short end of the stick. Today, he would have his men stage a false attack on a church with video footage while blaming white nationalists, so he could give the police the authority to shoot on sight. Such were his decisions when he felt the slightest dissent. He had his crew of cronies and puppet ministers on hand, and they took the podium with their emergency announcements ready.

"Dearest citizens, we have been there for you, and you have stood with us, but the threat today is far worse than any of us would have believed," he began.

Elsewhere, atop a communications tower, a couple of tattered and worn-down defenders of civil liberties had established contact with an unmarked prison. It was not on any map, and there was a genius there who had a workbench and a mini-lab and had a boatload of ideas and opinions on the way the world was going.

Trueborn continued, "The images we are about to show you are graphic and disheartening, but they are, uh, necessary, and we will show you today that we will not stand for hate anywhere, that we will not accept these hostilities and threats to our sovereignty and our peace. Today we will launch our uh, new policies, which will give uh, the police uh, power to uh, tear down this unholy collection of reprobates and dissenters. They are a threat to democracy!"

The monitors flickered and flashed a bit of screen snow, and the sound of a signal frequency was heard everywhere. Odd sounds were heard. *Ah-whee-Oh-woo-bzzzt!* Followed by a crackle, and then all the monitors all over the country that were on twenty-four hours a day to indoctrinate the people showed different footage. They showed people with flags chanting, "No more Trueborn" and "Stop the tyranny!"

People of all colors, races, and genders shouted obscenities toward the president. Trueborn lost his composure. His well-coiffed hair and "pretty boy" image now gave way to childish tantrums, and the monitors showed him in all his rage-induced panic. He swore at his staff and screeched orders to make the screens stop, and moments later they all went dark.

Doyle's plan from the prison had been to replace the Trueborn propaganda with some forbidden footage of all the protests the media kept buried deep within the hall of records. With all screens switched off, this could not take place, and so yet again a new plan was needed.

Molière was not as disappointed as most were about the shutdown of all monitors across the country. He knew the government had never been so weak. There were no protection robots, no prying spy monitors, and most of the human authorities were suffering from either radiation sickness or berylliosis from the microwave guns. If there was ever a time for revolt, it is now, but sadly, with all the fears people have beaten into them about worrying about money, food, and punishment from the government, the people have become far too meek. Any rebellion had to be performed by the robots, they had no fears, no financial rewards to lose, and no need for food. All the coercion's carrots and sticks were useless against them. The plan was to get the evil Trueborn to require robot activation before his rage subsided.

Molière was prodding Karen for ideas to prompt Trueborn into action.

"You know him, how can we get him to act?"

"Well, there was Gordon Mailer, his old campaign advisor, who has been gone for years. No one knows where he is."

"Who else?" Keith implored.

"Well, there is Amber Bierce, I know he had an affair with her, but she was disappointed somehow; maybe because he's married. Whenever she entered the building, his staff would whisper, 'Amber Alert!' If we could find her, I bet she could influence him."

The two looked down, realizing their options were next to none. They decided to approach the Parliament buildings to gauge things more closely. When they arrived, they saw that Jim Service, the man who had witnessed Molière's fight, had led a ragtag band of ill- equipped rebels wielding tasers toward one side of the Parliament buildings, while Daliyah Twain and the rest of her men wielding nonlethal blinding laser rifles were on the other. Their numbers were small, but their convictions were undaunted. The MPs that were left on the grounds were lacking as well. Many guards either resigned or faked being sick after the microwave gun fiasco took place. There was only a skeleton crew left as Secret Service agents huddled around the president and secured him in the Parliament buildings, which had endless tunnels and bunkers for security and doors that could not be broken down. The freedom fighters shouted and pounded on the doors, but it had no effect, as both sides recognized all the signs of a standoff.

Chapter Twelve

CHILDREN OF AUTHORITARIANISM

Four MPs had entered the prison and passed through identification checks as they marched toward Warden Lynette Dunsel's office, and they were in no mood to negotiate. All of them were in military greens with white helmets, clean-shaven, and terse in both mood and responses.

"We're here for prisoner 9944881, Doyle!"

Lynette didn't appreciate being barged in on or being treated as a subordinate.

"Wait a minute, I haven't heard anything about this," she started, but was cut off by the head guard." Check your palm device, and hand him over at once."

Lynette thought she'd point out her good standing with the "Human First" party, and as its leader, but much like her superiors and staff, no one was paying close attention to anything she said. She had difficulties getting out of her chair to accompany the guards, but they had a map on their devices and left to get him without her.

They opened his coded lock and were surprised to see how elaborate his workshop appeared, given that he was in prison.

"The president wishes to see you. Come with us. It's not a choice."

Doyle went willingly to meet the shady president and learn of his bidding. While the vehicle approached the Parliament buildings, they passed a group of kids on the street who had come to watch the rebellion take place. The driver shouted at the kids.

"Military Police! Get out of the way!"

The kids ambled and shuffled out of the vehicle's path. They didn't want to take part in or oppose any of it; they just wanted to record it on their devices and seemed to have strong opinions on either side of the issue.

Doyle spoke up with a bemused chuckle, "In my day, the young people would have been all over this kind of thing, they just don't seem to care one way or the other. It's baffling to me."

After a silent moment, the guard closest to him grumbled.

"They've had it beaten out of them, in a world where you get hung or baked over your opinion, you learn not to have one."

The other three turned and gave him a shared look of consternation. There was no conversation after that until they arrived at a secret entrance to the tunnels of the Parliament buildings. Trueborn was hiding in the lowest bunker of the building, watching internet reports.

"Oh, Doyle, it's you!" He said, "I've been thinking, and I've come to the uh realization that you may not have all the tools and access you need to keep that mind of yours active. I'm thinking of granting you some leave from the prison, so you can work here for a while, perhaps indefinitely. The food is much better, and you could see all the updated technology since you were incarcerated. Would you like that? There's just, uh, one thing you have to do for me first."

"There must be a price," Doyle said.

"There are insurrectionists, domestic terrorists, and seditionists all around, and we had to temporarily disable the robots, but some of our human military and police have taken ill lately, leaving us short on resources. You can switch the robots back on for me, can't you? I mean, you wouldn't want to, uh, be thrown into the main population or anything like that, I'm sure, right?"

Doyle always hesitated before he spoke, but his eyes darted around because his mind was always working faster than most, and he drew quickly from his knowledge base quickly.

"I'm out of practice on this sort of thing, I'm not up-to-date, and I would need the highest functioning laptop in the world to catch up. I'll work quickly, but you must provide me with the tools I need. I'd need to open the internet and decensor it for a few hours, and I'd need to get away from all government censors and algorithms, and even then I'd be hard-pressed to get it done in one fell swoop."

Trueborn frowned and finally said, "Whatever you need, but don't tarry." He was provided with the "Accelence 9000," the top drawer item for state-of-the-art laptop computers. He was assigned two MPs with cyber training to oversee all of his actions. Molière and Karen approached Daliyah at the Parliament buildings and asked for a few hands to go back to the site of the drone attack and bury the dead. Given how thin the MPs were spread, it was unlikely any measures had been taken on that count. Daliyah confiscated a truck and brought a few men with her to the temporarily sealed-shut Parliament buildings.

They arrived back at the scene to discover the roads had been torn up with large potholes from the exploded drones, and there was a mess of detached and bloody limbs, most with shoes still on, accompanied by flies. They braved the stench of the deceased and grumbled about how every government that inched toward authoritarianism resulted in countless dead bodies. Death had never been included among campaign promises of protection, but it never failed in delivery.

Molière decided that if he could expose Karen and Daliyah to each other, they would see the common ground between them and realize there was no reason to be enemies. If Karen was unusually quiet at times, then Daliyah was positively laconic. Karen decided to prove her worth by working hard with her hands to show that even a lawyer can prove physically useful when the chips are down. Daliyah had no rank among these people, but most just listened to her due to her fiery temper and the fact that she was usually right and didn't dwell on things. She spoke almost entirely with her face and eyes. Molière admired this because he relied on words so heavily that he was awestruck to see someone do it all with just glances or by turning her head away when she didn't want to speak. It helped that she had a pretty face, but he was more exhilarated by her minimalist communication style. Undoubtedly, many just turned away from her, thinking that there was no conversation to be had, but there was a depth to her that most overlooked, perhaps quite unfairly.

Later, she brought him a pressurized container of soup and simply said, "Here," and walked away.

"Hey, wait for a second."

She turned to face him, waiting to see what was on his mind.

"First, thank you; and second, I don't understand you. You hardly ever say a word, and I can't even imagine how you make that work for you, and... I'm a bit confused by it. I guess."

He shrugged with a half-grin.

She walked just a bit too close to him and raised one eyebrow, then stared hard at him in the eye, never dropping the one eyebrow. He knew there was a question being asked, but was uncertain what was being asked of him, so he returned her gaze; they just stood there searching each other's souls for answers in silence, and then she walked off again.

Karen had come to see him just as Daliyah walked right past her without so much as the slightest acknowledgment.

"Do you think some people can recognize each other without ever having met?" Karen asked.

"How so?"

"Well, I don't think either of us believes in past lives, but it does happen where you meet someone, and you look at them, and they look at you, and you feel like you know them somehow, even if it's impossible."

Molière sensed that lawyer-like tactic of starting slowly with innocuous questions before building up to a crescendo of accusations and reassured her.

"I've just never seen anyone who gets by on a maximum of three words a day without any difficulty. I always feel like I need more words, but sometimes they can get in the way."

Karen looked at his soup container and nodded.

"Strangers sometimes bond for the strangest reasons, I mean, you could have a six-foot-tall white guy and a short, shapely, and slim native girl with nothing in common, and suddenly he's watching out for her on the battlefield, and she's bringing him food. Maybe in a past life, you were her father, and in another, she was your mom, and that's why you are both so concerned with each other's well- being. What do you think about my theory?"

"Look, she brought an extra soup, and I was hungry, so I said thanks. Are you going to sue me over that?"

"No, but if she gets something stuck in her eye, I'd prefer that one of the other men run to her side to check."

"One of the things I was best at before this chip started acting up was regulating my emotions. Sometimes things get out of balance: jealousy, anger, sadness, biases, prejudices, and being too quick to judge. I learned to stuff those things down and never act on them because they aren't you. They are momentary, and the aftermath of decisions made under those emotional flare-ups will always come back to haunt you."

"You sound like one of those 'robots are better than people' idiots that led to Trueborn starting the so-called 'Human First' party," she countered.

"You don't think the strain of what we are dealing with right now isn't wreaking havoc with all of our emotions? If you date a robot, he'll never even look at another woman. Is it too late for you to switch parties and become the robot first leader?"

"You can look, but no thinking about it, OK?" Karen snickered. "New rules, *Missus* Trueborn?"

"Oh, come on. Do you really buy that silent girl act? I saw her writing in her journal."

"Maybe that's the only source she can trust these days." "You're defending her."

"You're attacking her."

"I'm not, but I don't like the way she looks at you."

"Oh, good! Now I have someone else who wants to control my thoughts, where I look, and maybe even what I eat. Are you sure you never worked for Trueborn? Oh, that's right! You did!"

"That's unfair."

They both collected themselves and apologized, as neither wanted an argument after such a day, but nagging thoughts crept into their psyches as they drifted off to sleep under the stars.

They were awakened by the sound of children playing games. Some approached them and asked questions about the goings-on at the Parliament buildings. Karen told a young girl that they were fighting for their children's rights and that they wanted them to experience freedom.

The girl, who had messy but very rich brown hair, just shrugged and said, "Oh, that's a racist thing, right?"

Karen tilted her neck and said, "No, freedom is not racist. Who told you that?"

"My teacher at school said it is, and we should report anybody who says differently."

Karen's face soured.

"Don't worry," the little girl added, "I won't tell on you; I don't like my teacher that much."

Karen was astonished and asked, "Who could blame you? 'Freedom is racist', what a stupid thought!"

The former attorney wanted to say more but feared she might get the girl into trouble at school.

Suddenly all the monitors were activated all at once as images from the "nonexistent" prisons showed famous politicians from opposing parties and trusted journalists the media had claimed committed suicide, were seen in prison attire. Never before seen images ran of treatment centers for people who had chip injuries or psychological problems after surgery, as well as those who committed suicide after being confronted with unpleasant memories they couldn't live with. Some became catatonic, and some became schizophrenic. Twenty percent of the population developed permanent problems or died. The government had invested too much money and permitted the Global Health Watch to label anything they chose as a pandemic and therefore could enforce lockdowns at any time, like when government officials wanted negative stories to die down. They could merely sentence almost everyone to become prisoners in their own homes. The shady people who funded these groups always presented themselves as beacons of hope, but they were permanently darkening the skies of all humanity's future one cloud at a time while people scrambled for new income sources. Karen and Keith were filled with hope that people would snap out of their mass formation psychosis, but by this time they had been beaten down financially, psychologically, and emotionally, and just like the children, they did not react in any meaningful way.

Doyle, the robot maker, was hard at work and had hacked many prison video feeds and played them into the nationwide monitor system. He coded the name as Trueborn's finest moments, so Doyle's overseers saw no wrongdoing as it was not showing on his laptop while it played outside. Next were clips of Trueborn wanting access to every bank account in the country and having the ability to not only freeze but also access the funds of any opponent he faced. Now that was real power because people never paid enough attention to sneaky bills being passed, like charging fines over opinions that didn't line up with Trueborn's views. If his opponents died or disappeared, few questioned the status of their frozen bank accounts. Doyle knew time was short, and he had to hurry. He typed in a deauthorization command that affected all automated flying devices, such as drones, self-flying fighter jets, and helicopters.

As it blocked access from everyone and labeled its source address as the target address, this powerful hack did not allow for any counter-hacks, requiring an unmanned unit to override it.

"What's that you are typing in there?" One cyber-security man demanded "What are you deauthorizing there? Why didn't you clear it with us first?"

Doyle shrugged.

"Well, you guys are in a hurry for the robots to get online, right? This means I'll have to cancel any old commands in case one was aiming a weapon, and it discharged while being reactivated. This is standard protocol before I can fix them. If we add the time it'll take to explain every move, we'll be here for days."

The MPs nodded, unaware that the command had nothing to do with the robots. As highly trained as they were, Doyle was a genius, and humans always underestimate geniuses. They watched him hacking away as images of Trueborn cutting ribbons to open hospitals played, and he gave rallying speeches to war veterans with missing limbs despite the fact he'd removed their funding and cut back hospital staff.

The images showed him at the best angles, as Doyle hoped to appeal to his narcissism. If he were caught admiring himself, it might buy more time for the public to watch his crimes on the monitors before they could be switched off.

Trueborn entered the room with several of his henchmen, unaware that his drones were down, his jet fighters, choppers, and the doors to the Parliament buildings were about to swing open and stay that way.

"Are the robots ready?" Trueborn asked testily.

"Just about, one more minute, and...that...should...do...it!"

Trueborn and his men had their palm devices go off in succession. Urgent messages about the display monitors were raging through the devices, and once again, all monitors went black. A flush of dark pink ran across Trueborn's face, and it was hard to determine whether it was from embarrassment, rage, or a combination of the two.

"Launch the drones! And kill any white person you see! All of them are racists!"

He was not actually prejudiced against his own kind but was certain such statements would always lure people of color into voting for him. If people had to die to cement his career, he could laugh it off.

Just then, two robot police stormed the room and still had microwave weapons and no fear of illness, so Trueborn's henchmen surrendered.

The drones had been issued a command by Doyle that just sent them straight skyward into the atmosphere until they burst from the pressure, but one had been spotted by a Peregrine falcon whose instinct was to defend its airspace. It swooped in with a jolt hard enough to break the command link, and the drone dropped over the building where it had launched and exploded.

Robots stripped MPs and the secret service of their weapons as the doors of the unmarked prisons opened. These held only the innocent who opposed the government's crimes. The real criminals stayed in public jails. The political prisoners were free to rejoin society. Trueborn screamed at his chief guard to kill Doyle, but the robots had disarmed them, and while they had a feature to never kill an elected leader, they could not prevent him from taking his own life. Trueborn's ego would never allow him to relinquish power. He took a microwave gun, which only had a *Kill* setting because of his decision, and put it to his chest, and The high-powered low-frequency weapon made an electronic humming sound as it began melting him to the floor. The gun was faulty, however, and he got a 6,000-volt shock that electrocuted him as his heated flesh and blood finished cooking him alive. They had been designed to make a tidy corpse for cleanup, and his case was no different. There was a small pile of his melted, burnt remains, but the only recognizable feature left was a bit of scalp with hair intact, which was only fitting as everyone had always admired his hair.

Robot cops typically stood about five feet tall so as not to appear intimidating, but when acting in unison, they were a force that couldn't be stopped. Suddenly, the monitors were all functioning correctly and revealed robots apprehending and disarming the authorities with rapid efficiency. Disarmed police, MPs, and secret service agents did not appear to enjoy the process of being escorted to off-the-grid prisons. Warden Lynette Dunsel knew things were going south when robots burst through the doors with highly official-looking prisoners. She asserted herself immediately, commanding them to "Stop! This instant!" The closest robot ordered her to stand down, and she turned to her loyal puppet, Bon, whose loyalty always waned in times of crisis and remained silent, not wanting to join her boss in being apprehended. It didn't matter because Sir Doyle had ordered the robots to detain anyone in a position of authority. For a time, society was without a leader, with only token authority in the hands of mild-mannered robots, as the all-too-human desire for power briefly remained outside of political circles.

The removal of this one component led to far less strife and conflict and caused much introspection. Even the most arrogant and deluded minds wondered if a robot-governed world with proper oversight might be better. It couldn't be worse than a system fueled by delusions of grandeur, narcissism, ego-feeding decisions, and constant corruption. The pool of leadership candidates was made up of the best lifelong liars who bought and sold votes with the most flimsy displays of staged charisma. Peace loomed for a few days, and the disabled monitors meant that people couldn't be tracked by their brainwaves anymore. This period of calm lasted for a week before the power-hungry, who always wanted to *protect us* from ourselves, agonized over the opportunity to seize power now that the playing field was wide open. Other members of the Human First Party stepped forward, as did their rivals; the People's Freedom Party hatched ways to sway people's minds by insisting they would do things differently, but their lead candidate was approaching his nineties and no one respected him. There was a strong female candidate, but there were wealthy organizations that lurked in the shadows opposed to her; as she might not just fall in line and be as subservient as her predecessors. She was Charlotte Gabbaro. A former military type with her own mind who couldn't be pushed around, the elites feared and smeared her at every opportunity.

The world was in political chaos, and no one had stepped forward until a coup had been planned by Trueborn's followers because, like him, they couldn't rest while power sat at the table in no one's hands. Many of them had been appointed to high-ranking positions in the military and the courts. This meant that a large contingent was granted injunctions and pardons and quickly returned to power, as once again the common people weren't paying enough attention. Doyle was captured, and he knew it. Eight men that had come from the prison surrounded him in the bunker armed with various weapons improvised from prison scrap in the workshops. Most were of the blunt-force bludgeoning variety. Pieces of pipe, a broken sledgehammer handle, and sharpened rebar were all being brandished before him, so he knew their goals would not be requests, The leader of the group was a man of about fifty with hardened features and the sturdy frame of a former muscle man who enjoyed a lot of beer regularly.

"We need those robots dead, not switched off, and you are going to tell us how to do it, and then make it happen. You wouldn't want to lose all those privileges, would you?"

He spoke like someone who was accustomed to issuing commands without any need for niceties. Sir Doyle knew he was in no position to bargain, as his options were at a minimum.

"They don't have a kill switch, and they are designed to withstand anything. They can't attack each other, so the best I can do for you is to turn them off again."

A silence fell over the men as they had envisioned some sort of self-destruct sequence and were flummoxed by this new information. Surprisingly, one of them announced an idea that would have been better served in private. "He could switch them off, and then we could switch him off, and that would solve things forever," a barren-eyed lackey said, looking quite pleased with himself.

Their leader mulled this over for a moment and offered a calming solution.

"You switch them off, and we won't kill you, OK?"

Sir Doyle was a genius, and one frustrating quality about power-lusting men was that they frequently imagined they were far smarter than the geniuses.

"Is that why you brought all the weapons, to let me live?" Sir Doyle asked nonchalantly.

The hard-faced man with the gut assured him, "We didn't know how much convincing you'd need."

Sir Doyle calmly went to his laptop and typed in a bunch of codes, but the last word was "reboot." The beer-bellied MP took notice and demanded in a gravelly voice, "What was that last command for? That Reboot? Tell me right now, or we'll bash your skull in."

Sir Doyle appeared bored and asked, "Do you know much about code or quantum physics?"

The man knew he'd been toyed with and raised his arm with a piece of sharpened rebar. Sir Doyle's defensive reflexes alarmed the military men, as he also displayed a speed and strength that belied his build and appearance. The calm-looking man of average build and relaxed body language was tossing the men around at will. Some of them flew into the walls with enough force that they were injured. One man had an intact sledgehammer and caught Doyle from behind with full force on the top of his skull, dropping him like a stone. Blood ran from both of his nostrils, while his unblinking eyes remained permanently in a frozen stare. A few of the angry men vindictively kicked and punched the unstirring body until they were tired and heaving deep breaths. Once satisfied, they high-fived each other as kids do after winning an after-school pick-up game of stickball.

Chapter Thirteen

CONFISCATED CONSENT

"Why? Did I say something wrong? I hate racism, so when the government does it, I'll call them out on it. What I said is true; Am I supposed to be jailed for being historically accurate?"

"People from your generation might have been allowed to say something like that, but nowadays they call that a rally for white racism," Keith offered.

"Because you've been brainwashed into it. If the monitor screen keeps hinting that whites are the only racists and the teachers are coerced into repeating that children are oppressors, they'll grow up with psychological problems. Has anybody ever said there is too much Chinese privilege in China and too much black privilege in Africa? Of course not, because China was settled by the Chinese, and Africa by Africans, and each became the establishment of the countries in which they were indigenous or settled. That doesn't make them bad or wrong in any way. When those countries were still thriving before the one-world government ruined everything, would you go over there and scream about how there aren't enough redheads like me in their governments or positions of power?

"Well, I am more concerned with the government hiding the adverse effects of these brain chips going wrong."

"People are dying, you know, and worse than that, they are going out of their minds. They are losing their appetite for both relationships and maintaining their mental health. They go numb in the head after a while, and some end up catatonic. Mental health problems are fine if there's money to be made off them, right?"

Molière gave the man a sharp glance,

"What about you? How many friends are you making by ranting about white people? How many friends do you have that are different from you?"

The old man laughed loudly in his face.

"My wife is black, does that help you out? Is a picture good enough, or will I have to bring her here and explain that she is black to you? Do you want to get a reaction out of her? You just tell her you think I'm a racist, that'll do it."

"I'm sorry," Molière said earnestly. "I just don't want to end up in jail if I am already slotted in for the wrong reasons. How do we tell people about these chips?"

"I'm doing my part, but only about ten people listen to me, That's why the feds don't care, To them, I'm just a nut yelling at the moon. It's the eighty-twenty rule; eighty percent of your sick days are used up by twenty percent of your staff, If you tell everyone all white people are racist, 80 percent will believe it. The same concept applies to brain chips, which is why everyone is getting one. It's a ticking time bomb, and they are fighting in line over who gets it first."

"I might have an idea, Thank you, you've been a big help!" Molière's face lit up for the first time since he'd had his chip implanted, and he bolted from the room to return to Karen as fast as he was able.

He eventually found her concluding a speech and pulled her aside.

"Karen! I've got it! We can get Doyle to hack into the brain chips and put a message in people's minds that they need to ditch these things right away! Even if it only works for half the people, it could be a huge start!"

Karen finally looked up at him, and he could see the strain on her face before she spoke.

"What is it?" he asked.

"I've been trying to reach Sir Doyle all day to no avail. It's not like he's gone fishing, it's a permanent residence, remember?"

Keith wanted to reassure her with a lame excuse, but They both knew Doyle was far too responsible to miss such an appointment.

"Who is running the prison right now?" Keith asked.

Karen hesitated as she tried to piece together the outcome of a regime change, a robot police takeover, and a secondary shutdown of all robots, and whether the authorities were still inside the prison or if they had been freed.

"The place might be abandoned for all I know," she said, raising her eyebrows in doubt before adding, "If you worked there and you discovered you could get locked in by a robot, would you stick around?"

"It's risky," he said.

They prepared for another trip on foot to the prison in an uneasy silence.

They arrived at the prison to see the residue of a revolt. Some of the inmates had unpleasant memories of the authority figures under lockup, and the prison had free movement during daylight hours. This led to a prison-wide brawl and a lot of carnage to wade through, but no doors were locked, and the building had been all but abandoned.

They rushed to the top floor and sprung through the gate to Doyle's lab cell.

"AGHHH! He's dead," Karen whimpered. "I knew it; I knew as soon as he didn't answer."

She had been so Stoic throughout this entire ordeal, until now. This, however, seemed to deflate her as she draped the top half of her body over Doyle's workbench and let out a beleaguered sigh.

Keith examined the body for long moments and this grated on Karen's nerves.

"Whatever in the world are you doing exactly?" "Well, he's not breathing, but he's not dead."

"Do you have, like, maladjusted chip disorder or something? What are you talking about?"

"Well, a fair bit of blood came out of his mouth and nose, but the biggest wound is on the back of his skull, and there is a clear square-shaped dent with a tracer line of blood around the perimeter of the wound. His pants were clean except for scuff marks. If he died from a blow to the head like that, there would be blood all over the place. When people die, all the food stored in their bodies gets released, yet there is no mess or smell. "There is no decomposing flesh, so either he can't die or he was a robot."

"Are you mad? They can't make a robot look that human, and the weight would be all wrong and the blood's real. It simply cannot be," she said.

"Do me a favor and go hit enter on his laptop, just a long shot." Karen obliged without any change on the screen.

"We've got to figure out what he was working on. How are your hacking skills?"

"What hacking skills? I'm a lawyer, you're the subversive."

"How am I subversive?"

"You wear black a lot, no one can ever get in touch with you, and you are lacking that pro-government attitude demanded from citizens. I've seen signs of being recalcitrant as well."

"That won't change my mind," Keith joked.

The laptop yielded a maze of complex coding beyond their comprehension.

"Can't you figure it out?" she urged.

He looked at her blankly and said, "I think the answer to the universe is 42, but I'm not sure. This is miles beyond my depth, I'm sorry."

Meanwhile, the government had re-established itself with Trueborn's right-hand man at the helm, and they had hired a group of high-end hackers to ensure they would never falter again. He was billionaire Willard Gertz, and he had just as much unctuous charm as Trueborn and could con the cheese out of a rat's mouth. There were good politicians out there, but many had been falsely accused of various smears to limit their success. Trueborn had made mistakes, but Gertz, with his meek bespectacled nerd look, was a master of the sweet and kind act but was also highly skilled in the cloak-and-dagger side of political games. He appeared so calm and mild, but his hackers were already at work coding all the brain chips to issue commands to control people. They sought to make them do anything they wished. As long as technology existed, someone could hack into it. Gertz had brought the best in for the job and couldn't wait. He had a long, dark brown mustache with ends that he liked to play with as he assumed it made him look deeper in thought. He toasted a picture of Trueborn every night, thanking him for paving his path to power. With all wills and minds at his whim, he would be more powerful than Caligula, Pol Pot, Ivan the Terrible, and all the rest. The idea set his eyes alight as he mused that all he had to do was praise democracy and the flag for a few years, and now the whole of humanity could be his plaything. It wasn't his fault that society handed over so much power to the government's leaders. They were fools, and he was the benefactor. The hackers had already begun making progress, and hackable humans with their brain chips were the appetizer, while the tasks he'd have them perform would be the feast. He could barely stand the adrenaline rush whetting his appetite. Sex slaves, murderers, humiliation experiments, and anything else he wanted, lurked just around the corner, and he was all but salivating in anticipation. A lusty, depraved smile crossed his face as the words "*Human toys!*" ran through his mind.

His eyes were all but dancing as he rationalized, *If you are all dumb enough to hand over all your ability to self-govern and give it to us, we'll of course take it from you. Hand over your weapons and clothing, and your ability to stand will be replaced by kneeling in front of me. It's for your safety! We'll protect you from school shooters and racial slurs, but not from us. How dumb can they be? I'll feed you your honeyed words,* he thought, *and then I will own every single last one of you.*

Chapter Fourteen

A DISTANT LIGHT SOURCE

In shock, Karen stood over Doyle's disabled robot. "They don't have the technology to make one of those resemble us so closely, they can't! If he's a robot, then who else is? Are they walking among us? What chance would we have against such an opponent? Can this even be happening?"

Keith recognized signs of growing paranoia and sought to keep her level-headed.

"Look at the detail and work that went into this. It wasn't made in a lab. Look at the situation that Doyle was in, people were hunting him to use his mind for their personal gains and to accrue power. This was a one-time prototype by a desperate man who saw the writing on the wall for his own demise. It was a Hail Mary pass and the end of the game. To avoid his undeserved fate, it's a dupe stand-in. He probably taxed himself without sleep for months to make such a sophisticated model. There is no way he would have had the time or resources to make more than one."

"In a court of law, we'd call that speculation," Karen said.

"Lucky for us, the courts have never been wrong, especially the ones Trueborn lined up with his former cabinet ministers," Molière remarked.

The disabled robot rose from the floor and grabbed a cloth to wipe its mouth and nose, regaining its previous composure.

"Are you OK?" Karen asked as though she were speaking to a child's toy, "No crossed wires or distorted commands? Not dead anymore?"

"Ah, Karen E. Howard, formerly of the firm Nolan and Johnson; barristers and solicitors, and then the 'Human First' party, I can understand your disappointment. The only good robot is a dead or disabled one, perhaps?" Doyle's robot replied with a lighthearted smile.

"That's Ms. to you! Now, how can you look so human and fool a group of military types into thinking you died at their hands?"

Doyle's decoy raised its eyebrows in a human-looking response and explained. "It was simply a one-hour reboot delay, If they saw me resist too much damage, I would have been undone. I am completely functional and only simulated death as it was the most predictable outcome."

Molière asked "So if you are the decoy, then where's the real Doyle? How can we restore order with the government acting every bit as crazy as when Trueborn ran things?"

"You have surrendered too many rights to the government to overtake them, they have all your weapons and all the laws on their side. This was unwise. Now they will exploit that weakness against you in no uncertain terms. The only peaceful solution is to escape."

"Escape to where? The whole world is under surveillance." Molière protested.

"Kepler 1638b." Doyle's robot stated nonchalantly. "Excuse me, but where?" asked Karen.

"Kepler 1638b, it's only four thousand, nine hundred, and seventy-three light-years away."

"Oh, good, I'll get my coat and radiation shield." Karen quipped.

"Oh, you understand about how we powered the vessel, that will save time. Doyle said if I found any worthy additions to the colony, I could invite them. Please consider yourselves invited."

Molière was desperate for solutions to this untenable situation but could scarcely believe that the robot was functioning correctly with these preposterous solutions.

"How would we even get past the deep space radiation, and in what craft, and how would we get past that tiny little problem of exceeding the speed of light? Where exactly would we be going? Is that in the Proxima Centauri system, Shall we just wish ourselves there, or can you explain any of this?" he pressed.

"Time is short, so I'll explain this in terms you might understand, but we mustn't dwell on the particulars or risk being wiped out by the remnants of Trueborn's authorities. Within the Cygnus star system is a red dwarf star called Kepler 452, and the exoplanet orbiting it is called Kepler 452b. This is larger than Earth but similar, it orbits its star faster than Earth, but it should be highly adaptable with some obvious adjustments. The first is about travel, and Doyle had spent a lot of time working with his colleague Dr. Bradbury on developing a radiation-proof warp drive. They designed and built the ship to exceed the speed of light by expanding the space behind it compressing the space before it. Objects can not exceed the speed of light, but space itself can. At this very moment, space is carrying entire solar systems beyond the speed of light. I'm sure you'd agree that if it can move an entire solar system, it can move a ship. Space is bendable, and one can arc and curve it to suit one's purposes. As for propulsion, the radiation from space itself will be the fuel. Rather than using exotic matter or negative energy, they've constructed a radiation pulverizer that destroys radiation, thereby converting it into heat and using that heat to propel the ship forward. "It creates massive reserves, so fuel is never an issue," the simulated human explained.

"You cannot simply destroy radiation. It comes in various forms, the waves move too fast and have vastly differing properties. The alpha and beta waves move too quickly to be isolated, and the gamma goes through almost anything but lead. Under what possible execution could you wipe out all of that, leaving only heat, and how would it be enough heat to propel a craft a distance that might as well be beyond infinity? If your ship is made of lead, it isn't going very far," Molière said.

"The craft, as you call it, is made from a polymer of plants, metallic alloys, and basalt left over from the ancient volcanic residue of Mars. It is reliably durable, has a dual reservoir to collect and store the radiation, and a shield between the reservoir and the ship itself. It is completely safe and can exceed the speed of light by immeasurable amounts. The entire trip should be less than a month by our time measurements," it said.

Karen asked, "What do you mean by our time measurements? Are you going to be using a different system that's going to be a month here and a year there in a different system, I want a universal standard in place."

"If I were to ask you what time it is, you would look at the palm device on your wrist, and tell me something based on Eastern Standard Time. Our standard is partly based on daylight savings time, an artificial standard that has provided incorrect information about the passage of time since the 1800s. It is based on maintaining the comfort of the night being dark and the day being light. What's more, our complete understanding of time is incorrect. We see it as being based on the number of revolutions of our planet. This has no bearing on deep space. If one revolution of the planet constitutes a full 24-hour day, and three hundred and sixty-five and a quarter revolutions constitute a year because it orbits the sun, then what possible bearing could that have if one is on Saturn, Jupiter, or Tea Garden, let alone if you were en route between them? What time is it in space between planets if one is too far from Earth to know how many times it's turning, or if the sun supernovates and nothing can be measured by the revolutions that are no longer occurring? If the planet revolves around its own sun in a week, that means it is a year using your faulty method of comprehending time. The time-space continuum has very little to do with your understanding of the time of day but more to do with space itself," Doyle's substitute said.

"I think my brain's about to explode, I need a drink." Karen bemoaned.

Molière was about to ask more questions, but Doyle's clone spoke first.

"You can bring about 12 more friends, there will be room for them. You may have further concerns, but your friends may also require time to weigh their options as your government will pursue absolute power over its subjects and enslave your people entirely. Once the ship leaves, a return is unlikely for safety reasons."

Karen and Keith made their way to the shambles of the Parliament buildings, which had been pelted with rocks and paint and had their windows broken. They found the freedom fighters on both sides of the buildings. There was the group led by Jim and the fighters from the truck. Others followed Daliyah on the opposite side, neither venturing near the other's recently claimed territory of the Parliament grounds. Keith had his doubts about this fantastic idea of escaping via the space that moved galaxies; it was a lot to ponder and difficult to accept, let alone believe, or sign-up for.

Still, he wanted off of a planet full of world leaders that promised protection and safety every single time they tightened the shackles on their constituents. The few true leaders who made bold decisions were painted as crackpots, racists, or other defamatory labels without ever being held accountable. This left the glad-handers and the baby kissers, who secretly wished for corporate slavery and peasant subjects, at the helm, praising their own virtues and criminalizing anyone who disagreed. Molière desperately wanted out of this cycle of insanity. The solutions offered by a damaged robot seemed so outlandish that it was easier to believe that one of Trueborn's hackers had programmed it to steer them wrong. If he couldn't convince Karen to take it seriously, how might Daliyah and Jim accept this far-fetched interplanetary escape route? It would be like selling a cross-world voyage to sailors who thought the world was flat and feared they'd sail off the edge of the world, ironically enough, into deep space.

With all that was happening, becoming the spokesperson to pitch a potential death ride into space wasn't enticing, but Karen approached him first.

"Keith, what did you think about that crazy story from the mangled robot?"

"Well, I am not sure if he was malfunctioning in any way, but that was a far-fetched story. We are like drowning people on a sinking ship being offered safety on a high rise if we would only make wings from the feathers of the surrounding vultures. Not a lot of choices."

"Come swing to safety on this strand of spider's silk, you'll be fine." She grinned.

"Do you think Doyle could have actually made such a ship, somehow fueled by radiation heat? They banned space travel after Mars, if the Feds knew about this, they would have tested it on him."

"Maybe they did, and that's why no one has seen him in years. I know that all the people who claimed he wasn't bright were the stupidest ones. That guy was bloody brilliant in ways that normal people can't understand, so they pretend he's dumb to make themselves feel better. It's classic gas lighting. If anyone could make such a ship, it'd be him."

"So you want to ask the freedom fighters?"

"They have the right to decide for themselves, even if they think we are nuts."

"You aren't seriously thinking of joining that robot in his radiation dance to the stars, are you?" Karen asked with a tone of incredulity.

"Do you wish to remain here? A criminal if the bad guys win, or a slave if the good guys win, what's the difference?" he replied.

"Well, I'm not going to commit suicide and die of radiation poisoning over the ramblings of a dented robot."

"What if we could establish communication with Kepler fifty-seven or whatever it is?"

"It's a little far for that, don't you think?"

"Yes, it is, but if a guy was smart enough to get there, it wouldn't be too far a stretch to think he might figure out a way to communicate."

"You are dreaming, do you think radio waves are going to get their own spaceship too?"

"I want out. Life is dead here, there is no life, no compassion, no rising above prejudice; no better government that won't inch towards totalitarianism the moment the opportunity presents itself."

"It's risky, but at the very least we can give those who fought on the right side the same option that we did."

"Okay, you go find Jim, and I'll talk to Daliyah."

Karen went to make her proposal, but Daliyah wasn't far from his sight line at the top of the steps.

He approached her and noticed the intensity of being battle-ready running from her face to that of a relaxed friend. She was such an odd mixture of qualities, she looked far younger than her years and had more of a girl's face and body than that of a woman in her mid-thirties. Her brown eyes, which had been steeled in the wake of nearly constant conflict, exuded a seriousness that invited pause from even the surliest of individuals. When she relaxed, though, all that disappeared, and she instead emanated a lightheartedness that most failed to see.

"Hey, how are you keeping these days?"

"Fine," she said in her typically minimalist style, but allowed a coy smile.

"I've got a proposal of sorts for you and your men."

She widened her eyes and raised her eyebrows, holding the expression but saying nothing.

"OK, this is going to sound pretty absurd, but if you could hear me out, I'd appreciate it."

She gave a single downward half-nod but didn't take her eyes off of his the whole time.

He relayed his story, but she gave no reaction one way or the other. He looked at her blankly with widened eyes, silently seeking a response. This was her preferred language; speaking with one's facial expression. It was so different, but he liked it, and it could be very effective in keeping one from saying the wrong thing.

She looked down for a second, and said, "It sounds iffy."

"Well, thanks for not telling me I'm crazy, If you could tell the men, "I'll be done with it."

"Are you gonna go?"

"I don't know yet, there's a lot to think about, a lot of risks mixed with a lot of not wanting to stay here."

She nodded and went to tell the men, He noted that her abbreviated speech style always left one with the feeling that there was more to talk about while also revealing the value of being economical with words. He was her opposite but enjoyed their interactions nonetheless. No overreactions, no objections, no criticism, she just evaluated his message and made a decision. There was a rare power in that, and he admired it.

He had someone else, though, and she would be returning with Jim's message, and he dared to hope for one moment that they might escape this ill-begotten government and its illegitimate claim to power.

"Did you talk to him? What did he say?" Karen gave him a look of exhaustion.

"He said they are interested, but not if Daliyah's men are going."

"What?!"

"They support the new members of the 'Human First' party, and they don't like robots. Daliyah's men never want to see anyone from Trueborn's government again, and they think the robots helped overthrow him, so they want the robots to stay in case this ever happens again. The two sides don't like each other."

"You have got to be kidding!"

"They don't want any robots on the ship, and none of Daliyah's men, that's their condition, if it's met, seven of them will go."

"We are *all* on the same side! What is *wrong* with everybody?"

"I'll let you tell Daliyah. If I didn't know better, I'd say she dislikes me." Karen said.

Keith left and discovered Daliyah at an improvised food tent. "I feel like I owe you dinner or at least a decent bowl of soup."

She gave her head a dismissive half-shake.

"Some guys from the other side want to get off this rock, but they are worried about robots and 'wrong-way' voters."

She looked up at him, waiting for him to finish his point.

"I'd like to speak to the men on both sides and see if I can get everyone on the same page."

"You talked to them?" "No, we split the duties." "Oh, your lawyer friend."

"We're more than friends, and yes, she was good enough to find out their thoughts."

"Now that they don't want to go with us because of how some people voted, I wonder how they got that idea."

"Oh, you don't think Karen is out there trying to influence them, do you?"

"Yeah."

"She wouldn't do that; she just wants to get her life back, the same as everyone else."

"We never had a problem with them before. I told you before she's playing you."

"Why do you keep saying that? What have you got against her?"

"She doesn't want me on that ship; she doesn't want our men; she just wants people she can control, just like all the other people in that 'Human First' cesspool. Are you going to marry her too? What's that going to look like if things don't work out? She'll take you for everything you ever had and say you mistreated her, and then she gets all the money you'll ever earn. She's that type, I can tell. Once certain people start playing the political games, they can't stop; you'll see."

"Those are some pretty large accusations; how can you possibly be so sure?"

"We have white guys, black guys, First Nations, and a few women. Their side has Latinos, white guys, black guys, and some women. There's no cultural war here, but leave it to a politician or a lawyer to find one that doesn't exist, and five minutes later we're all enemies."

"OK, let me talk to both sides and if she objects to or contradicts one thing I say, we'll know she's playing crooked, okay?"

"Fine," she said, curious about his approach.

"Some of you already know what we are looking at here. There's a chance we could get off this crazed planet forever. We still have a lot of checking to do, but we need an idea of who wants to go, and I want to stress that it's open to everyone. I don't care about your religion, skin color, past, or if you've taken drugs or gotten too drunk. It's not about anything like that. It's about rescuing humanity from the dregs of society, not judging each other. If we can't learn to get along, we are done as a species. Are we so infinitely stupid that we can't rise above our petty differences, that we must cultivate and exaggerate the prejudices that every single living person has? Do you want to know where black-and-white discrimination comes from? It comes from only listening to our own kind and thinking our people are the only ones who have got it right. It comes from judging people, putting them in a box in our minds, and never letting them out of that box, which is called preconceived notions. So if you can prove you can rise above that, I say you are in. Every one of you is in a mixed group of all different races, genders, and religions, but we aren't going to hate each other because of that, instead, we will hate each other over how someone voted in the last election. No one can have been wrong or swayed the wrong way because they are morally inferior due to their voting decisions, right? Do you know what you get when you get rid of all the wrong-way voters? You get one government that keeps getting reelected even if it goes wrong, even if it is corrupt, and even if it becomes so comfortable that it will follow the dictates of wealthy organizations that want to experiment on its population and want to kill off the middle class and make them poor in order to reduce competition. They want to decrease the size of the human race with disease and famine because they truly believe that the carbon footprint from people walking around is more dangerous than industry. Global warming is real, she continued, but it's been worse, and we've had a nuclear winter, hot volcanoes erupting with lava, and an ice age. We'll be OK; we don't have to kill off millions of people, so the corrupt elites can laugh at us. We just need to make better fuels and reduce pollution. If we can have air conditioners, we can invent earth coolants as well. Why are we taking health advice from wealthy men who aren't even doctors? Why are we in a civil war with Morgania when they are the same people who just voted differently? The manufacturers of military equipment fund election campaigns and lean on them to wage war. Remember when they said the one-world government would mean no more wars? They just flipped the chessboard around and had us attack ourselves. Let us stop being their pawns today and allow anyone who wants to leave this island and is willing to take the risk to do so. Let's say we can be brothers and sisters, If we can usurp the worst government in the world at least temporarily, we can share a bus ride across the stars, can't we? Does anyone have a problem with that? The reason equality is such an important goal is that if you favor one side, the other has to suffer. Let's prove we can travel as a group just because we fought for these grounds as a group. It's up to you!"

The men and women deliberated, and while some stayed within their camps and beat the drums of fear and hostility, most relaxed their stances as reason seemed to win the day for a few on each side at least.

Karen looked at him differently than she ever had before. It was a mixture of surprise and uneasiness.

"What's the matter?" he asked.

"Oh, I don't know. Here I was thinking I'd met this nice quiet dilettante who'd dabbled in a lot of different things—the arts, music, maybe some sports—and kept moving on, never finding his niche." I can see now, that isn't you at all. Without any legal background, you got my son's property switched into a land trust and buried us from prying eyes without so much as a signature, or video conference from me, the owner. With your strange but very clever light trick, you got us into that prison, and now I'm watching you calm an intensely paranoid crowd and give half of them enough hope to become astronauts. If they don't first radiate themselves to death on their way to Utopia. I don't think you are some bumbling lost soul who never found his niche, I think you are a highly competent expert of some sort. You get out of jams like they're nothing, and you have a dead-zero panic threshold. C'mon, out with it. Who the hell are you?" She demanded.

"I am an incomplete person, a mistake artist, a screw-up who trusted the wrong people and wrote off too many salt-of-the-earth types. I embraced a career when I should have stuck with my friends and vice versa. I am someone who has enjoyed great personal triumphs and stood on a few precipices that others have never looked upon. My life has been a journey of wrong exit ramps and 'use at your own risk' dirt roads. I've loved and left, and I've been left. I am as every man is because I've been proud of stupid things and ashamed of things that weren't my fault. Perhaps foolhardy enough to think being involved with a former attorney didn't have to mean I'd be judged with such scrutiny that I'd have to answer for all I've done and not done, or else pay the price of suspicion and accusation over nothing. Does that help you out?"

"You're angry."

"Is this the part where we ask each other how many people we've slept with?"

"OK, very angry."

"Not angry enough to be suspicious."

"You don't like that, do you? Did someone have reasons to ask you a lot of questions about your past? I didn't mean to strike such a nerve."

"I'm just saying that if I were the suspicious type, I might have a few questions for you, too."

"Fire away."

"I don't ask people accusatory questions without a proper reason."

"Where did you get that habit, from your new friend Daliyah? I bet you'd like her, she hardly says a word, she'd never ask where you were last night, she probably wouldn't even care, and she probably wouldn't think you were worth the waste of words. The perfect woman, right?

She keeps her mouth shut and puts food in front of you. Oh!... Or is she offering you something more than that, too?"

"Well, she is not insecure, I'll give her that."

Karen glared at him and facetiously added, "Thanks for putting my fears to rest so aptly."

"Thanks for the sarcasm."

"Oh, don't worry about that. "I'm never sarcastic on purpose; it's always accidental."

"Maybe your lawyer can get you a deal on some insurance for that."

"So *that's* what's eating you? The lawyer thing you mentioned. You don't have a '*thing*' about lawyers, you *hate* them. I am a lawyer, paired up with a lawyer hater. You despise all lawyers, so you despise me, is that it?"

"No, but I wouldn't like it if you saw an avenue to exclude someone from this trip because you didn't like their hair or speech pattern. Leaving someone here for a future of slavery is tantamount to murder."

This ended the conversation as they went to sleep in different areas for the first time since they'd met and wondered what tomorrow would bring as the only ship headed for Kepler was set to leave. Keith tucked himself into a sleeping bag from the freedom fighters, but before he could close his eyes, he thought he saw something in the sky, but it was dark. He turned over for comfort but heard the sound of a nearby explosion as a swarm of rapidly approaching fighter jets came streaking through the sky.

Chapter Fifteen

HYPERSONIC TENSION

Explosions rocked the grounds and lit the skies from the temporary medic and food camps all the way to the Parliament buildings. Jim ran up to Molière, stating," It's Morgania attacking Hornsbridge, and they've upped the ante!"

The explosions grew louder and then fell silent, save for the burning of buildings and newly formed fiery craters as dismembered police robot parts flew apart in all directions. In true overkill fashion, there were some human casualties as well, as the city appeared on the verge of collapse.

"I think that was the Trueborn government attacking its own robots," Molière speculated.

Jim looked baffled. "But, he's dead, isn't he?" he asked, with wide eyes.

"How much do you know about his second-in-command?" Molière asked rhetorically.

"I didn't even see the fighters!" Jim admitted.

Molière looked resigned and brought his would-be military accomplice up to speed.

"Those were likely F-97s, the red-tailed hawks; they use scramjet technology and can reach a speed of Mach 9 and hold it. That's almost seven thousand miles per hour; no robot can stop that. They've got hypersonic smart missiles that will beat Mach 7. The crafts are unmanned and could be used as a final note of destruction if it weren't for the cost."

Jim looked perplexed, shouting something, but a deafening, thunderous roar drowned out their voices.

"What the hell was that?" he asked with profound confusion.

"That's them approaching, but it's OK; they are gone now. Once they get that far past the sound barrier, we'll hear them after they're gone, not before."

Two robots climbed a tower and tried to down one of the fighter jets but were hit by a missile for their trouble. The tower was blown open, and the top half fell on scattering bystanders. As advanced as their strength and speed were against a human, the robots were mere pylons for the fighter jets to obliterate, and they had destroyed every single walking machine in Hornsbridge. It was a foregone conclusion that similar results were occurring in every major city.

Jim shuffled his feet.

"I'm thinking about joining you guys on your never-ending trip to the other end of the universe," he said.

"We'd be lucky to have you."

Molière went to see if he could mend fences with Karen, as few things could add perspective to a disagreement like a near-death experience.

It wasn't her that he found, but to his surprise, it was Daliyah. "She's not here," Daliyah said in anticipation of his question.

"Oh, well, I'm glad you are still with us. Will you be making the trip too?"

"There's not going to be much left here to stick around for."

"Yeah, if you vote the wrong way, you'll be labeled a conspiracy theorist or a white supremacist. You'd look pretty funny as a white supremacist, don't you think?"

Daliyah didn't often smile, rather she mostly maintained a deadly serious air about her, but when she did smile, it was inescapable, and she was unable to suppress it. Suddenly, he understood why she didn't reveal it often. If she did, men would likely follow her around in droves, and she had no interest in that.

"I don't think your girlfriend likes me much," she said.

"She's a bit out of her element around here, but I'm sure there's nothing to it."

"A lot of women don't like me because I fight sometimes; women or men, I don't care."

"Well, sometimes people are assholes, and if you never take a stand, they'll run right over you. We see it in nature all the time. We don't blame the badger, the snake, or the squirrel when they do it. Governments get more lethal weapons every day, and we don't oppose that, but if a person does it, people pretend that there is something wrong with them for standing their ground physically. I don't have any problem with someone who stands up for themselves, even if it means they've had a dust-up or two. That goes for women too; I've never bought into the whole 'girls don't fight' nonsense. They just do it a bit differently, but some, like you, have the warrior gene or fiery blood; they say that about Native Americans, Latinos, Irish, redheads, and really almost everyone. I just think everybody has it in them somewhere. I respect it, and I respect pacifists too, but that's only a part-time solution that works among other pacifists. In the wrong neighborhood, pacifism will get you killed. Under the wrong government, pacifism lands you in jail. The other side of the coin, however, is that we need people like Karen. She isn't ever going to fight someone with her fists but uses a courtroom and believes in the system so strongly that she will take on the whole world despite boring rules, excessive reading, and Trueborn's crooked judges. If not for a few lawsuits that snuck through, he'd have had us shambling around in chains by now. If you give her a chance, I think you'll find a good person there."

"MM-mm" That was as much of an acknowledgment as Daliyah would give him on the subject of Karen, and he took it as the world's smallest victory in hopes of making peace between them.

Jim and his crew dug holes within the missile craters to avoid being targeted in the future. Daliyah's men gathered what food and supplies they could in preparation for the trip, but only Doyle knew where the spacecraft was stored. The prison that held Doyle's robot had been destroyed by the airstrike. Jim finished digging for the day and ran into Molière on his way to clean up.

"Hey! Where's your girlfriend? People are starting to worry about whether the ship will survive or if there even is a ship."

"I'm looking for her right now."

Daliyah came out of the food tent and heard the tail end of the conversation. She looked at Molière but said nothing. She didn't have to. Keith was picking up on the silent language, and he knew what she meant with her glance. "So, when you need her most, she disappears on you, just like a typical lawyer." For a person who rarely spoke, her messages were coming in loud and clear; any more so, and they'd be deafening.

Twenty-four hours later, the skeleton crew of military police had retaken the Parliament grounds, and with the air support available to them, no one ventured near. The ragtag crew of defeated and demoralized freedom fighters was desperate for a source of hope and growing skeptical about Molière's story of a secret ship that could break the speed of light. Suspicious glances and people not moving out of the way when he tried to navigate a narrow passage were becoming commonplace. A large man with long red hair and a handlebar mustache in a leather jacket smugly confronted him by the food tent.

"Hey! it's the man with the spaceship, sposably. Say, your girlfriend used to work for Trueborn, din't she?"

Molière nodded, awaiting a quick deterioration in conversation that might prompt an attack.

"Well, I'm not seeing her around anywheres, am I? Int she the one with the keys to the ship? She knows where it's hidden, dun't she?" Dun't she trust you enough to tell you? Or maybe she thinks she shoun't trust you. Maybe she got herself a seat on that ship with sum'n else and took off without cha?"

"Yeah, or maybe she caught a whiff of your breath and ran for the hills."

"She might like it, ekspecially."

"You were hoping to be her costar in 'Beauty and the Uncouth Slug'?"

"Enough!" Daliyah said, marching up between the men.

"Go get the food boxes!" She barked.

The man stood his ground, raising his jaw at Molière but not speaking. He wasn't up for a duel of wits, but resentment of the permanent kind was building in his eyes, and his temper was rising.

"Go!" She insisted.

Daliyah raised her voice and took her two palms and lunged into the man, pushing his chest, and while he was big enough to prevent her from moving him, he looked down and left to get the boxes.

"This ain't over," he said as he walked away.

"Not till you learn about mouthwash."

Daliyah turned and lowered her forehead frowning upward at Molière.

"Sorry," he said.

Karen appeared from the top of a hill nearby, looking disheveled and dirty. Her dress was marred and torn, she had earth stains on her face, and her hair was unkempt.

"What happened?" Several people asked her, echoing each other almost in unison.

"I went to find Doyle or his tin can copy anyway. The missiles hit us before we even knew they were coming. That stupid robot stuck me in the mini shelter in the basement, but it knew they were after him and led them away before they blew him into a billion pieces. He did provide the location of the ship, but no one's going to like it. Doyle's tin can had a great processor, and he was able to reprogram the Parliament robots to make adjustments to the ship, the 'Alacrity II'. He says that Doyle is safe on Kepler with a handful of people and some bots, and they're colonizing it." she said.

"So where is it?"

"Oh, just for fun, he put it on the roof of the Parliamentary building and only gave access to the roof to the robots working on it. They were programmed to say it was on Trueborn's orders. This means we won't have much time before it's discovered by the new management. If anybody has any really shiny ideas about how to get up there, I am all ears."

A lot of eyes drifted or took to looking at the tops of their boots. "We'll have to fake bringing in a prisoner," Molière announced.

"We can get some uniforms from the mayhem on the lawn, and we can bring Karen as the fake prisoner; then, once we have access to the roof, we bolt for it before the fighters come. Does this ship have any defenses?"

Molière turned to Karen, hoping for a yes but receiving only a weary stare.

"I didn't ask for the blueprints due to time constraints, sorry."

They quickly gathered uniforms and white helmets to fool the remaining security personnel. They also noticed a path that led straight past two ground guards, then to the Parliament steps, which meant only two guards to fool before gaining access inside. Molière and Jim took the lead, with Karen in tow, and as they approached the doors, Molière couldn't help but notice the retina scanners both men wore. If a few property cameras had been damaged in the assault on the robots, the ones at the doors were repaired and functioning perfectly. Keith forced himself to look straight ahead, and then meet the eyes of the closest guard.

"I haven't slept in two days, but we got her! This is Karen E. Howard, the white supremacist leader of the revolt," Molière said. The guards both perked up after hearing the name.

"Can I tell you something though? It wasn't for credit, just duty of state, and I seriously need to get some sleep. If you want to take her in and get the credit, I don't even care. I'll fall over if I don't get some sleep soon. Is it OK?" he asked.

The first guard's face lit up eagerly, but his strict partner remained grim.

"We need to scan each one of you first; you know the rules!" The second guard was older and more experienced but wanted to get some appreciation and said, "OK, you do that with them, and I'll take her in."

Molière tried to stall, as the second guard extended the scanner attached to his palm device and raised it to Keith's eye. There was a brief delay as it scanned him while the other guard opened his door by code. The reading announced a fail, but Molière's crew seized the guard that held Karen and entered as Daliyah's crew wrestled the scanning guard to the ground and placed him in a choke hold that rendered him unconscious. Karen knew the way to the fire escape as it was the shortest distance, and the alarm wouldn't be any louder than the one already ringing. They had to run like mad, as even being within range of a Taser or microwave gun might end the whole mission.

They ran noisily, took an elevator to the top floor, and then went to the stairs to the roof. Daliyah left last and the electronic doors closed on her and could not be flung open.

"Grab Me!"

Keith yelled at Daliyah, and she wrapped her arms around his neck and shoulder as he pushed his legs against the elevator doors, prying her out, all but one boot getting caught between the doors and stuck in the elevator.

Karen led the way to the fire exit and botched the code on the first try as everyone's adrenaline, which was already high, ran even higher. They held their tongues, but everyone's eyes urged, "Hurry up!"

They only had one more try before it would lock for an hour over a failed code. Karen took a breath, and the door beeped and opened automatically. Shots were heard in the distance as the guards had taken another elevator and were running at full speed, ready to kill on sight. The craft was covered in a tarp that had a detailed painting of the roof over it. It appeared exactly like the roof if viewed from above. Jim sealed the fire exit door and bought them a few more seconds. His men pulled off the tarp as Karen unlocked the ship with a code and gave the launch code to Keith.

"What are you doing?" His puzzled voice surprised her.

"Well, I'm not going. My fight is here, and I will use the legal system to bring them down. I will face my punishment and battle them out in court."

Molière stared in disbelief.

Daliyah tried to find the pilot area, and to her surprise, a robot was in the cockpit and asked her for the start code.

"The Code!" She shouted. "I've got it," Molière answered.

"Bye love, good luck." She kissed him and looked down before turning away.

"They'll kill you! You have to come with us!" He shouted intensely. "Jim! Grab her and bring her. I have to get this thing off the ground."

Jim made a move toward her, but she just shook her head and ran back across the roof toward the fire escape. Molière gave the code to the robot pilot and dashed back to the side entrance, only to see the guards break through the fire escape door as the craft rose into the sky, leaving only a portal for him to watch as Karen struggled futilely to pull her wrists free from the heavy-handed guards. He unwittingly pressed his face right against the portal as the mounting feeling of helplessness grew stronger and the sight of her struggling shrunk to that of a tiny speck in the distance.

Daliyah looked at him and then at the portal, and in her inimitable way, just said one single word;

"Why?"

This time, it was he who didn't answer. Unexpected moments, he once told a friend, were one of the things that made life worthwhile.

Right now, he was emotionally processing all that he just witnessed and wasn't sure how many more unexpected moments he cared to endure.

Was it the argument? Had he not spent enough time convincing her, had he assumed too much?

Of all the times Trueborn's sleazy moves frustrated him, made his world smaller, made him depressed, annoyed, and confounded him, there was no preparation for a moment like this.

Here he was; in just the second vessel to make the longest journey in human history, and he could barely appreciate it. The craft was shuttle-shaped but had an aerodynamic appearance as if it could slice through the air. The hull was sleek, and there was a freezer full of compressed food. There was running water to expand the food. The lighting was a pale blue tube that ran around the interior with a soft glow that would allow clear vision. There was a small recreation room and sleeping quarters. There were computer chess and card games, and a history application that played simulated footage of every scenario in recorded history. Ironically, Trueborn's grip on the news and the web had no impact here, and he was listed as a corrupt criminal in power with a database of all the statutes and laws he had circumvented or broken.

Daliyah came over to him and just sat quietly. She was unobtrusive and not about to invade his private thoughts, but she was still there should he wish to talk. He was so grateful to her for giving him that time to compose his thoughts. He was raised to believe that failing to acknowledge someone nearby was rude, so he pushed his anguished thoughts aside.

"I'm sorry about your boot," he said. She looked down at her bare feet.

"Time for some toe jewelry," she said, offering half a grin.

After giving the thought some space to breathe, she admitted a mistake.

"I was wrong about her."

Keith appreciated the acknowledgment, given how few people own up to their mistakes.

"I am not a religious person, so I can't speak about a leap of faith, but I will say that for her, it was too big a leap of logic to cross the stars faster than matter can travel."

The man with the big brownish-red mustache heard this and took exception.

"There's no such thing as a 'leap of logic!' he said in a loud, aggravated tone with challenging eyes.

Molière was torn between ignoring him and putting him in his place, but Karen's decision had left his diplomacy skill reservoir on E.

"Wow! Are you ever smart! You must be one of them guys with book-learnin!" Molière jeered.

Doubt ran over the man's face as he knew he'd been insulted but was uncertain how to respond, and he left annoyed.

Daliyah's eyes lit up while she covered her wide grin with both of her hands.

Molière excused himself and went to the dormitory, and he thought of the story of Moses being led to the promised land, being God's right-hand man, and then not being allowed to enter, after all his sacrifices. He was allowed to look as if that was a boon. Keith felt this was one of the best and worst biblical stories. It sums up the price of over yearning and how one has to acknowledge their failed goals without condemning the road to them.

Conversely, if God loved everyone and punished his right-hand man so harshly for experiencing a single moment of doubt, there was a capacity for cruelty and capriciousness there, that didn't remotely fit the story of all that unconditional love from heaven.

He identified with Moses at this moment. He felt he was doing humanity an enormous favor by leading an escape to the heavens and out of the clutches of an elected slave master in noble disguise. In reality, many people had become so cowed that they had no desire to leave at all. What favor had he done for Karen, who would have wanted him to stay but didn't want to dampen his dreams by telling him so? Now he would continue away from all he had ever known, touched, or cared about. He would never forget a single longing or regret, thanks to his memory-boosting chip. It would all remain in perfect color and detail, and like Moses, who could not enter the promised land, he could only replay those memories in his mind but couldn't touch a single one of them as they were all now buried millions of light-years into the past.

Chapter Sixteen

THE PANICKED HERD MENTALITY

The concept of time had always nagged at Molière, but the idea of being mere hours away from a planet where everyone he'd known would have either had grandchildren by now or been dead for years troubled him immensely. The last time he saw Karen alive, she was being taken away by armed guards. She will have lived out her life and been laid to rest while he shot through space beyond the speed of light and was not even one hour removed from that moment. The entire crew was experiencing unsettling thoughts and questions, while all he wished for was to grieve this odd passage of time alone.

Jim had some natural leadership traits and the courage to match his size, but it was clear that he was beginning to regret his decision to join the crew.

"Why can't we see the stars, and what's all this light? I think that robot's off his lithium battery and veered into the Milky Way or something!" He grumbled.

"It's the Doppler effect," Keith told him reassuringly. "The *what* effect?"

"Think of it like this, Jim, you see one of your old buddies, a trucker, or a farmer, let's say; you are on the sidewalk grabbing a bite from a street vendor. Your buddy spots you, honks the horn, and lets it ring out in a long, steady single note. As his vehicle gets closer to you, the sound becomes louder on the approach, but as he goes past you at the same distance, the sound fades faster. This is because the sound waves coming from the moving vehicle change frequency relative to where you are standing." Keith said.

"It works with light too. You are seeing white light from out of the portals rather than stars because of the rate at which we are moving. The frequency of the light waves has changed so much because of our speed that the light emitting from past stars has been changed to below that of infrared meaning, we can't see them. Conversely, there is something called a gravitational redshift, which means that stars or any other visible thing will change color depending on how close it is to you. The waves at this intensity and frequency are moving towards blue light, which is extending the way we see them, so it might look like the Milky Way, but it's actually the abundant microwave radiation all through space that we are seeing as a constant bright blue light."

"Are you some kind of physics geek or something?" Jim asked.

"The only thing I learned about physics is how to hit the ketchup bottle from underneath to get the ketchup out faster."

"R-ii-ight. Well better watch it, Here comes that Daliyah chick, looking meaner than usual."

"I hear that from people, but I just don't see it. I see someone who might have had an accelerated childhood and doesn't want anyone to know her inner child is alive and well. I get that no one would want to piss her off, but if you don't give her proper reason, she's quite fine." Keith said.

"Your call," Jim said with raised eyebrows as he walked away.

Daliyah came and sat about eight feet from him and wordlessly turned her head away.

Keith learned from her that when someone has a lot on their mind, it can be most refreshing to forego the need to address them immediately and simply allow room for better thoughts to emerge.

Initially, he imagined this silent routine would be offensive to most, but he was discovering there was an odd beauty about people just giving each other time to simply be a touch truer to the moment they were in. There was a certain comfort in knowing he could take his time before addressing her. Any silence could last all day as far as she cared, but he felt this silent supportive presence was a small gift, and he wanted to acknowledge it. He walked over to the table she was seated at, and on the opposite side, he stretched out his frame across three seats to lie down as she sat upright on the other side. He was learning her unspoken language. Keith knew she wouldn't judge him for being so uninhibited, and he wanted her to know that on a ship full of people who saw her as a potential loose cannon, he was entirely comfortable with her being in his personal space. It wasn't flirtatious but a show of acceptance, and she read it correctly.

He wanted nothing to do with another romance after two epic fails in a row, but he could appreciate a friend who'd rarely interrupt, rant, or ramble, if ever. If only he could say the same for himself. She turned slightly and put her feet on the chair next to her. This was her answer; she was entirely at ease just lying there without any words spoken. It was so foreign to him but very comfortable during a time when nothing else was. After about an hour, some crew members were grumbling about the unknown length of the trip. Questions reigned about the exact velocity of the craft; whether it had weapons, and how repopulating the new planet might occur given the considerable imbalance in the number of men and women.

"Why's that robot all sealed off in the cockpit? What if he doesn't know where he is going or pops a piston or something?" A raspy voice asked in protest.

"Why, are you going to replace him?" one of the female crew members shot back.

"I just want to know how long I'll be in this tub before we all get cabin fever and start killing each other in our sleep."

"Maybe we should start with you, and cut your throat just to keep your mouth shut." A voice hollered from the back.

"Well, it sure didn't take long to descend into prison rules, now, did it?" A harsh voice boomed above the rest. Jim challenged the room with an icy stare and added, "Anyone gets cabin fever, and they have to take me on with this knife, right here! Any takers?"

A lot of begrudging eyes were deadlocked, but calm was restored. Keith liked what Jim did but also knew it couldn't last for months with mixed company and no official leader that anyone had to follow, so he approached Jim.

"Is that going to be the new government? Your hunting knife?" Molière asked with a grin.

"I just don't want this to go sideways on the first day. If you have any suggestions, I'm all ears," he admitted.

"These guys are worried about the ship having built-in weapons when we all might have to watch each other with one eye open in our sleep. I knew an MP on a big aircraft carrier once. He said it was like a city on the high seas. Stabbings, murders, gambling debts, and drug use are all taking place in uniform by trained men with a common goal. The officers had options like court-martial, dishonorable discharges, cleaning the bathroom with a toothbrush, and the brig. What do we have? Your hunting knife and some half-remembered speeches from the annals of democracy. Do you think that'll be enough for some uptight rebels after the collective mood swings take full effect?" Keith asked glumly, as Jim rubbed his chin.

"I don't know, but let's make a pact to stick together, I've seen you fight, and I want you on my side. I've got some size, and I know how to use my dukes. What do you say?"

"I'm hoping that reason will prevail, but if it hits the fan, I've got your back."

The two men shook hands and retired to their respective dorm areas, where they slept very lightly. In the morning, little pockets of like-minded people formed cliques as a troubling sense of tribalism grew. Traits like openly whispering to each other, so the wrong people couldn't overhear were followed by disapproving glares from the opposing groups. Territorial behavior grew as sections of the two dormitories were barricaded with overturned mattresses and a lookout on each side. One camp believed in following the robot pilot, and the other distrusted it and wanted to overtake the ship. As time rolled on, the rebel spirit that had been so desperately needed to break free from the shackles of the Trueborn government's tyranny was blooming into a descent toward mutiny, if not all-out piracy.

There were four women on the ship. Two were Donita and Bridget, both level-headed and reasonable. Daliyah was loyal and strong, and while some worried she could be lured down the wrong spiritual path, Molière believed in her implicitly. Then there was Barb. She had a duplicitous nature and an appetite for inciting conflict and drama. A terrific instigator who showed a proven skill for starting fights between two strangers. She was undoubtedly a strong voice in the undermining of the ship's pilot. This was not so much over concerns about the robot's integrity or programming, but she craved a good fight between any two sides, provided she could take a back seat. If Bon from the prison had a sister, it would have been Barb. She had been in the company of the man with the red handlebar mustache and the mercenary with the scratchy beard. Lines were being drawn, and the numbers weren't amounting to any favorable advantage for reasonable discourse.

Jim approached Keith with his concerns regarding a brewing feud. "We've got to do something before things get out of hand."

"What's your best hunch?"

"If we sleep on this, we wake up dead, or worse, we can either put a beating on one of the ringleaders, which could backfire entirely, or we can try to talk them out of their crazy misgivings. What do you think?"

"We are two, Daliyah, and the other two make five, against eleven. If we trounce one of them now, that could cement their need to get their frustrations out. I am a civil libertarian, and I'm not interested in the 'iron fist' approach. I do agree that we cannot delay any further."

"You talk to them then, because if I do it, I'm going to want to smash one of them in the mouth if they lip off to me. It sure isn't going to be Daliyah, because she doesn't talk. The other two women are facing a lot of peer pressure right now, and I'm not sure they want to wear the bull's eye." Jim fumed.

"So you'll generously hand it to me, is that it?"

"Rational discourse, right? That's your thing, so prove it. Prove to me that human beings are worth saving as a species; demonstrate to me that every form of government does not secretly desire totalitarianism; does not hunger for god-like power over the masses; and, even in this microcosm, catering to our lowest animal instincts will not rule the day."

"Well, thanks for the pep talk, I feel so light and cheery suddenly."

Molière walked over to the dorm, where most people acted territorial, and stragglers followed him in.

"I was hoping to speak to everybody. I wanted to say that I am noticing a lot of team spirit around here. I like people who are loyal and stand by their friends no matter what. When we opposed Trueborn and his cronies, we put aside all judgments. We didn't care who anybody was or what they believed as long as they had the guts to oppose a dictatorship disguised as democracy. It took courage, and everyone who dared to face this trip knew we'd be up against the unknown. We knew we'd leave everything behind to go into the abyss and find our chance to self-govern and be free from oppression. If we choose that, or we can copy all the things we fought so hard against. We can operate on rumor and become so afraid of it that they ban freedom of speech and call any innocent question misinformation, so some ass gets to decide what is true, what's a rumor, what's banned, and what thoughts are to be labeled 'word crimes'. Let's not have that. If there are people who think the robot is drunk at the wheel, then we should hear them out. I don't buy that, but I'll listen to anyone who does. It's important to remember if we did overrule the metal man, none of us could even fly this ship. I know I can't. If we deviate from our course by even one degree, we could end up in a completely different solar system until we run out of food. What if we end up in a black hole where the gravity is so strong that even light cannot escape and time stops cold altogether? I don't like how long this is taking or all the uncertainties about a planet so far away that no one but Doyle could even imagine getting there."

The crowd took turns interrupting to vent their annoyance. "Why'd we have to go so far?"

"Why didn't we go to Mars instead?"

"Why is it so bright out the portals? "It looks like we went the wrong way!"

If chaos were music, someone would need to control the volume.

"Mars was a bluff, Doyle knew the government would take it over from him, so he used it as a decoy to send the first ship from there, and then the government blocked any more ships from going there. This is why we have such a long trip, we can't risk the government sticking its nose in and ruining everything like they always do. The portal views look weird because we are going so fast that it creates a sort of optical illusion where things look incredibly misshapen. I am no expert, but a wave of light or sound changes depending on how it is approached or how it is approaching. The further from mass we are, the weaker the waves of visible light. We have a scale of waves; radio waves, microwaves, infrared, ultraviolet x-rays, and gamma rays. They go from red to blue, and some cannot be seen depending on the frequency. We are messing with time dilation here; did anyone think everything would look like what we are accustomed to? Do you want to kick the robot out of the pilot's chair and reassemble it at a table? What if something goes wrong? Who is going to fix it? Let's feel good about escaping that dreadful government and look forward to building a new world and finally getting to breathe easily rather than turning on each other. I am not in charge, I have no authority over anyone, I am just asking that you give it some time and give the ship a chance to prove its worth."

"Sounds like a bunch of technical mumbo-jumbo to me!"

A voice called out as others chimed in with similar objections.

"You can't hide behind your light show of ten-dollar words and fool us, you know!"

"It's probably his robot!" another shouted.

"Look, I just want to get there in one piece, just like you. I don't know if the planet is safe if Doyle's radiation buggy exploded on impact or anything else that you don't know. I just know we have got to ride this out if we are to survive. You can make up your minds about that all you want; I'm done."

Molière walked away with his faith in free speech taking yet another hit. Its value depended entirely on the other side's willingness to listen, and humans so often failed at that. It's easier to silence and condemn than to listen and self-question. It hadn't been enough to sway the small crowd, but it caused dissent. The merc with the scratchy beard argued with some of his brethren and seemed to have abandoned any ideas concerning a revolt. It wasn't much, but the five soon became six, and the remaining majority paid less attention to their dormitory divisions.

The merc with the scratchy beard was Byron, and he was welcomed to the group and seemed pleased to be in the company of Bridget and her best friend Donita. If Byron hadn't fallen ill, he would have appreciated his welcome. At first, he complained about feeling weak, wouldn't get out of bed, and frequently looked pale and sweaty. A lot of the freedom fighters had been forced to learn first aid on the fly, but none were doctors, and nobody could properly help him.

One self-appointed expert from the ranks shouted, "It's radiation sickness."

Without a doctor to confirm how that even looked, people just avoided him and demanded that he sleep away from the dorm. Donita was a chesty woman with dark skin and a kind nature, and most people liked her right away. It was a morale crusher when she had a pair of her earrings stolen while she slept, and no one confessed despite repeated inquiries. Her best friend had been with her for many years, and Daliyah didn't wear jewelry or makeup, so Barb was suspected but went into such histrionic denials that people acquiesced. The days that followed were trying, but there was a relief when Byron recovered from whatever bug had affected him. Then one night, as most were sleeping, there was an obvious shift in the trajectory of the craft that everyone felt with a careening jolt. Some went back to bed, while others went to investigate. Barb came from the bathroom, asking what had happened.

Jim shouted, "Up here! It's the robot!"

The robot had been disabled somehow and was completely unresponsive. This resulted in a course change, as the entire group was now on its way to food exhaustion while hurling across the universe faster than any ship had ever traveled to a likely destination of nowhere. The crew frantically pulled the robot out of its seat for examination and tried to reactivate it without success. Daliyah pointed to a button with the letter A on it and struck it fiercely with her hand. A second jolt took place, and the craft veered wildly before settling on what felt like its prior course.

"How did you know?"

Jim asked, but she didn't answer him. She bent down on her hands and knees and shimmied as far into the crawl space as the feet of the robot went. She stood up and gave Donita one of her missing earrings back. A wide-eyed Donita thanked her but forgot to close her mouth because she was so surprised. Back at the dorm, Daliyah walked past Barb and used a tool to break open her personal footlocker while Barb wailed in protest.

"What are you doing? You can't go in there!"

Daliyah popped open the lid and removed the second earring belonging to Donita, then punched Barb hard enough in the mouth to send her reeling.

"Don't steal!" she hissed through gritted teeth and gave her a second wallop as Barb, who was heavyset, openly sobbed in pain and shame before a hushed room of silent observers. They marveled at the sight of a slight and petite woman besting someone fifteen years her senior and easily twice her size. No one took exception or showed much sympathy, and no one tried to break it up.

Bridget turned to Jim and said, "She deserved it." Jim nodded, adding, "It looks good on her; I'm fine with it."

Donita said, "Good and evil are *not* gender-specific, and sometimes the largest consequences can come from the smallest source."

Jim asked Keith to find out how Daliyah knew how to correct the ship, as it was on everyone's mind.

Keith saw her later in the common room and was eager for answers.

"I don't suppose it would do any good to tell you to ice up that hand, so instead I'd rather ask you about that engineering degree you don't have, which probably saved the lives of everyone on board."

She turned her head upward toward him with her eyebrows raised slightly and said nothing for a few seconds. Keith wondered if he had offended her, but she then spoke freely.

"The button was different from all the rest; it was bigger and had a big "A" on it. The robots don't need that. It had to be for us dumb humans. I figured we needed an autopilot button if something went wrong with the robot. It seemed like an obvious choice, so I hit it, that's all."

"That's all? You could have killed us, but instead, you've become a hero overnight! Ha Ha! Half the crew didn't trust you and thought you were bad news, and now we all owe you their lives! Good for you! Maybe now people will learn a little about how if someone comes schmoozing up to you, playing to your ego with their charm, it's rarely for your benefit, and sometimes the real gems are right in front of us hidden in plain sight. I sure don't believe in touching instruments when I am unsure of their purpose, but you came along and saved everyone. Thank you, and every little silent thought in your head. You were brilliant. Excellent deduction skills there."

She gave him an elated but semi-confused-looking smile and held that same expression for several seconds, and he nodded to her that he really meant it and walked away, expecting the others to act similarly, but they didn't. Instead, most thanked her for setting Barb straight and reminded her that it was well deserved. The respect for Daliyah had risen substantially, and morale gradually returned, but Molière privately wondered if the crowd needed to sate their appetite for any justified violence when they were scared and angry before they could indulge in civility again.

"I think I see it!" Donita roared excitedly.

Donita was not one for seeking undue attention, still, everyone clamored around her. Most of the portals were still blocked by gleaming light, but one had a crescent-shaped arc of black space that could be seen through. Donita had been filling her time wishing on an unseen star, but now they spotted a star being orbited by a planet larger than Earth that was a combination of beige and gray, and after months of just looking at light, everyone took turns craning their necks and twisting their faces against portals for closer examination.

Chapter Seventeen

A HOLE IN YOUR THEORY

"You'd better go look at that radiation pulverizer," Daliyah said, walking right up to his face, so he'd know it was urgent. He was about to reply to her indignantly. *What did she expect him to do about whatever the issue was?* He'd never seen such a thing in his life. For Daliyah to use three words or more in a sentence meant it was crucial, so he nodded and rushed down to examine the pulverizer. Doyle had invented it to destroy all radiation and convert it into fuel. He found some crew members in distress. A Frenchman nicknamed "La Rochefoucauld" kept pointing at the warning meters by the control panel in front of the chamber.

"Mon Dieu!" he said repeatedly.

Above the console was a series of meter readings with needles, and all were pointing past the safety zone and were well into the green area, which meant radiation contamination. A few were in the "red zone," which meant a critical reading. The needles began swinging wildly from one end of the dial to the other.

"Everyone out of this room! Now!" Molière angrily shouted.

Everyone funneled into the dorm, perhaps because they felt safer there. Confusion reigned once again.

"What's going on?

"Are we all going to die?"

"Is that thing malfunctioning?"

"Maybe it's a false reading!"

The collective commentary was unhelpful and interrupted Molière's thoughts. "Bridget and Donita! You both worked in a robot assembly at some point, right? I need to go to the cockpit and examine that robot and see if you can reactivate him somehow. If not, I need to know how they disabled it!" Bridget ran for the cockpit, but Donita stayed while Jim questioned Barb. Jim looked at Keith and pointed out the grim facts.

"She doesn't have the technical knowledge to disable one of those things, and, for that matter, I don't think anyone on this ship does. Do you want me to get her, anyway?"

"No, forget it."

Donita had a habit of opening her eyes very wide when she spoke to people. It was a sign of honesty that con artists often tried to mimic, but when it was inauthentic, it showed. One of the reasons everyone liked Donita was due to her honesty, so when she objected to Molière, he knew she wasn't lying.

"Those robots can't be disabled; once activated, you'd need a missile or a tank gun or something like that to stop them. There is no off switch, and they can't be reprogrammed. It should be working; we can examine it all day, and there is no slot for a flash drive, no disc slot, no bios, and no way to disable it at all." Molière appreciated the helpful thought, but it only compounded the problem.

"I am a little out of my depth here. The robot is the only one on board that would have a clue, and now you tell me our disabled robot cannot be disabled. What can I do with that news?"

Donita bulged her eyes even wider than usual.

"I don't know, I am just relating this new wrinkle, and it's a bad one."

"Fair enough."

Molière sighed and made his way to the one portal that revealed a bit of space, and he asked Jim to keep his eyes glued on it for any kind of anomaly. Keith needed answers. "Donita," he asked,

"Can you think of any way a layperson could mess with a robot? A person with no skills at all, how could they do it?"

Donita shook her head as she searched her mind for an answer.

"The only way it could have happened is if Trueborn ordered it, and he's dead, or Doyle, who's on Kepler 452b."

"Remember when Trueborn went on all the two-way monitors and commanded the robot to shut down? What if someone recorded that and played it for the robot while we slept?" Molière asked.

Donita's eyes bulged wider than he'd ever seen them as she nodded vigorously.

"Yes! That would work! Barb could have used her palm device!" Molière slumped his shoulders down, looking resigned, and said,

"So without a voice recording, no one has to reactivate the robot, it is dead to us forever then." Donita nodded in silence.

Bridget had red hair and green eyes, but she didn't fit the temperamental stereotype until today. She had returned and overheard the conversation, so she charged over to confront Barb.

"You stupid cow! Look at what you've done! You screwed us all to death because of your petty racism. You petty idiot!" Bridget's eyes were flared and the whites all but glowing as she tore into Barb without relenting.

"It wasn't racism!" Barb insisted.

"Yeah, then what the hell was it then? You stole from the only black woman on board, and now you're trying to pretend you aren't a racist! Do you ever tell the truth? You bloody pathetic psycho."

Barb had already earned the wrath of the crew and didn't want to be on the wrong end of another civil beating, so she started to talk fast.

"It wasn't racism, OK? Look, it could have just as easily been YOUR earrings. All the men are looking at you two all the time. It's pretty clear Daliyah's made her choice; she only talks to one person on the crew. I wanted to start a fight between you both because of the outrageous popularity you two share."

I wanted people to realize that maybe you two aren't the golden sisters; they all think you are OK. Look at me, I'm old, fat, and gray, and my hair is turning white. I know no one will ever look at me again. What are you going to do, beat up an old lady for a second time? Go ahead and show your true colors! "

Bridget was steaming mad but collected herself.

"No, I am not going to sink to your level. You were caught for thieving and sabotage, and all you can do is go virtue-signaling instead of apologizing. You are so pathetic! If you do one more stupid thing to hurt this crew in any way, I'll shove you in that radiation room myself. Do you *get* me?"

A long silence hung in the air afterward as Donita stared Barb down with a far less kindly bulge in her eyes this time. Barb put on her best game face but failed to conceal a shudder at the last moment. The two respected women stormed off, leaving Barb to start sobbing with no shoulder to cry on. The man with the reddish-brown handlebar mustache was named Trevor Molletteski, and he decided that he too, needed a friend. When most of the people had gone to see what they could do to help with the radiation problem, he approached Barb and told her he didn't have a problem with what she'd done and felt that the ship was being run by a popularity contest. He added that if the same people were going to be put on a pedestal when they got down to the planet, life might not be so comfortable for the two of them, and that if something went wrong under the leadership of the "brainiacs," it might create a more level playing field for the less accepted people. Barb smirked as he spoke, because finally, at long last, there was someone on board who spoke her language and understood what the *real* problems were.

Molière had returned to the portal with a partial view to find people taking turns trying to tilt their faces for a better glimpse of deep space.

"Keith! What do you make of this? It looks like a black hole!" Jim called out.

Daliyah asked, "Is that shooting radiation at us?"

Donita assured everyone that black holes sucked things in and didn't let them out. Hardly anything with mass could escape the high gravity, not even light or radiation. She confirmed.

Jim asked, "OK then, what's jacking the radiation levels? Let's ask our part-time pacifist here."

Bridget then queried, "If the radiation is so high in the black hole, could it mess up our instruments and readings?"

Molière said, "There is another possibility. It might be a white hole." "A what? What the heck is a white hole?" Jim asked.

"Well, a black hole has enough gravity to pull in entire suns, and it is so dense that almost nothing escapes, not even light, On the inside of one, time and space actually become each other," Molière said, looking downward, realizing how most wouldn't be very accepting of this news.

"What the hell are you talking about?" Bridget asked with a look of immense confusion.

"It gets worse. If a black hole pulls everything into it, a white hole shoots things out, and that could mean gamma rays to the tune of a million suns, and nothing we know of could withstand that level of radiation. Not an ozone layer, and not a small ship's pulverizer designed for deep space levels of radiation. A gamma-ray burst from a white hole would cook us and an entire planet behind us even if it missed the target.

Mustachioed Trevor had heard enough.

"You are so full of it, just makin' it up as you go, eh? Has anyone here ever heard of a white hole? There is no such thing, and he's just tryin' to freak yas all out."

Molière knew Trevor was the sort of guy who always played up to the crowd like he was on their side but really just wanted to start trouble under the guise of looking out for everyone, not unlike the former crime minister. He had this maudlin way of endearing himself to people, earning their trust, then waiting for just the right moment to take advantage.

"Really, Trevor? Then what happens after a black hole dies? Maybe you can set us all straight. I'm sure you were just about to point out that gravity is a field all through space, and it is affected by both space and time. That's the reason a rocket can leave the gravimetric pull of Earth. It's not due to its power but due to its speed, right? And, how fast does it have to go to avoid gravity? I'm sorry, I didn't hear you. What was that? Eleven kilometers per second? Why, that's correct, Trevor, I'd have never pegged you as a man of science, but I guess I misjudged you, my apologies." Keith allowed him time to rebut, but only silence fell.

Trevor glared at Molière while oozing enough hatred and vindictiveness to promise a future meeting soaked in violence.

He would not allow himself to be mocked again without dire repercussions.

Molière continued speaking to a suddenly engrossed audience.

Donita asked, "Can we all just let him speak in an unbroken train of thought, please?"

Keith started again.

"Look, I'm no expert; it's just a theory because the faster you go through space, the slower time goes. We could be looking at something long after it's dead, just like when we look at stars; they've been dead and burned out for eons, but the nova is long gone. We're actually looking at something that takes so long to reach us from a past, so far gone that the sight is from another era in time."

Jim came up to Molière quietly muttering.

"We're going to have problems with that Trevor guy, you know. Maybe we should do something, preemptively."

Molière looked up at his towering friend, who looked beleaguered.

"Like what? Doyle said the trip would be open to anyone who wanted to escape. He said he didn't consider any criminal records under Trueborn legitimate. I doubt he'd welcome our in-ship rewriting of the criminal code."

Jim scoffed and then asked, "How do you know so much about all this bloody space stuff anyway?"

"So much?" I am clueless. I know just enough to keep a physics professor from wanting to kill me on sight. The only thing I learned from physics was to hold a hammer at the bottom of the handle so you save your arm strength."

"Do you want to go over that shit about space and time becoming each other for me?"

"I'd rather hang out in the radiation room."

Jim laughed and repeated his prior concerns. "So about that Trevor guy?"

"Ugh, maybe he'll just find a nice settlement on the other side of the planet."

Just then, Byron entered the room.

"Hey guys, guess what? Trevor just asked me if I'd still be willing to be a mercenary when we got to the planet. I hope he doesn't want Doyle dead because it was his ideas that got us here in the first place." His bemused grin disappeared as he was greeted with sour looks of consternation.

"Oh, don't worry about him," Byron casually mentioned. "He's a true coward. He acts tough when he is on the side with numbers, but one on one, he'll duck out every time. He has no character. You have to watch him when your back is turned, but he's never gone after anybody up front. He'd be more likely to put something in your drink or unload your weapon before a gunfight. No morals and no guts at all."

Keith facetiously added, "I'll sleep better tonight knowing that."

Jim and Byron left to revisit the portal when Daliyah approached the systems room.

"Whoa, hey, hey, hey, where are ya goin' there, Daliyah?" Keith asked with some trepidation.

"No one's checked the radiation levels," she said without turning her head or breaking stride.

"Nah, nah, now wait just a second there, will you?"

She didn't answer, but she turned and spun her head so that her hair swung in front of her face momentarily before resuming its proper setting. This meant she was awaiting further explanation.

"Um, you are smaller in stature than most people here, so there's a chance you could be more at risk than someone with a larger build."

She squinted at him in doubt.

Realizing he was getting nowhere, he reached for absurdities.

"There's a pit bull behind that door, and he hasn't eaten in three days."

A more skeptical squint followed one that resembled the look a person gets when they've just tasted spoiled food.

"If you go in there, it could mess up your ovaries, and you might not be able to have kids."

She gave him the stern look of a teacher when presented with the 'dog ate my homework' excuse. Then a slow, knowing grin arose and stayed on her face for some time.

"Yes, exactly. Your ovaries are in grave danger, and you shouldn't even be in this room; now go run away somewhere safe or your kids will come out funny. Go! Go on."

She stopped defiantly and looked directly into his eyes with the brewing confidence of a surehanded poker player, before finally turning away. He hung his head down, feeling ashamed for exposing his concern for her and the fact that she now knew what he didn't even want to admit to himself. She did eventually leave, but not after looking toward the systems room door, as if to suggest that if no one checked the levels, they could be at risk.

"I'm hoping that if we put some distance behind us, we're going fast enough to avert any radiation damage."

He said this, hoping to escape the momentary tension.

"It's OK, we can wait," She added and left the room.

Did she mean wait to check the levels or wait for a better moment between them?

He thought to himself, *The woman says six words a year, and now she's giving me double entendres.*

Despite any embarrassment over exposing a protective streak toward her, she refused to gloat or make him squirm in it, and he was grateful for that.

"Land Ho!" Jim howled in a booming voice as they neared the atmosphere on Kepler 452b.

The planet looked massive compared to Earth. There were shouts of "Hooray!" and "Hot Damn! We made it!"

The atmosphere surrounding the beige and grey planet was coated in dense clouds, and penetrating through it jarred the ship roughly.

"Slow it down!" a voice hollered.

People started shouting from various places on board. The ship had been built on Earth to exit its atmosphere, but the larger planet had stronger gravity that was pulling the ship faster to the ground than anyone was ready for.

"We are nosediving!" Bridget hollered "Will the reverse thrust be enough to stop us from exploding on contact?"

"Everyone get to the dorm and surround yourselves with mattresses!" Molière shouted.

Jim stood a few mattresses upright and fastened them to bed frames, preferring to "pinball" around rather than get compressed. Daliyah crawled between the mattress and tied the sheet on top of it so that the entire mattress would elevate and land on the floor surface with her cocooned on top. Molière contemplated the irony of being pulverized to death on a ship with a massive pulverizer on board. The idea almost amused him. He just stood off to the side, wondering if the last year and a half of his life had just been a series of missteps with no end in sight and that this might just be the promised land he'd never get to see. A flurry of thoughts whizzed through his mind. *What did they say about the planet? It was rocky, like Colorado, it could retain its oceans and had lots of active volcanoes. Surely Doyle would have mapped out a safe landing spot. Had any of those jolts thrown off the targeting?* He looked out the portal and saw small, rocky hills surrounded by water. They looked like egg cartons floating in shallow water. So much for any ideas about landing in an ocean. There was a deafening thud that echoed throughout the ship as it shook. Mattresses and people went flying into the air, some bouncing and landing on each other.

Molière was tossed back toward the cockpit and bruised his arms while unceremoniously breaking his fall.

"Where are we?"

"What now?"

Voices quieted as the dismal thought dawned on the group. They were stuck underground; stuffed deep into clay and rock. The surrounding ground pressure locked the exit doors tightly into place.

Chapter Eighteen

BROKEN SHACKLES AND STILTED DREAMS

After some initial panic, the crew became somber and silent. The Alacrity II had a rough landing and was buried in the planet's surface; no one even knew how deep. The portals were all black, and most of the crew wondered if they had escaped the oppressive governments of Earth, broken the light-speed barrier, and dodged being drawn into a black hole only to reach a new planet and die there. It was millions of years away in time, and to die in a confined tomb without so much as a glance outside drained the energy out of them all. They'd expended all of their fear and panic in getting here, and now most sat solemnly in reflection of their perilous bid for freedom, and they'd beaten the odds all the way to the finish line, as only silence hung in the air for long minutes. Daliyah walked up to Molière, looking him in the eye, and then turned to the side and turned further in a slight beckoning motion. He followed her to the top of a coolant compressor, and there was just enough space for two to sit privately and converse.

She stared him squarely in the eye and said, "If we're gonna die, I want to know some things."

"OK, shoot."

"What's string theory?"

"That's what you want to know, at a time like this?" She nodded.

"Well, I'm not the best person to ask, but as near as I can say; when scientists study the big everything out there, they break things down to the tiniest parts like atoms and even smaller particles. The trouble is, they are so tiny you can't see them. When looking at the time-space continuum and gravity and things like that, they can tell a lot by what the particles are doing. Because time and space are complex as hell, they shrink things down to a single particle, like being one single point on the map of spacetime. The problem is that the math breaks down when you look at things this way. Physics geeks absolutely lose their friggin' *potatoes* whenever the math doesn't work, so the next best thing is to imagine the point connected to another point or a series of points on a line; a string, if you will. The problem is that while the math seems happier under string theory, the proof doesn't quite line up as well as hoped. So it's just a theory that hasn't been proven conclusively. Why in the hell would you be concerned about that now?"

She tilted her head to one side and shrugged.

"You think there is something off with me, what is it?" "I don't think--"

Daliyah interrupted and cut him off mid-sentence, for the first time ever, and it surprised him.

"Don't say there's nothing wrong with me; you know weird stuff about people; they don't even know themselves. You understand things about me that other people don't get, so then you must know what's *wrong* with me too." Her look was piercing but vulnerable at the same time, almost desperate.

"Well, I don't think anything is broken, if that's what you mean, and every person alive has things they can work on to be a better person. I haven't done a perfect job in my life, and I've made a boatload of mistakes. I try to learn from them, but there are kernels of wisdom that I just flat-out reject. That's probably why some people call me a recalcitrant. A stubborn nonconformist, if you will. As far as I can see, you have an image problem. You are petite but an absolute pistol, not a firecracker, more like a stick of dynamite. You are not a derringer but a Glock with hollow points. People have said things to me like, 'Wow, does she ever look mean!' The other women go to hug you, and you start to cough so as not to spread a cold, but you are always better five seconds later. I've heard it said that poodles bite more often than any other dog because people don't take them seriously. This makes sense to me, if people are always dismissing them and denying them their due respect, any dog will get angry. If humans are constantly trying to con, seduce, and manipulate, I can see how a person might feel the need to return the hostilities in kind. The media always shows confrontational women as 'strong women," but patience, kindness, and levelheadedness are better strengths to have. I certainly don't see a foolishly confrontational nature in you. Maybe everyone else does, but I see someone who grew up way too fast and didn't get to develop their innocent side so much. I see it come out when you laugh; then you look like a happy twelve-year-old, you know, like you were meant to instead of growing up overnight.

When you share things and give people medicine, you don't even stick around for the 'Thank you'. I think there is a kind, understanding person buried beneath a breathtakingly feisty exterior. For someone who finds being feared more comfortable than being appreciated or cared for, it's safer. There are no betrayals to worry about. No false hopes or broken promises. The only problem is that it's not you at all. It's a comfort zone that denies you all the best joys in life. A shared trust, being part of a team, and someone standing and being in awe of you just doesn't happen to a lot of angry people. I know; I've had my share of forgettable moments days being a hothead too. You are a leader, you are incredibly considerate and very deep. If there is anything wrong, it isn't functionally wrong. Life has taught you bad lessons, and unlearning that code is never easy. This cheap tough guy act might be authentic, but I don't think it reflects the real you. I think you are an absolute treasure of a human being who is utterly terrified someone will find out."

"So what's *your* interest in me, then?" she asked.

"You mean apart from the fact we all owe you our lives no matter how things might end? Do you mean apart from seeing all the good in you that you often won't let anyone else see? I think I feel a bit protective of you, like an older brother, sort of. Obviously, you can take care of yourself, but I just feel like everyone sees the wrong picture," he said.

Daliyah's eyes closed to a half-squint, and she firmly stated, "I call bullshit on that one."

A wide-eyed Molière asked, "What?...Why?"

"You like me just as much as I like you, and it's not because you want to be my big brother. You want to climb all over me, and you feel guilty about it because I look half my age. I was *still* getting asked for ID last year, at thirty-six years old. That's why guys make references to my being twelve years old. They are trying to exaggerate how young I look, and that gives them a pass for getting up the nerve to ask, or they're scared people will think I am far younger than I am when they pass us on the street. I have seen that movie before! I've been watching it my whole life, and I don't like the ending.'

Molière squirmed in his chair a little.

"Nothing like a near-death experience to bring out the secret confessions, huh?"

She gave a half-nod.

"Yeah, I like you a lot, and maybe I haven't sorted it all out yet. I am fascinated by your secretly delicate side. I haven't been top-drawer boyfriend material lately, and I didn't want to screw things up between us because being a disappointment to you would use up the absolute last of the good stuff left in me. OK?"

She had no fear of men, and her face had been getting closer to his every time he saw her, but it never felt too close. He went to kiss her, and she was ready. A loud clanging reverberated just above their heads, interfering with any privacy.

"Hey! Anybody in there?" a robotic voice called.

"Are you alive? Bang on the ship's exterior if you are breathing properly."

The two confessors looked at each other and burst out laughing.

"All crew members must avoid the ship's exterior! We are cutting in. All crew members avoid the ship's exterior!"

Several robots made short work of digging around the vessel and cutting through the hull with laser drills. Once the crew made it outside, they shouted with glee but were struck by the increase in gravity. Kepler 452b was roughly six times the circumference of the Earth. This meant the pull from gravity was almost double. The sun was brighter and revealed that nature was untarnished and beautiful. The air was fresh while the land was rocky. There were walls of rock and cliffs in most directions, with some light brush and woods. There were cone-shaped rock hills with beds of water between them, surrounded by small pockets of farmable land. They had to hike a fair distance from the wreckage of the ship, but they didn't mind as most were feeling lucky to be alive. There was a series of two-story buildings within a group about the size of a shopping center with a big sign that read "Blossom Town."

There were about twenty residents on the new planet, and some aging had taken effect among the first who'd landed. Most of the crew were eager to chat with Doyle and probe his superior intelligence ad nauseam. Trevor and Barb wasted no time offering skewed versions of how they'd been mistreated aboard the "Alacrity II" before it planted itself within the soil of its new home. Jim met a girl he liked, and there was a lot of pairing off in a remarkably short time. It felt like a hippie commune, with everyone working together for the greater good. This was infinitely better than being oppressed, but without certain police-style checks and balances in place, completely free societies rarely stayed that way. Policing could also be easily mishandled and misused. Thankfully, there were robots on hand to perform construction work and maintain a modicum of authority if trouble broke out. The people were friendly and seemed genuine. For once, Molière felt he could let his guard down and relax. He carried Daliyah around on the back of his neck totem style to spare her the effects of the heavy gravity during hikes, and she loved being up there, so he convincingly hid the fact that his back was occasionally sore when they returned. Her favorite move was placing a palm over one of his eyes while giggling because he knew it meant she wanted to turn. He grew a beard and lit campfires for Daliyah and himself, as they often avoided all the political town hall discussions and contemplated the idea of breaking away from the group to fully explore the new land.

One night Keith awakened by Daliyah's muttering in her sleep. He rubbed her hand slowly in case she was having a nightmare, as she'd never done so before.

"You were having quite a dream, are you alright?" he asked.

"A spirit came to me in the dream; Azeban, with a warning," she said.

"Look, I have all the spiritual depth of a used pizza box, I am a reality slave. If I can't see it, measure it, or gauge it, I don't buy it. I'm still curious, though; what did it say?" Keith asked.

"He had an animal's face and told me that 'When two warriors meet, and quiet each other's souls; they often die together; shoulder to shoulder, or arm in arm, it makes no difference. Lone wolves don't travel in pairs.'

Then he pointed to this edge of the planet with a cliff that led to a star-filled abyss, trying to frighten me. I said 'What do you care?' and then told him that if this was the death he was offering me, I not only accept it but demand it. If I should die a sooner tomorrow, with you, I'll take it, no other path suits me. If he should return to me with any *other* offer of death, I'll spit in his face. He turned away, then I woke up," she said.

Molière's face creased a little as he drank in the foreboding message.

"That's a *very* sour dream, Maybe there's something negative here, you or your subconscious is picking up on, do you think a change of scenery might help?"

She gave a single downward nod, and they gathered some compressed food and rucksacks with improvised bedrolls when a visitor came to their chamber section.

"Hi, I'm Jay," a long-haired man of stocky build with an honest face said upon entering. I'm here to extend an invitation to Sir Doyle's residence. "He wants to meet you!"

Daliyah shrugged as if to say, "Why not?" Molière's enthusiasm for meeting the genius had waned a little, and after living through Trueborn's corruption, he sought a more remote destination as he didn't want to watch any form of government grow. Out of a sense of debt and obligation, he renewed his curiosity and agreed to visit the real version of Doyle.

At his home, Sir Doyle came down some stairs, and his face lit up at the sight of the couple.

"Welcome, Please feel welcome, to sit anywhere before gravity pulls one of us to the ground.

I understand many thanks are due. First, to Miss Daliyah here for rerouting the ship's trajectory, and to Mr. Molière for a host of reasons! I'd like to hear all about the episode from both of your perspectives."

Daliyah turned to Keith and gave him a blank look, meaning she wasn't going to be the one talking.

"Daliyah's a little economical in her speech, so I'll fill in what I can, fire away."

"Well, I've heard the crew was quite divided many times, and you were a calming force, and that there were some shenanigans with people's property and threats, and yet you all made it here in one piece. I'm told both of you showed tremendous leadership. We have a pretty peaceful group here: scientists, botanists, academics, and the like, but your group was more diverse and a more hunted troop. Here we have mercenaries, moderates, and radicals; not an easy group to keep unified. That said, I can already sense the germ of tension between the rougher types and the bookish ones. You kept these men from turning on each other and descending into anarchy. I'd like to ask you to do it again. You could be a sheriff of sorts, perhaps.

We don't have anything to pay you with, but I'm certain I could offer some pretty special perks. Would you like that? "

"I think you have me confused with someone else. Part of the reason we came here today was to thank you, of course, and to inform you that we are leaving the group to explore the planet," Molière said firmly.

"Understandable," Doyle replied.

"For starters, I can provide two robots as deputies, but on Earth, we saw how there are certain nuances of human understanding and group dynamics that eluded our high-functioning bots. No one wants to see any such errors, no matter how slight. If you two wanted to go on sojourns to explore, the robots could manage things till you got back. Our little society might be small, but we have a lot of resources unavailable elsewhere. Will you consider it?"

Daliyah had no expression on her face, which indicated ambivalence, but Keith grew weary of having to placate egos and settle arguments by channeling diplomacy skills that weren't his first calling.

"Mr. Doyle, I'd be more interested in learning about how you achieved so many things. I have grown cynical in my outlook, and I don't want the headaches. If I can help with irrigation, wall building, or such in the short term, I'd be fine with that. I owe you that. I've been falsely accused, hunted, and criminalized because I wanted control over my own body. That's my big crime, and I've lived as a fugitive over it. I have a chance to go and lay under the stars with the quietest woman I've ever known. That quiet has been music to my soul, and I can listen to it all day, every day. That's my plan, and given the trouble it took to get to this moment, there is nothing anyone could offer me to top that."

"The first humans that ever saw a thunderous waterfall might have run from the sound or feared the weight and speed of the water. It takes a man of vision to recognize that it's the very same water that will keep humanity alive. It feeds the plants, it's our drinking water, and hopefully one day it will become hydropower. You've found your still waters that run deep in Daliyah, and that cannot be underappreciated, but governing a serious matter." Doyle replied undaunted. Keith looked closer at the man but said nothing.

"You seemed shocked by my white hair, and I suppose my prototype lookalike was a vanity project in that I could not make it age. Making that particular robot drained and taxed my energy, and I couldn't do it again. I need someone who won't fall into corrupt habits, or the sordid history of Earth will just repeat itself. If we don't want dark-spirited forces running the government, we might have to ensure that by leading it ourselves. Please tell me you'll think about it."

"I'd rather throw Jim's hat into the ring. He's a merc yet has no problem delegating or taking turns at leading; he's not power-hungry, and he knows his shortcomings. He plays to his strengths, and he's a giant at six foot six. What's even more fun is that he doesn't pronounce the word 'escape' as 'ex-cape.' Kieth said.

"-and despite his fine diction, he stumbled all the way through his experience, and said had it not been for you, no one would have made it here alive. He also said your friend Daliyah surprised everyone with her leadership. Jim told me the experience left him somewhat bitter, and he knows he would use his position to settle scores and recused himself for that reason."

He also suspects your backstory would have more to it than meets the eye, but mentioned that he'd trust you with his life. He added that; if I chose anyone other than you, I'd be dooming our new society to failure. Strong words! Now you say the two very best prospects are running off together into the wilderness forever."

Molière shook Doyle's hand warmly.

"I want to thank you for your genius and service to humanity, and I'm not trying to come off like Diogenes here thumbing my nose at society. I know it's easier to throw rocks at the home team from the sidelines than it is to go out and win the game. Anyone can point out flaws, but few can fix them. I'm not your guy for that. I'm sorry."

"Well, I'll have to respect your decision. That only leaves me with Walt Kerouac, and he is almost as old as I am."

They said their goodbyes, gathered the rest of their supplies, and left that evening. As they made their way toward building a new life, they were mostly comforted by the certainty that comes with new love and hopes for tomorrow, but Keith had visions at night of the new world turning into the old one. They built a cottage that overlooked a lake far from the town and enjoyed an intimate life of privacy and serenity for a year and a half before it became routine and predictable. Once they grew accustomed to the sound of large dragonfly-type insects flying in V-formations of five that sounded like helicopters whenever they approached, other than a few bloated bullfrogs and hand-sized lizards, there wasn't a lot of wildlife. They enjoyed cerulean blue sunsets with gradient tinges of lavender and magenta. They dined on a variety of wide-mouthed and scaly fish and took full advantage of any surrounding vegetation they could find.

"We should exchange poems," she said one afternoon just beaming with cheer.

"I don't know how to write poetry, not a clue," he confessed.

"Me neither, so what? Bad poetry is the best!" she grinned at him until he agreed.

They went off and crafted some jumbled lines and exchanged them. "This is because I feel like I've imagined you sometimes," he said.

Although she was silent

She gave birth of color to all that was grey

Her soul was an island

Like a single drop of rain on a sunny day

Yet her spirit seemed free of anguish

A light and elusive breeze in a summer's field

Her body spoke a humble language

The image was frozen in my mind and sealed

Then she danced through the field

without a care

A child of the sun;

with youth granted forever

As a slow realization made me aware

This girl was no one and her name was

Never

He had no knowledge of meter or rhyme schemes, but she treasured it nonetheless. She looked at him differently now; her cynical squint was gone, it had been replaced with a more youthful wide-eyed openness. Her guard was down, and he saw her warmth of heart; naked, pure, and unflinching.

"This means so much, I wrote you two and wanted to save one for your birthday but...here," she said.

I sing sugar-coated, she'll say

She'll feel your heroism today

The harder you try, the more you care

She'll stick into you, and pull out what's there

She'll love you just for a minute

And then be on her way

And yeah, but I'm not like that.

He smiled at the sentiment and reassurance even if it felt a bit off the mark, as he had no doubts about her loyalty in the least. The range of her second effort, however, surprised him.

A man goes down to the sea

To try to figure out his own complexity

A roaring wave splashed his face

He thinks of another place

Now has his whole life been a waste

In fates struggles he had fared so well

One day turned sour, in a tale too sad to tell

He sits down between the rocks

The water rushes in and the boats leave the docks

He has to step back to believe how hard he fell

Climbing back so high

Tired, but you've got to try

Enough to make you cry

Mistakes will always be your plight

Fighting's hard when the target's out of sight

Hurts twice as much if you find that you are wrong

And it'll hurt again because the road is so long

Dream long into the night

For only time will tell if you are wrong or right

The voice at the mountain of time

Could never tell a lie

He could be twenty-five for as long as he's alive

He stands up feeling very old

His back it cracks, his hands are very cold

He picks up his sack that used to hurt his back

But a strange feeling had taken hold

For the first time in an eternity

There was a glimmer in his eye that no one had ever seen

He swung his sack of chains and memories

And cast them into the sea

A younger man's hair blew in the wind

He cried aloud, raised his arms and he was strong again

Like a part in a play, he walked away

A man among all men

Keith looked at her "It's about the tests of humanity, the journey, our new life, redemption, new love?" He asked.

"It means anything you want it to," she said beaming with a coy smile.

"We've liberated each other's innocence and calm. We make each other better people, and we can die knowing we failed at things and missed out on a great deal but found what most will live out their lives and never even glimpse. In essence, we are the cure to the other's ails, and the very embodiment of unlikely," he replied.

"-and free," she added.

The next morning, Daliyah saw him by the water and noticed his mind was elsewhere, then asked him a two-word question.

"Not happy?"

"Well, I am not unhappy with you, that much is certain, but I wonder if we have fallen into a sort of paradise myth."

"How so?"

"Well, when you think about what we want from life versus what we think we want, sometimes they don't line up."

She widened her eyes to hear more.

"Well, you have these two businessmen, overworked, maybe they are lawyers trying to make partners, but they can't get there," Moliere continued.

"They want to win the lottery and drink Mai Thais on the beach all day and be served girls in jiggly bikinis, and that is the snapshot they put in their minds. They busted their asses to make life meet that snapshot. Then one day they get there, they can buy all the lottery tickets they want, and they strike gold. With money to burn, they get everything they want. Now they are on the beach day after day, getting drunk, getting fat, and getting cirrhosis of the liver. They see the girls strutting around in their bikinis and flirting, but they realize they are doing this with all the fat, wealthy men for tip money and likely voice disgust and contempt toward them in the change rooms. The girls go home at night to younger, fitter men who exercise. The snapshot is a fantasy and a motivator, but the reality is a sad, pathetic existence on the periphery of life. Paying people to feed their egos and fantasies is a phony form of play-acting in which the cast mocks them with false flattery in exchange for tip money. Their dream doesn't align with reality. What is left to dream for once the dream meets reality? One has stolen the very ability to dream by achieving it. What is the substitute? A bigger island with more girls and a flashier car than the last one? Do you remember how excited we were when we built this place? When we had to make sure we'd have running water? We knocked ourselves out, and we fought so hard to make it like this. To make it peaceful, with no one bothering us, judging us, or making our lives difficult, and we've achieved it. Only now there is no one to tell us about their life lessons, no new jokes to hear, and no problems. With no problems to solve, our minds will invariably decay. We need hurdles to cross for a sense of accomplishment. If we don't have something to challenge us, something to overcome, we will stagnate. We fell for the fantasy snapshot, but like a prisoner who escapes from jail and is so focused on getting over the wall, there is no plan to build a life with no money, no contacts, and no prospects, so he robs a store, gets caught stealing, and goes back to jail for even longer."

Daliyah put her head down for a moment and spoke without lifting it.

"You probably wanted kids, and I'm not sure I can have them. I've had a few bad bounces in life, and I'm scared I might have damaged the factory. Now all I want is to have kids with you, and I don't know if I can," she said.

"Well, even if we did have kids, they'd probably see us as a form of government and never listen to anything we said. If we have some, great, and if not, we won't have to worry about them becoming politicians."

They laughed. Daliyah added, "I'll go any place in the world with you; I don't even care. I think we should go back and see if Doyle's offer is still on the table."

They packed what they needed and made the trek back to town, but it was not as they left it.

There were a lot of posters with a mustachioed Trevor's face as the sheriff and Barb as the mayor.

Daliyah looked at Molière with an unsettled sideward glance.

"I don't think this was the snapshot of our fantasy," she said.

Chapter Nineteen

EDEN, OR THE DEVIL'S PLAYGROUND

The town had grown quiet; Not many people were working on development or scrounging for resources. Many of Doyle's robots were conspicuously absent. The natural exuberance of new hopes and promises of tomorrow seemed muted and the town felt all but desolate.

"Where is everyone?" Keith asked Daliyah.

She tilted her head to the side and squinted at him with one eye. They approached some of the more frequented buildings first. They found Donita and Bridget together and were greeted warmly.

"So what's been happening here?" Keith asked, smiling.

"We thought you two had walked right off to the edge of the world or tried to salvage the ship wreckage and took off for another planet." Donita teased.

"Naw, we just got tired of skinny dipping with no audience; it defeats the purpose entirely."

The women smirked at him in mock disapproval but quickly shifted the conversation toward the new culture on Kepler 452b.

"Well, we had some town hall meetings, and we decided not to have any prisons so that Trueborn's world law could never be repeated. That also meant no police action for Barb's sabotage. I think we might have opted to rethink that one, as she runs the town now, with Trevor as her armed lapdog."

Donita explained.

"How?"

"Look, if you want to have a good government, you need to be part of it, if you leave it to whomever, then you get whatever. We aren't blaming you, of course, but things have gone south here, and fast. At first, we noticed that some robots and laser drills were missing. Then Elsie Parker and that John Benchley friend of hers went missing, and we knew something was up. It looks like right after Doyle died, Trevor somehow found himself equipped with a laser gun, the only one on the planet, and now he thinks he's Lord, God, and King of the Land. People let him get away with it because that laser will reduce a full person to ash in one shot, and no one wants to be next. He followed Trueborn's lead and banned all weapons except those that controlled people. He's getting more ornery by the day, and this is none of anybody's business, but Bridget and I aren't into men in any romantic way at all, and there is a shortage of women here. Do you see the problem?"

"Yes, I sure do, and where's Jim been all during this?"

"He chased after that elegant botanist Monica Talbot, and then they went to see if they could find you two. Maybe they lost sight of how big a planet this is."

"Did you really think you'd be safe without some kind of police?"

"We are escapees from tyranny, refugees from an oppressed world. Do you think anyone wanted to be a cop or a governor after that?"

"So, what now?" Molière inquired.

"Lay low, Trevor's ego has run amok, and if he sees either of you, he might do something stupid, and there are no robots left to protect anyone. We did find a few piles of ash, so it looks like he vaporized them with his new gun."

"How did Doyle die?"

"I think he was killed; he left no further instructions, and he was someone who planned every last detail in all that he did. Mayor Barb has copied Trueborn's gag order policy, and anyone who says Doyle was killed will be charged with disinformation and conspiracy theory. No one wants to find out what heavy punishments might accompany such a foolish charge."

Keith turned to Daliyah, and she revealed a slow downward blink and drew a long breath, absorbing the weight of the situation.

"We can't even break the atmosphere due to dense gravity, even if we could fix the ship. So now it's sinister government round two, and I didn't come this far to play out a life like that again." Molière stated.

They bid their friends goodbye and walked with heavy steps to Doyle's lab. It was boarded up with a sign that read that any trespassers would face the full brunt of the law.

"Law!" Daliyah sneered.

"The first sign of tyranny is always government overreach, even *here*," he muttered back.

They pried off the nailed-up boards easily enough and decided to explore the lab for any clues about the laser weapon or a way to disable it.

"Hey, what are you guys doing there?"

A voice called out to them. It was the pale mercenary with the dark features and the permanent five-o'clock shadow. His loyalties were unknown. Molière answered, hiding any doubt in his tone of voice.

"Doyle said he'd fix my robot legs when I came back; I am just checking to see if he kept his word."

"Look, I don't really care, but if Trevor finds out, he'll zap you on the spot, so you better be quick."

Nods were exchanged, and the couple raced to examine the lab. "Everything's coded," Daliyah groaned.

"Doyle wouldn't have sealed it all up without some sort of clue, would he?"

Daliyah pinched her shoulders and showed her palms.

They each searched different parts of the lab, and Keith found a broken, open footlocker that had added bolts for protection.

"Well, this is where he kept his secret weapon. For a peace lover, he sure made a badass cooker," Keith surmised. "What was he expecting, dinosaurs?"

"Here!" Daliyah shouted.

"Shhhh!" If I'd known you were going to be such a loudmouth, I would have stayed on Earth."

She squinted, jutting her chin at him, and while mocking a scornful expression, she said, "It's a flash drive, a tiny one; it looks like it might fit into a Palm device. Take it!"

"Where'd you find it?"

She pointed to a computer with a side panel loose from its housing. "OK, let's get out of here."

He didn't want to dwell in a risky environment without first examining the drive, so they retreated to their old quarters and set to work. The drive revealed a network of complex calculations that were so far beyond Molière's understanding that they might as well have been in a foreign language. There was an endless series of subfolders that had notes on everything from aqueducts and nuclear fission to rocket propulsion. Time ticked by, and Daliyah suggested popping the locks and staying in Jim's vacant abode to avoid detection. This proved wise, as he needed two full days to find a folder that might help him.

"Daliyah, I think I've got something!" She rushed over to him with alert eyes.

"There's a design here for a *Gauss pistol*," he said, almost in disbelief. "A what?"

"It's a projectile-launching handgun. It uses coil-wrapped capacitors to propel an electromagnetically charged slug that gains speed by moving from one capacitor to the next before it's fired. It's like the maglev system on the Hyperloop. The bullet never touches the barrel; it sort of levitates in there as it gains velocity. Once it goes, it's lethal. If Trevor goes crazy on everyone with his laser, I'm hoping we could destroy it in one shot and level the playing field. We'll have to go back to his lab and try to make one."

In the meantime, Mayor Barb had ordered a new dress code. No one was allowed to wear anything other than a t-shirt and shorts in order to avoid concealing any weapons such as knives or garrotes. She said it was to ensure Trevor's protection and respect for law and order, but Bridget and Donita felt she liked the humiliation of the other females being leered at by wandering eyes. Both regretted their "no police" stance, but not entirely because that all depended on how the police might be used. If they were to become strong-arm puppets for the authorities, they might just as well be a paid street gang.

The door creaked, and the handle turned slowly as the couple's eyes widened with fear. Donita came in the back, with Bridget standing lookout.

"They're going to kill you! Barb put it in Trevor's head that you've got it in for them, and they aim to hang you both!"

She informed them, stifling a quiver in her voice.

Keith and Daliyah were not having much luck in Doyle's lab, and Trevor and his mustachioed crew were building a small jailhouse with one cell. They put a sign up that read, "His and Hers." They also started building gallows, complete with a dangling noose.

Daliyah stared out through a window slit and watched in disbelief as the structure gained stability. Trevor joked about people trying to talk with stretched necks as they were dying.

"Don't worry, Keith, we're making sure it's safe for ya!" Trevor hollered out loud, amusing his friends.

"We even got a shorter rope for your little whore!" Another called out as they laughed.

"Course, she might have some duties before she squawks!"

Another bray of laughter rang out as the men seemed pleased and proud of their handiwork.

The hunted couple weren't as far away as their hunters imagined and had to work quietly as they raced against time to finish their Gauss pistol, there was no way it could beat a laser. It required an initial charge time of five seconds before it was ready to fire and a two-second charge between each shot. Molière and Daliyah frantically searched the lab for anything that might help their cause.

"Got something!"

Molière didn't want to be interrupted, and time was working against them as at any moment a band of henchmen just outside might burst through the lab doors.

"What is it?" he muttered.

"It's the housing for a second laser gun, but there's no guts."

"Guts?"

"Yeah, there's no tinkery things inside, you men like to play with."

"Tinkery!"

She smirked at him, then spoke in a sobering tone.

"You are going to have to challenge him to a gunfight with an empty weapon, and I'll shoot the Gauss at his laser and break it; it's our only chance."

"You want me to get into a draw against a laser fumer with an empty toy?"

"I'll go if you want," she said flatly.

"No!" He said louder than he intended.

"There's no robots left."

"Fine, then," Molière sighed, resigning himself to being the bait.

"If you get nervous and your hands start to shake, they'll know your weapon is a fake."

"Any other cheery advice?"

"I know you think it should all be about free speech and civil discourse, but if they kill you, I'm going to shoot dead every single one I can, before they get me, just so you know,"

He nodded wordlessly.

In the year and a half spent away from people, the side of Daliyah that was gentle and considerate was all he saw. Day after day, she was like a personal angel in his presence. It was startling to see how quickly her ruthless, violent side, which had long since vanished, could brew up at a moment's notice. She was never this way toward him, and he was grateful. His gratitude was not merely for her having a kinder nature than many would have even imagined, but at this particular moment, a softer personality would undoubtedly have wilted or dodged the problem. He was grateful for every bit of fire that burned deep within her soul, as he could trust no one else to perform this daunting task. There couldn't be another person as gentle as she was ruthless, who sat so comfortably in her own skin without ever revealing mood swings or overreactions. If he died, he could take comfort in knowing that his new friends were steadfast. He couldn't have asked for better, even if only star-crossed misfortune had firmly placed him among them.

He thought about people's integrity and how nearly everyone would have called Mick a better choice of friend, but in a situation such as this, Mick would have rolled over faster than a two-dollar hooker who had just been thrown a fiver. He was more socially acceptable, more refined, and well-read, but if any sort of risk emerged, he'd change his colors like a chameleon. Jim and Daliyah were rougher around the edges but were also far truer people who could always be taken at their word, no matter the situation. They couldn't be coerced or cowed into deviating from their values. These frequently misjudged people, seen as flawed or less than politically correct, often made for better friends, he decided. He felt so much more comfortable about spending his last hours among people who were putting their lives at stake for what they believed in than anyone who compliantly empowered corrupt governments by soullessly marching to their whims.

There was no time for weighing internal philosophical debates now, and Daliyah insisted on testing out the new weapon to adjust to its aim. She went outside the lab on the opposite side of where the gallows were being built and experimented with little round tube-shaped pieces of lead. The charge made a very faint buzzing sound, and the mechanism was not particularly loud, but when the slug hit the target, there was an audible crack. It sounded more like a crossbow than anything sophisticated. Four audible cracks rang out, separated by a few seconds between each charge, alerting him that showdown time was upon him. He thought about the ash piles left behind from the incinerated robots and wondered if he'd die screaming or if it would be so quick he might not feel it at all. This was his latest conflicting thought among a sea of others; abortion, gun control, altruism, and policing. He'd lived his life trying to be open-minded and shunning hypocrisy. If he could successfully disarm Trevor, he was certain that he would not kill him, probably not maim him, and hopefully not do anything barbaric at all. If Trevor were to kill him, however, hypocritical concerns had little bearing as death whistled between his eardrums as a silent countdown emptied his personal hourglass. He took solace in the certainty that Daliyah would instantly avenge him, should he fail.

"OK, I'm good," she said.

How did he end up with such a volatile and fiery woman who had the opposite effect on him in that she always left him feeling calm and relaxed and never caused him a single moment of stress? If her "just deal with it" attitude proved a petite female could stare death in the face with all the calm of someone reading a newspaper, then surely he could out bluff a hostile coward. He walked out of the lab and into the street, just a few doors up from where the gallows were being completed. He spotted Trevor, pointed the hollow shell of the empty laser pistol, and shouted:

"I've got one of those too, you know. If you drop yours on the ground, I might not have to turn you into an ashtray."

"That don't work!" Trevor scoffed.

Barb called out to him after her careful examination of the gallows.

"It was in his notes, and he only ever made one in case of dangerous wildlife or an uprising," she bellowed.

The two men locked into a stare-down as a trace of doubt ran across both of their faces. Molière knew he'd been exposed for using a fake weapon, and Trevor was plagued by "What if?" thoughts. The doubts faded as quickly as they came, and Trevor pulled out his weapon and shouted, "Take that!"

Amidst all the tension, Molière never heard the gentle buzz of the charging Gauss pistol. Daliyah had aimed for the body of Trevor's laser weapon, over his hand and beneath the nozzle. They had made their Gauss pistol hastily, and its sights were off. Few heard the sound as Daliyah fired the quickly crafted weapon. Shh-kt! The projectile dropped slightly on its trajectory, and as a result, it connected right against Trevor's index finger and broke the laser's trigger, severing his finger from his hand, as it and the trigger were sent flying. Trevor screamed long and loud, mostly from pain and the horror of disbelief.

The laser flew across the avenue and bounced as blood gushed from Trevor's hand. No one knew that Daliyah had shot him or that she had partly missed her target. They all seemed to believe this was a precision shot from a sniper as people dropped to the ground, theorizing that Jim had come back and crafted a weapon of his own.

Daliyah emerged from the lab and went looking for Barb, but it was too late for any discussion to take place. After Trevor's instant surrender, Barb looked up at the gallows of her design. She then envisioned herself dangling and being laughed at, as she fought for air. She knew this could happen because the drop was purposefully low to discourage any necks from breaking too quickly, as she had wanted to enjoy a drawn-out display.

She had never imagined that others might have the capacity for compassion or understanding in order to issue her community hours or some milder penance. Their exhaustion from strife and disinterest in tyranny was beyond her dark imagination. In her haste to flee her past, she fled to live alone on the run from people who would never bother pursuing her. Barb ran because she had no such compassion toward others and could never imagine fairness or mercy in her mind's eye because it was so foreign to her, and she had no moral reservoir to compare it with. Had Barb been in charge, she would be beating drums to hunt the prey. When she searched her soul, she could only find delight in the suffering of others. In the absence of a conscience, she imagined that's what others would do in the same position because she only looked for the very worst in people, even if she had to falsely paint them that way. Based on her flawed logic, she inadvertently banished herself to an egress of sorts on an unknown planet. Kepler 452b might have offered her wonder and discovery. Instead, it only offered her panic, loneliness, and despair. Blind to human decency, she ran too fast and too far in fear, exhausting herself to a staggering and stumbling pace in the wake of Kepler's increased gravity. She suffered a fatal heart attack just twenty-two miles from the town.

Had she stayed, she would have seen her gallows dismantled and used for the construction of more beneficial developments. Keith seized the laser, which was no longer functional, and walked up to Trevor, who was clasping his bleeding finger stump. Molière tore off part of his sleeve for him to use as a tourniquet.

"I can't fight! I can't fight! I'm injured!"

Trevor shrieked as the wheel of his moral compass swayed, rocked, and spun faster than usual. Molière looked at him slowly, studying him like a riddle. He genuinely wondered what events in a person's life go so wrong that they don't care who they kill, who they cross, what innocence is lost, and live their lives with no semblance of principle except profit and nihilism.

Molière was not religious, but he was a big believer in forgiveness. Trevor, without any superior weapon, was no threat to anyone. He was a paper gunboat that couldn't stay afloat. He was an unsophisticated shadow of the Trueborn persona without the refined manipulative skills. Molière had read about prisons where they teach people skills and how to solve their issues constructively, and he wished he could implement such a system if only he knew more about it.

"What do you think your punishment should be?" He asked Trevor.

"I dunno, kill me? Let me off with a warning maybe?"

"That's quite a leap of decision-making there, Trevor. I think you lack character and ethics. You can't see the good in people around you. I think I am going to have you build an additional room for each person on the planet without asking for any help. You might notice that if they offer you some food or try to help you despite your character. They might be better people than you thought, and serve better purposes than being used as mere subjects.

"That's it?"

"That's all."

"Wow, are you ever dumb, I would have killed you for sure," Trevor said, grinning.

"Maybe so, but I think there is something worthwhile in you that deserves saving. You helped people get away from Trueborn's evil government machine, so there must be *some* good in you. A bespectacled man dressed in black came up and introduced himself.

"Hi, I am Father Henry." "Hello."

"What you just did took quite some restraint. Are you a man of God?"

"Nope, I am a card-carrying atheist; I am afraid." "Oh! I see, well, God's house is open to everyone."

"What do you think about the story of Moses?" Keith asked.

"Most people ask me about Jesus, first."

"Oh, I like the story of Jesus; it's a warning that if people ignore bad governments abusing their authority, they might kill anyone, even a savior, or son of the almighty."

The two men laughed and engaged in many religious and philosophical discussions while never losing respect for each other's point of view. They embraced the idea of people sorting their differences through long verbal exchanges and came away with a new respect for the other's perspective. They never did change each other's beliefs, but they enjoyed a friendship based on diving into some of the deepest questions ever put before humanity. This was how opposing sides were meant to learn from each other and improve their viewpoints by listening on a deeper level and examining the other person's perspective. Daliyah and Keith settled a little closer to the town but still kept their privacy intact. Jim did eventually return, and when he discovered some of his belongings missing, he searched the town for the culprit. Trevor followed in Barb's footsteps and took off for safety in a panic, and that was how Barb's remains were discovered. He collected the nerve to return and seek a burial for her. Jim was returned to a calmer state, and his belongings were returned.

Eventually, the two sides did separate, with more of the scientists in one camp and more of the mercenaries in the other. Before discovering a tracking device in Doyle's workshop, they had no idea that the Earth had engaged in nuclear war and that the planet had been destroyed by the corporations that funded war machines and presidential campaigns. Even under one world government, the right and the left couldn't stand the thought of the other being allowed to live out their lives in peace. The left continued to grossly exaggerate the presence of white supremacy groups and teach schoolchildren to feel guilt over past events they had nothing to do with. While the right clung desperately to money and resource-hoarding principles that left the majority of the population in poverty and overbuilt the military, they continued this when there was only one world society and no one to fight with, so both sides started a civil war. They could never imagine walking in each other's shoes, so the feud never stopped, and the earth was blown into a million tiny pieces with no winner. On one planet, two camps arose: one formed a left-wing party to protect the rights of gingers, who were red or red and brown-haired white people who felt they were being treated unfairly. The right pushed back with an "Equality is for Everyone" party.

Soon, schisms appeared, but this time the prospect of a planet's annihilation served as a stark warning about the over-protection of certain groups. Titled people become entitled in personality, and it failed so badly on Earth that the titles of Lord, Lady, Count, Countess, Baron, and Baroness faded into history. This was due to the misconceived benefit of anointing a nobler presence among the commoners, which soon descended into expressions such as "Drunk as a Lord." The myth of superiority was revealed, and the culprits of pomposity and pretentiousness were exposed as the true purpose of giving out such preferential titles. They became so pompous and smug that it made them unlikable. The larger part of the Kepler population from both sides announced they would leave the power players to themselves and live without any political parties to decide matters for them. This eventually left both sides with only one manipulative figure without any real power. They abandoned the idea of governance and lived quite peacefully from that point on.

They made a statue of Doyle and one robot because they too were to be lost in history. Trevor learned to act responsibly, perhaps more out of concern for Jim's wild-eyed glares at him than any personal growth. Donita and Bridget left to make their way to explore the land. Jim got married to Monica and became the unofficial and untitled leader. Daliyah and Keith left once again to chase the serenity of sunsets and calm. Gradually, Daliyah lost her feisty edge completely and became the delicate and gentle person that she was meant to be. Keith and Daliyah lived out the remainder of their days without regrets. They grew stronger due to gravity and their odd calming effect on each other. They died, arm in arm, old and gray, having lived out rich, content lives. Molière wrote out his memoirs about the journey from Earth, but they died in peaceful seclusion, so other than Daliyah, no one ever read a single word he'd written.

ABOUT THE AUTHOR

R. Scott Reath is a free speech advocate and a strong believer in the right to privacy, constitutional compliance, individuality, and bringing people together via uncensored and honest dialogue. A former freelance writer turned author was so impacted by certain literature that he felt obligated to attempt to invigorate readers in the way he had been inspired by those who came before us.